Roped In

Strings #2

J.C. Hayden

Contents

TRADEMARK ACKNOWLEDGEMENTS

The author acknowledges the trademarked status and trademark owners of the following trademarks mentioned in this work of fiction:

Harry Potter series
La Bohème
Netflix
Facebook
Judge Judy
Instagram
Bridget Jones series
BMW
Toyota
Bailey's
Kaluha
Milanos
Boston Public Radio
XBox
The Little Mermaid
Disney
The Addams Family
Hey! Arnold
Superman
Wicked
Law & Order
The Wizard of Oz
Moana

To all the women I know who have had their hearts broken before. Don't be afraid to love again.

Roped In

J.C. Hayden

Chapter 1

“**G**ood set tonight, Talia.”

I looked up at a set of bright white teeth set in a wide, pink mouth surrounded by smooth dark brown skin.

Don't you dare blush, Talia, I warned myself. *And don't answer him in that stupid, high-pitched voice you always use every time he talks to you.*

“Thanks, Eric,” I breathed, in that stupid, high-pitched voice I always used every time he talked to me. My voice was so high I sounded like that actress who plays Moaning damn Myrtle in Harry Potter.

“Cat didn't come by tonight?” Eric, the bartender at Standards asked, wiping a glass with a white cloth before putting it somewhere underneath the bar out of my line of sight. “Love the hair, by the way,” he said as he leaned on his elbows on the bar, his smile warm and welcoming.

Eric was absolutely my type, despite that fact that I didn't even believe I really had one. But so many of the dudes I'd dated were just like Eric. Big, sexy, cocky, and utterly unavailable. I glanced briefly at the gold wedding band on his finger before shaking my head and taking a deep breath to get myself under control.

It wasn't like I really wanted to be with him, especially since he was easily fifteen years older than me and had four kids, but he was just so charming and sweet that I turned into a pathetic mess around him. I was like a preteen with a crush on her cute teacher because even though I knew nothing would ever come of it, I could still stare at him and think he was dreamy.

Get a grip, Talia.

“Thanks,” I said, grateful for the dimness of the bar covering up the completely unlike me blush at Eric's compliment. I ran a hand through my recently cut hair, trying to get used to the shorter cut. I'd been growing it out since college, but when I went in for a trim about a week ago, my stylist—who was actually my cousin Raven—convinced me to lop a bunch of it off. It was at my shoulders and not nearly as short as it was six years ago while I was at Klein, but it was still an adjustment after growing it down to the middle of my

1

back over all this time. "But yeah, no, not tonight. She has rehearsal early tomorrow morning."

"What show is she doing now?" Eric asked politely, his eyes focused on me. He was always so attentive and genuinely interested when he asked a question. Hence, the stupid crush.

The venue the band and I were at tonight was one we played often. They hired us to come every Wednesday night to play our usual bluesy set. My best friend, Catrina Murphy, often came to the shows, but since she had to be off book by tomorrow morning, she was holed up in her apartment with her husband, Brody Galen, not actually rehearsing and probably letting him distract her with his pouty grin. Catrina and I had been best friends since we were freshmen in college at a small liberal arts university called Klein that was in the suburbs of Boston. We'd both majored in music, and while Catrina went on to become, basically, a world-renowned Broadway and Opera star, I was still playing mostly local gigs with the band I'd been in since the year after we left school while also working as a waitress at a small Italian restaurant in my neighborhood.

"*La Bohème*," I told Eric. "The opening show is in three weeks so they're definitely in major prep mode. But she'll be great in it. She's always amazing."

Just then, I felt my phone vibrate in my pocket, and I pulled it out to look at the screen before I showed it to Eric.

"Speak of the devil," I said.

"Tell her I said hi," Eric said with another sexy grin before I grabbed the glass of pinot noir he'd put down for me and turned to lean against the bar before answering my friend's call.

"Hey, Kitty Cat."

"Hey, Tal—"

"Hi, Talia!" I heard shouted in the background.

"Brody says hi," Cat said, a smile apparent in her voice. Sometimes—and I was totally secure and self-aware enough to admit this—I envied the relationship Catrina had with Brody. They'd started seeing each other while we were seniors at Klein and after some of the typical twenty-two-year-old drama, they'd been inseparable ever since. Even when Cat and I had continued to live together after college, Brody was a regular fixture in our lives, so much so that he and I had even grown close over the years. Every time he looked at my best friend I could see how much he adored her, and every time they were together in my presence I was reminded about the profound love those two had for each other. I would watch the quiet, unspoken moments between them—how they could communicate so clearly without words. I would watch the subtle displays of love and affection—a touch on the arm, a tucking of hair behind the ear, a hand on the lower back—and some deep, hidden part of me would wish I could find something like that.

Even if I didn't believe that existed much beyond Cat and Brody.

"What are you guys doing?"

"Just finished an episode of that docuseries on Netflix you told me about," Catrina said. I could hear the rustling of something that sounded like a bag of popcorn. "Brody's been helping me run lines all night and both of us are pretty over *La Bohème* at the moment."

I laughed, and Cat continued, jumping straight to her purpose in calling.

"You aren't going to go home with Isaac, are you?"

Isaac Blake, the drummer in our band, Flora and Fauna, was a tall, slender hipster who I'd been hooking up with on and off for the past year or so. It was casual and I knew it would never be anything more than that, but Catrina had made it clear many times over that she didn't approve. She thought Isaac was a slimeball I was wasting my time on while I could be out there finding the guy I was meant to be with. Her words, of course.

One thing I hated about my best friend—ever since she'd fallen in love with Brody, she had become a hopeless romantic who believed everyone's perfect mate was out there just waiting for us to come along.

I didn't have the heart to tell her that I didn't think that was in the cards for me.

"Not tonight," I told her, trying to keep the edge out of my voice. "So stand down, sergeant." I loved Cat, but her judgment over whatever *thing* I had with Isaac always made me bristle.

"Anyway, how was the show?" she asked a moment later.

"It was good. Usual crowd. Wish you were here, though."

Catrina sighed. "Me, too, Tal. I hate missing your shows."

"Sorry, I didn't want to make you feel guilty," I said, suddenly feeling weird and vulnerable. "I just like having my bestie here, that's all."

There was a pause for a moment when I almost told Catrina I had to go, but then she said, "Everything else okay?" I heard more rustling and assumed she was getting up to go into another room so Brody couldn't hear.

One thing I loved about my best friend—how much she valued our friendship and respected stuff that was just between us despite being married to Brody for almost four years.

I wasn't even planning on telling her about what had happened last night, but hearing her voice made me change my mind. Ever since I'd started playing shows with my band there was something about throwing myself into the music that always left me feeling raw and exposed. If Catrina was there for a show I could come back to myself from just talking and laughing with her, but without her here to ground me I felt flayed wide open.

Catrina was right to guess that something was going on with me. I'd planned to take what happened, shove it to the back of my mind, and never think about it again, but now the need to tell her was an ache in my gut.

"Jack messaged me."

There was a long pause.

"Catrina?"

"Jack," she repeated blankly.

"Jack," I reiterated with a bit more emphasis.

"Wait, Jack *Harding*?" She sounded shocked, but also like she was trying (and failing) to temper her reaction.

"Yeah."

Back at Klein, Jack Harding and I had casually dated—or casual as I thought—for almost a year. He was everything I wanted in a guy. He was huge—at least ten inches taller than my five foot four with a body that was so big and muscley that he made even Brody, who was also tall with wide shoulders and muscles, look small. He was cocky at the right moments and sweet in others. He laughed at all my stupid jokes and, in turn, made me laugh so hard that I could hardly breathe. Not to mention that in the six years since I'd ended things a few weeks after graduation, I'd never had sex as good as the sex I'd had with him. It was like he knew every bend and curve of my body, every erogenous zone, every place that made me out of my head with lust. Even at twenty-two he could read me like a book. I could only imagine how much better he'd gotten over the years.

But I *couldn't* imagine it. Because I refused to let myself ever think about him. Ever.

Because Jack was also everything I never wanted. He came from money. Like a lot of it. His family was *the* Harding family. Like Warren G. Like the twenty-ninth President of the United States. *Those* Hardings. I was raised by a single mom who owned a diner in Vermont and who, before that, was a waitress in Queens who had been on food stamps. Jack might have been kind and funny and sweet and fantastic in bed, but he and I had never been meant for each other.

"What did he say?"

"Hang on," I said, walking away from the bar away from possibly listening ears. "I'll read it." I found a small high top table in the corner of the bar and slid onto a stool as I pushed the *speaker* button on my phone.

It only took me about five seconds to pull up the Facebook Messenger app to open what Jack had sent me. He'd actually sent the message three weeks ago, but since he and I weren't Facebook friends, it had gone to a separate inbox that I didn't look into all that often. It wasn't until last night that I'd finally opened it and been in a tailspin ever since.

"Hey Talia,'" I started reading. "'I hope this message doesn't completely catch you off guard. I've just been thinking about you a lot recently and wanted to send you a message to see how you are. I saw Flora and Fauna's page a few months ago and I've listened to a ton of your music. You guys are seriously awesome. I'm so happy for you. Maybe this is out of the blue and maybe even inappropriate, but I'd love to take you out to lunch sometime. Just to catch up. If you don't want to, I understand. If you don't, I just want you to know how much I care about you and how much I valued our friendship. Take care, Talia. Jack.'"

I didn't say anything after I finished reading it. The shock of the message hit me all over again, and for a moment, I felt like I couldn't catch my breath.

"Wow," I heard Cat say.

"Yeah," was all I could manage to choke out as my eyes scanned over the message again before I took the phone off speaker and pressed it to my ear.

"He sounds really sincere," Cat said quietly.

He did. Of course he did. Jack had always been one of the most genuine people I'd ever met. He almost never minced words. He said exactly what he meant and expressed exactly what he wanted. When he'd wanted to get more serious and exclusive in college, it was the only time he wasn't upfront right from the start, and that was only because he knew I'd get spooked. Which, of course, I had. But even then, I'd wanted him more than I wanted to keep a distance between us, so I let it go on until I felt myself slipping—slipping into something I hadn't fallen into since I was eighteen. Since I'd been deceived and royally screwed over. Since I'd vowed to myself I would never let a guy take advantage of me like that ever again. When I felt myself start to slip, I ended it for good.

And I hadn't seen or heard from him since.

"Well, it doesn't matter." I tried to shake myself out of my melancholic thoughts. There was no use dwelling on the past, on what could have been, on choices I'd made six years ago.

"What do you mean?"

"It's not like I'm going to message him back."

Catrina made an indignant noise. "What? Talia, why not?"

"What could there possibly be to say?" I felt a tightness in my chest that had me instinctively bringing my hand up to it.

"That you care about him, too. That you appreciate what he said about Flora and Fauna. That you want to catch up, too."

"Catrina—"

"He..."

She cut me off like she wanted to say something, but then trailed off. I frowned.

"What?" I said. "He what?"

"He got engaged last year."

Her words were like an icy knife to my heart. *Fuck.* Even after all this damn time there was something about him that still got to me. I rubbed my chest again and tried for a nonchalant tone.

"Great, so you want to me to have lunch with an almost-married guy."

"They broke it off two months ago."

The icy knife twisted. I didn't know why, but just knowing that terrified me.

"Talia," Catrina said, her voice quiet and urgent. "Maybe this is fate. Maybe he's messaging you because he misses what you had. Maybe he broke it off with his fiancée because he still has feelings for you—"

"Catrina, stop," I said quickly. My chest was getting tighter and tighter, the ache of her words was starting to radiate out from my chest to my limbs and I couldn't stand it. "You sound delusional. We haven't seen each other in six years. He hasn't been pining over me. He doesn't even think about me."

"Well, that message tells you that he does."

"He probably just wants to fuck," I said, hoping to get Cat off this topic. She hated when I spoke so bluntly about sex. "He broke up with his fiancée and he wants to get laid, and he thinks, 'I know who's D.T.F.'—"

"Stop it."

"It's true. You know how men are—or I guess you don't since you've got a hubby now, but Cat, men are trash. All they think about his sex. And all I ever was to Jack was a good fuck—"

Cat scoffed. "You and I both know that's a lie."

Dammit. She always had my number.

"Whatever." I looked up from the table I was sitting at to see our drummer, Isaac, looking in my direction. Leering, really. Yes. That's what I needed. He would be the perfect distraction. I flashed him a smile, and as he started walking toward me, I wrapped up my conversation with Catrina.

"Look, I gotta go. Isaac's walking over and—"

6

"Don't hook up with him, Tal—"

"Take off your judgey pants, Judge Judy," I said, feeling the ache in my chest start to settle now that we were no longer talking about my ex. "We're still on for girls' night tomorrow night, right?"

"Of course," she said, voice getting a bit softer. "I'm kicking Brody out at seven, so be here then."

"Okay," I said, just as Isaac got to my table, his look of intent clear on his face. "Love you, Kitty Cat."

"Love you, too, Tal." Then she raised her voice, almost yelling through the phone when she said, "And don't sleep with—"

I hung up the phone before she could finish.

Isaac continued his leering and flashed a smirk.

"Don't sleep with who?"

God, Catrina was so fucking right. Isaac *was* a total slimeball, despite being a talented as hell drummer. Most of the time he was my friend, but when we hooked up, I realized how gross he could make me feel. He wasn't even that good looking. He was cute enough, but his face and nose were too long, his facial hair was unkempt, his hair was kind of stringy, and he was thin in a way that I hated in bed—nothing to grab onto when he was moving inside me, no ass, no muscles, nothing. But he was decent and definitely willing, and sometimes I just needed to scratch an itch.

Despite how much I wanted to get Jack Harding and my conversation with Catrina—"*maybe he broke it off with his fiancée because he still has feelings for you*"—out of my head, I knew there was no way in hell I was going to be able to go home with Isaac tonight. Not when the image of dark green eyes and a chiseled jaw kept swimming into my consciousness.

"Catrina isn't your biggest fan," I said flirtatiously, hoping that I could humor him a bit before gathering up my stuff in the back room and slipping out the side door.

"Oh, no?" he said, leaning his elbow against my table and bringing his face wickedly close to mine. "I've always been a fan of red heads."

I sighed inwardly and gave him another flirty look. "Maybe they aren't fans of you."

Isaac threw his head back and laughed, and I cringed inwardly. Guys like Isaac, they always commented on loving how "blunt" and "honest" I was. They said they thought it was sexy and funny and charming. They almost never liked it when the bluntness and honesty became about them, though. One thing I'd learned about men over the last couple years—they wanted you to be just right. Reserved but not too shy, sexual but not slutty, honest but never when it applied to them. It was why every guy I dated since college ended up kicked to the curb before things could even get serious. It was why I'd never make things serious with Isaac, who always threw a fit when I corrected him or gave him constructive criticism during our rehearsals.

I stood up from the stool.

"Don't worry," he said. "I'm a fan of *dirty* blondes, too," he said, obviously thinking his emphasis on the word dirty would make me drop my panties.

Little did he know, that tack wasn't going to work on me because it just reminded me that I hated my new hair color. Raven had convinced me to go lighter for the last month of the summer. She'd lightened it with ashy blonde highlights that I wasn't at all used to, and I couldn't stop myself before I ran my hand through the choppy layers. I missed my natural deep brown that bordered on black. And even though Raven kept trying to convince me to give it a chance, that it would look good with my olive skin tone, I just couldn't get used to it.

"I'm sure you are," I said to Isaac, who had taken my standing as an invitation to move closer.

"You heading home?" he asked, intention clear in his eyes.

"Yep."

"Think I could join you?"

A memory of the last time he'd been at my place flashed quickly through my mind. He'd pounded into me fast and hard for about four minutes before he came, rolled off me, threw the condom in the trash, and promptly fell asleep without even asking if I'd finished. I'd gone to my bathroom, stared at my caramel-colored, bloodshot eyes and wished I could kick him out. Instead I'd hopped in the shower before getting back into bed next to him. He'd tried to go down on me in the morning, but he wasn't figuring out where to put his tongue or his fingers so I'd just laid there for what felt like an eternity before I decided to fake a moan to get him to hurry up and finish down there. Then I finished him off with my hand and told him I'd see him at our rehearsal later that night. He'd kissed me sloppily at my front door, and I'd told myself I would never hook up with him again.

"Sorry, not tonight," I said with a pasted-on smile. "Have to be up super early to take my abuela to the doctor." Of course, he'd never bothered to ask me about my family and didn't know that my abuela lived in New York.

He nodded in understanding and ran a hand down my bare arm. "Next time then."

I nodded and felt like I was swallowing down vomit. "Next time."

Chapter 2

I washed the smell of the bar and the lingering sweat from being on stage off me when I got back to my apartment a little while later. I lived in a studio apartment in Back Bay with exposed brick and a fireplace I had no idea how to light. It cost me a fortune for the size, but I loved it so much I didn't care. It was adorable and the neighborhood was my favorite in the city, so if I had to pay a limb for it, then I would.

I switched the lamp on that sat on my end table and switched off the overhead lights before I slid into bed in just my underwear. Usually I wore a large t-shirt or something to bed, but I had a pile of laundry sitting by my front door that I planned to lug to the laundromat while I waited until I was ready to go meet Catrina the next day. So tonight I would just be sleeping in old, rarely worn underwear. *The life of glamor you lead, Talia Emery.*

When I got under my warm, heavy covers, I picked up my phone off the end table and immediately opened Instagram. I scrolled through for a while, saving a bunch of pictures of makeup looks that I liked and wanted to try before I looked through a few more apps.

That was until my skin started to itch with the need to read Jack's message again. I kept telling myself no over and over, but before I even knew what I was doing, I was opening messenger and reading every word even though I'd basically already memorized it.

Cat was ridiculous. Jack didn't break up with his fiancée because he still had feelings for me. I hadn't seen or talked him in over six years. The only glimpse I'd gotten of him since that morning I broke things off was the small icon of his picture next to his message.

God, I wanted to see more of him. I wanted to enlarge the picture, zoom in, take in every single feature of his face that I'd managed to forget over the years. Which, if I was being honest, probably wasn't much. He was a difficult guy to forget.

Just like when I was in the bar with Isaac and I remembered the night we spent together, a memory of my last night with Jack came blazing into my consciousness in a way I hadn't allowed it to since then.

Cat and I had just moved into our new apartment, but she was over at Brody's for the night. She'd just texted me that she wouldn't be back until the morning when I heard a knock at my door. He'd

9

barely gotten in before Jack was all over me. He'd turned me against the door so he could rub his front against my back. We didn't say a word as he peeled every stitch of clothing off me and then sank to his knees.

I'd been a quivering mess against my brand new front door, gasping and moaning his name and practically begging when I'd heard the rip of a foil packet. He was still fully clothed when he slid inside me, and just the thought of that had me racing toward orgasm. But he didn't let me come. In fact, that night, he'd brought me to the brink so many times that it started to hurt. I'd felt tears sting my eyes as I was begging him—begging him for more, begging him to stop, begging him to let me come, begging him to end his torture.

Somehow, we'd made it to my bedroom, and it was almost midnight before he turned me on my back and sank deep, deep, deep inside me. He never took his eyes off me—not when I came, not when he followed only seconds later, not when he pulled out and threw the condom away, not when he rolled to his side to watch me until he fell asleep.

I knew I was in too deep. I knew I'd fallen.

So the next morning I told him I didn't want to see him anymore.

He hadn't even been angry. It was almost like he was expecting it, like he knew that the night before would be the end, and that's why he dragged it out for as long as he had.

It was like he knew it was goodbye.

And when he kissed me goodbye, I knew this time he wouldn't come back, not like all the other times I told him we couldn't see each other anymore and he came back and convinced me to keep going for a little while longer. This time it was different. This time was the end.

I was mindless as I searched his name on Facebook. My hands were shaking as I tried to push the memory of that last night out of my mind. And when he popped up, I clicked on his profile picture, knowing I shouldn't.

If possible, he was about ten times sexier than he'd been in college. His hair was slightly longer on top and buzzed on the sides, while in college it had been buzzed all over. Somehow—impossibly so—it looked like he'd gotten even bigger and taller. His face had shaped and molded with age, making the lines of his face sharper and cleaner, the prominence of his jaw more stunning than ever. I couldn't stop staring at the picture. It was just a simple picture—it looked like someone had snapped it while he was at a bar—his fiancée maybe?

I clicked through more profile pictures and when I got a little bit further back I saw the picture of him with a woman. They were standing next to each other, arms around each other's waists standing in front of a Christmas tree. She was tall and thin with long, brown, wavy hair and classic features. She was wearing a green, long-sleeved, turtleneck dress that showed off her long legs—legs I couldn't possibly compete with. He was wearing an almost matching green sweater, tight around his muscular arms and chest, and a pair of khakis.

They looked happy, smiling at the camera, in matching green. I clicked through a few more of them together until I got to the one that made my stomach flop uncomfortably.

Jack was wearing a suit that fit him perfectly. She—Rachel, I'd learned from scrolling—was wearing what looked like a very expensive black evening gown. They were at an event of some sort, a few people milling around and looking at the them all dressed similarly, white table-clothed tables all around them, a chandelier in the middle of the room, and Jack was down on one knee.

I closed out of my Facebook app quickly and laid there for a while, staring at the ceiling.

Dammit.

Shit.

I should have brought Isaac home.

I knew it would have been a bad idea. I knew I would've regretted it. But if he was here at least I'd be getting laid instead of laying here thinking about Jack.

◆ ◆ ◆

I tossed and turned for what felt like hours, but when I looked at my phone I saw only about an hour and half had passed since I'd put my phone down.

Images of Jack kept floating in and out of my mind. The morning I'd ended things. The night he took me ice skating and looked so happy that I hadn't stopped smiling for a week. The night he asked me to his sister's wedding and I'd flipped out. The look on his face when I told him it was over for good. Him down on one knee.

Fuck, why was I still thinking about him? I'd been successfully blocking him from my memory for six years. I never let thoughts of him creep up, but one fucking Facebook message and I was off the rails.

I knew what it was.

It was the unknown. It was wonder about what he wanted or why he wanted to reconnect. The wonder about how he was.

11

I just needed to eliminate the unknowns so I could move on.

I pulled my phone to me again and pulled up Messenger.

Jack, I wrote.

No, this is stupid.

I put my phone back down, stared at the ceiling for another ten minutes, and then picked it up again.

Jack,

It's good to hear from you. I'd love to grab lunch. You still live in Boston, right? How's Sunday? I know a place.

"Fuck!" I shouted in the silence of my apartment. I felt like an idiot. A stupid, stupid, stupid, pathetic idiot who couldn't stop thinking about her ex and who was lying in her underwear Facebook messaging him at two o'clock in the morning.

A few seconds later, I was still berating myself when my phone binged.

Talia, I'm so happy to hear from you. Thank you so much for responding. To be honest, I didn't think you would, so this is a really nice surprise. Sunday is great. I'm still in Boston. You name the time and the place and I'll be there.

Shit.

Chapter 3

I was sitting cross-legged on Cat's couch, staring at the credits screen of *Bridget Jones' Diary* when Cat walked back into the room, grinning at me and holding two mugs and a bag of cookies between her teeth.

Our girls' nights always went something like this. I'd go to her place or she'd schlep to Back Bay from Brookline (although it wasn't really schlepping because Brody always insisted she drive his BMW rather than her beat up Toyota Camry), we'd cozy up on the couch and giggle and watch movies that our other best friends, Callum and Carver, hated and would never allow when it was the four of us hanging out.

On tonight's agenda was the entire *Bridget Jones* series, which were, hands down, Cat and my favorite movies, although I was still somewhat a skeptic when it came to *Bridget Jones' Baby*.

Cat dropped the cookies between us, handed me a mug, and sat so she was also cross-legged and facing me. There was a box of unfinished pizza crusts on the coffee table, my empty wine glass, her empty glass of passionfruit juice that she *only* drank when Brody wasn't around because he couldn't stand the smell of it, and the DVD cases of the *Bridget Jones* movies.

I sniffed at my mug and arched an eyebrow at Cat over it. "You're trying to get me drunk aren't you?"

"Please," Cat said, feigning annoyance. "As if either of us could get drunk off Bailey's and Kahlua."

I leaned forward to smell the contents of Cat's mug before she could pull it back with an unabashed grin on her face.

"I have rehearsal in the morning," she said with a shrug, as if that was an enough of an explanation as to why her drink was entirely devoid of booze.

"Whatever, Murphy," I said before taking a big swallow.

"So?" she said before she tore into the Milanos. She dunked one into her hot chocolate as I reached for one. "Did you go home with Isaac last night?"

I shook my head. "Seriously, what is your deal with Isaac? Can't you just let me get some?"

13

"Of course I'll let you get some," she said, feigning incredulity. "But obviously you forgot what you told me the last time you guys slept together."

"I know, I know—"

"Because your exact words were, 'never again, Cat.' And as your best friend, it's my job to hold you to that."

"Fine," I conceded. "But you're the one always going on and on and on about me finding someone."

"Someone you deserve," she said matter-of-factly.

Someone I deserve. God, how sad was it that I wouldn't even know what that looked like at this point?

"Yeah, well," was all I could manage in response.

"So..." Cat started slowly. And before she even got the question out, I knew exactly where it was going. "Did you respond to Jack?"

"Yes," I mumbled without looking up at her.

"YES?!" she shouted, bouncing on the couch cushion under her. "Yes? Oh, my god, Tal, and you kept it in this long? That should've been the first thing you said when you walked in the door, like, hey I'm here to watch *Bridget Jones*, also I messaged Jack back."

"Oh, my god."

"Tell me everything."

With a sigh, I pulled out my phone and handed it to her so she could read my message and the ones that followed. After Jack had told me to name the time and the place, I suggested this café in Cambridge that had amazing vegetarian sandwiches and was big enough that we would be able to have a small modicum of privacy while we talked. I'd thought about going somewhere in my neighborhood or even taking him to the little Italian restaurant, Gia's, I worked at part-time, but I was terrified about Jack being on my "turf." What if things went sour and all I could remember at my job or at any of the places I loved to go was him being there? So, it would be the Green Hornet because I only went there maybe twice a year and I could live without it if Jack's presence inside it ruined it for me for all eternity.

"Green Hornet?" Cat asked after she read through the messages and handed me back my phone. "I love that place, but it's super out of the way for you."

I shrugged, and before I could reply, she said, "But I get that. Can't have him sullying your favorite spots if this lunch date goes south."

"It's not a date," I said quickly, ignoring how well my best friend understood me and my reasons why I'd chosen where I had.

"Relax, it's just a figure of speech."

"Whatever," I said. And after a pause, "It's not a date."

Catrina rolled her eyes at me. "It's like you're allergic to that word."

I faked a shudder. "Maybe I am."

She rolled her eyes again and then sat up straighter. "So, what are you gonna wear?"

"Probably nothing," I said dryly. "I was thinking of showing up to this super hipster place in nothing but my birthday gear."

Cat laughed loudly and shook her head. "Okay, seriously though. You have to look good, but not too good like you're trying too hard. And you have to look sexy but not like you're *trying* to be sexy. And you have to look sophisticated like you put thought into your look but you aren't trying to impress him. You have to look like you're secure and confident and like you totally don't care what he thinks but that if he thinks you look good that's fine."

"Jesus Christ, are you hearing yourself?"

Cat giggled. "Okay, that definitely sounded crazy."

"And you know how I hate how women have to be perfectly perfect for men."

"Okay, you're so right," Cat said, trying and failing to put a serious face on. "Feminism. Women's empowerment. All that. So screw it, just show up in a trash bag and he can deal with it."

Both of us rolled with laughter at that, and the subject was effectively changed. I wouldn't dare tell Catrina that I had been thinking all day about what I was going to wear to lunch with Jack. When I'd gone to the laundromat to wash my clothes, I'd been mentally and physically sorting through them and mixing and matching to see what might look good, and all those things Cat said—confident and secure but not like I was trying too hard—had been at the forefront of my thoughts.

It had also been at the forefront of my thoughts to message Jack and cancel, but every time I opened Messenger I forced myself to toss my phone to the side. I could do this. It was just lunch.

Hours later, we'd finished *Bridget Jones' Edge of Reason*, a second mug of hot chocolate, and the entire bag of Milanos. We were about halfway through *Bridget Jones' Baby*, and I could feel my eyes getting heavy when I heard a lock turn in the front door.

Cat and I were cozied together on the couch under a big fleece blanket when her husband Brody walked around the couch to look at us, a big, easy grin on his face.

His blonde hair looked messy like he'd run his hair through it a bunch of times and his gray eyes were shining like he'd maybe had one too many drinks. He was also wearing a really tight button down and when I glanced over at Cat, she was totally checking him out.

"You two look so cute."

15

Yep, definitely drunk.

"Hey, baby," Cat said, sitting up and smiling back at her man. "You're home early."

"It's almost midnight, and as much as Gabe loves you, I think he was sick of hearing me talk about you."

Gabe Keaton was Brody's best friend, who also happened to be Catrina's cousin. He and Brody had been on the soccer team together at Klein, and Gabe had gone on to play professional soccer while Brody went to grad school for creative writing. A few months ago, Gabe had gotten a bad injury and despite his young age had been forced to retire from professional soccer. Cat told me he was still devastated but trying to put on a brave face, so I was sure Brody's night with him was as much to try and cheer up his friend as it was just to spend some time with him.

Brody nudged his way onto the couch so that Catrina was in between him and I, and he leaned over to look at me.

"Hi, Talia."

I chuckled. "Hey, Brody. Did you guys have fun?"

"Not as much fun as you two," he said, gesturing to the pizza and cookies and glasses littered on the coffee table.

Catrina snuggled up to him, wrapping her arms around his waist as he lifted an arm around her shoulder.

"How's Gabe?" she asked, seeming to not even register how easily she'd wrapped herself around her husband like it was so routine that it was part of her.

"He's okay," Brody said, looking a little sadder. "He misses playing. Hell, I miss it, too, sometimes, but he's getting better."

Catrina was staring up at Brody and he was looking down at her as they talked about Gabe. Catrina and Brody always did this. They always unintentionally got lost in their own world. I knew they didn't do it on purpose, and if I ever said anything to Catrina, she would apologize profusely and try to change her behavior, but it was like for several moments, the world around them ceased to exist. They entered into this bubble that was just the two of them, their shared language, their shared movement, their shared air. And nothing could pull them from it.

When we left Klein and Cat and Brody slipped into their honeymoon phase, I always thought that things would ease up with their obsession with each other, with their weird connectedness and their googly eyes. Somehow, though, the bond and the love and the honeymoon and the googlies had only gotten stronger as time went on. They got more connected, fell more in love, slipped into the bubble even easier than they had before.

16

Part of me wanted to make gagging noises and joke about how lovey dovey they were, but the other part of me never wanted to break this spell they fell into. It felt sacred somehow. Sometimes I would go crazy thinking about how badly I wanted what they had.

Other times I knew I would never be brave enough to get it.

Rather than try and break the spell, I got up to the go to the bathroom. As I was walking down the hall I heard Cat murmur all dreamily, "You smell so good. Like beer and Old Spice." The gagging noises won out and I shouted, "get a room!" over my shoulder before closing the bathroom door to the sounds of their laughter.

After going to the bathroom, I splashed some water on my face and stared at my reflection. I didn't know if I would say that I was pretty. I definitely wasn't as pretty as Catrina, who had long, beautiful red hair, and a bone structure I would literally kill for. But I was attractive in a sort of girl-down-the-block way. I had a heart-shaped face and full red lips I got from my mom's Puerto Rican side of the family, but while my mom's eyes were a dark, deep brown, she always told me my eyes looked just like my dad's. Caramel-colored, almost with a golden yellow tinge, and almond shapes that tilted slightly upwards at the sides giving me what dudes always called an "exotic" look, a term that I loathed.

When I looked in the mirror, I tried to imagine what Jack might see when he looked at me. Would he find me attractive? Would he wish I was ten pounds lighter in my thighs and ass like I'd been in college? Or would there be something he liked? Maybe even something he wanted to see more of.

I shook my head vigorously, trying to shake the thoughts out of my head before I went back to Cat and Brody's living room.

Only to find my friend and her husband right in the middle of a pretty intense makeout session.

"So, yeah, I'm gonna head out."

Cat practically leapt off Brody, who looked dazed and like he hardly knew where he was.

"Oh, my god, Talia, I'm so sorry. Please don't go. I'll make Brody go in our room so we can finish the movie."

I just shook my head with a smile.

"Nah, don't worry about it. You two crazy kids have fun."

I gathered up my stuff and when Cat walked me to the door she was frowning.

"Tal, I'm really sorry. I don't want you to think I tried to cut our girls' night short for some dude."

"Um, that 'some dude' happens to be your husband," I said, arching an eyebrow at her.

She shrugged with a small smile. "Sisters before misters."

"You're such a dork."

Her smile widened before it fell a bit. "Seriously, Talia. You aren't mad?"

"No."

"You'd tell me if you were, right?"

"Have you ever known me not to tell you when you're being an asshole?" Catrina laughed and shook her head, and I said, "Plus, it's after midnight. I'm exhausted and I have to work early in the morning."

"Okay, fine."

Catrina pulled me into a big hug and held me for what I thought was a few seconds longer than she normally would have. When she pulled back, she kept her hands on my arms.

"Call me on Sunday after the lunch, okay?" she said, her voice quiet so Brody wouldn't hear. "I want to hear everything that happened."

"Okay."

"Everything!" she hissed. "Word for word. Don't forget a thing."

Yeah, I definitely won't.

"Okay!"

"Okay."

She gave me another quick hug, and I pushed her off me.

"Okay, go bang your drunk husband."

She smirked. "I'm totally gonna take advantage of him."

I practically guffawed at her words. "Yeah, from the way he's been staring at your ass the entire time we've been standing here, I don't think there will be any advantage taken." I looked over her shoulder. "Bye, Brody."

He looked up from Cat's ass. "Bye, Talia!" He waved happily. "Come over any time."

As I walked out into the night, I couldn't help but love those two loons.

Chapter 4

I stood in an alleyway a block away from the Green Hornet until 12:22. Jack and I were scheduled to have lunch at noon.

I'd watched him go in at 11:54 from my stalkery spot down the block. I'd panicked until 12:05, played a game on my phone, panicked when I saw it was 12:11 when I checked again, and then I'd called Catrina who'd calmly and supportively told me I was an idiot and to just go inside.

I pushed into the doors of the Green Hornet at 12:23, and I stopped in the doorway for a full minute just taking in the sight of Jack.

He was just as gorgeous as he'd been six years ago, more gorgeous than his Facebook photos showed. His dark hair was long on top just like in the picture of him and his ex-fiancée. The sleeves of his long-sleeved Henley were shoved up to his biceps, making his arms look deliciously huge.

I always said I didn't have a type. I liked big, muscular, preppy guys like Jack. I liked thin, edgy hipsters like Isaac. I liked pudgy nerds. I liked jocks. I liked them old, young, any race, any occupation. As long as I felt that spark, I was into him. But Jack... If I had a *type*, my type would be Jack Harding.

Even looking at him rang every single one of my bells. Although he was sitting, I could see he was—like I'd suspected from his photos—even more cut than in college. He looked more mature—aged, but in that distinguished way that only men could age.

I drank in every bit of him, knowing I couldn't—*shouldn't*—admire him when he could catch me doing so, and as I moved toward the table he was at in the corner, I watched as he glanced at his watch—Jesus, I loved a man who wore a wrist watch—and then looked up in the direction of the door.

His entire face shifted when he saw me. The way his expression went from mildly worried and annoyed to joyfully content in the span of three seconds made my heart stop. Despite all the shit I'd put him through, dragging him along when I knew how he felt and I knew I wouldn't change my mind—even though I was too greedy to give him up the way I knew I should long before I actually did, he still lit up when he laid eyes on me the way he always had. The memories of him assaulted me—of him grinning when he saw me walk into a bar, when he opened the door to his apartment and saw me standing over the threshold, the day at Marmaduke's—a diner just off campus—during the spring festival when I knew I couldn't keep doing this to him and he looked up and saw me walking back to our table with two iced mochas. He still looked at me that way.

He still looked at me like he only had eyes for me.

"Talia."

"Hi," I was barely able to get out.

I hadn't fully appreciated what seeing him would do to me. I felt winded and overwhelmed. I felt like I couldn't breathe, like if I spoke I might do something idiotic like start crying.

"I thought you weren't coming," he said when he stood to greet me.

"The Red Line was delayed," I lied. "Sorry I'm late."

We were standing next to the table where he'd been sitting. He towered over me as he stood close, looking down to meet my eyes. I didn't know what to do. I desperately wanted him to hug me, but I was afraid it would kill me if he did.

"It's okay," he said quietly. Almost reverently. Fuck, I didn't know if I could do this. Jack had always been awful at hiding his feelings. He had never wanted to. Not like me. I was a fucking pro at it. I was so practiced at hiding how I really felt that I was even able to hide my feelings from myself. Not Jack. Jack was open and honest and true to himself to the end, which was proven by his next words that nearly gutted me. "I'm really glad you're here, Talia. God, I missed you," he finished on a heavy breath.

Before I could think better of it, I reached up and wrapped my arms around his neck. He responded immediately, bending slightly to put his arms around my waist. He held me so tightly that I went up to my tiptoes. I inhaled deeply, my face in the crook of his neck, and I felt the tears sting the backs of my eyes when I realized he smelled exactly the same. He still smelled like the piney aroma of either his soap or deodorant with the combined smell that was just him, just the delicious scent that lingered on his skin and his alone.

I couldn't tell him the truth—that I missed him, too, with a fierceness I hadn't realized until this moment—but I could do this. I could put my arms around him and breathe him in until it became inappropriate in a public space.

"You smell the same," he whispered in my ear, his breath tickling me and turning me on as he echoed my thoughts. It was like we'd had no time apart. He was still the same Jack. I was still the same Talia. We could have been standing inside Marmaduke's holding onto each other after another one of our fights about where we were going and how he wanted more. It was so familiar in his arms, so right, so vital.

Once, when Catrina and I had been sitting on her couch, late at night, just talking about everything and nothing, she'd said—quietly, like a prayer—that being in Brody's arms was like coming home. I didn't know what she meant, didn't know what it was like to have another person be so necessary that their existence felt so safe that it was like the peace and purity of being home. I had no idea what she meant until now, standing in the middle of the Green Hornet with Jack's arms around me after so long.

Finally, I leaned back to look at him, but we stayed in each other's embrace.

He smiled, and my heart pounded.

"Hi," he said gently.

"Hey," I replied, almost a whisper, unable to do anything but that.

"Do you want to have lunch?"

I nodded.

"Do you want to sit down?"

He was grinning and I just wanted to scream. How could it be like this? So easy and casual and *good*?

I took a step back and his arms slid down and away from me as I dropped my arms from his shoulders.

We sat down across from each other and just sort of stared at one another for a long time. Eventually, we ordered lunch—I got this fancy California sandwich with avocado and sprouts and he got a grilled cheese and tomato sandwich, which caused an unexpected rush of affection to flood me when he told the server—and we still didn't do much more than watch each other. He sipped his iced tea, I sipped my club soda. His eyes traced over my face like he was learning me all over again. I found myself doing the same thing.

He smiled.

I ached.

When the server brought our food, Jack ordered a beer and asked me if I wanted a drink. I said no at first, but as soon as the server started walking away I blurted that I'd have a Bloody Mary.

We kept sitting in relative silence as we ate, but it was the comfortable silence of old friends. It didn't feel tense. It felt sacred, like we needed the silence to fully appreciate just being in each other's presence again.

After a while, the server took away our empty plates, and Jack regarded me over his beer. He took a sip and then set the bottle on the table between us.

"You look really good, Talia," he said. "I love your hair."

I self-consciously ran my hair through the lighter colored locks that I wasn't quite used to yet.

"Thanks," I replied.

"So, tell me about what you're doing now," he said, sounding so genuinely interested that I wanted to hug him again.

I told him about Flora and Fauna as well as my job at Gia's. He asked all the right questions about both, and I responded by asking him about his work. He said he worked at his dad's law firm and then promptly changed the subject.

"How's Catrina? You two still thick as thieves?"

I couldn't help but smile. "You could say that. She's doing really great. Her and Brody have been married for a few years now, and they're really happy. Her career is obviously incredible."

"Wow, yeah, she's really making a name for herself, isn't she?" Jack said, looking impressed. "I heard there was *Tony* buzz around her *La Bohème* performance."

"I know! And she hasn't even had a show yet. Everyone just knows she's going to be that good." I was so proud of my friend I could shout it to everyone around me. She was so talented and deserved every bit of success she got.

"That's amazing. She's super talented," Jack paused for a moment. "How's your mom?"

My heart fluttered at his question. He was so kind. I'd forgotten how kind he was, and all it took was a simple question to remind me. Jack had never actually met my mom since she'd never come up to Boston while we were at Klein except on graduation, but that day had been so hectic that she and Jack had never crossed paths. She worked her ass off every minute of pretty much every day so she could save every penny, which is why she'd never been able to come to town "just because." I'd grown up in Queens, New York, where my mom had lived up until five years ago.

"She's really good," I told him. "She moved to Vermont the year after we graduated. Opened up a diner of her own and business is doing really well. It's always been her dream."

"Talia, that's incredible," Jack said genuinely. "Wow."

"I know," I agreed. "I'm so proud of her. She's always worked so hard. She deserves it. How's Julianna?"

Jack's face lit up at the mention of his sister. "She's great. Pregnant with her third baby."

"Seriously?" I said with a laugh. Jack's sister was five years older than us. I'd met her once when she'd come to Klein for Homecoming right before Jack and I had started hooking up. She was tall and thin and elegant, and she looked like she could scare the pants off the strongest of people when in actuality she was one of the sweetest

22

and most down to earth people I'd ever met, despite still being tough as nails. When I'd met her she'd been a few months away from marrying her now-husband Elliot and swore they would never have kids.

"Yep." Jack looked pleased. "I have two amazing nieces, Sophia and Ainsley. They're three and four and they're the most amazing human beings I've ever met."

Hearing him talk about his family made my insides stir with butterflies. I knew how fun and goofy Jack could be, and I could just imagine how much his nieces probably adored him and loved spending time with their uncle. The craving to see him in that setting was powerful, but I didn't want to completely acknowledge that. I wondered if he ever read them bedtime stories or had tea parties with them or took them to the park.

We chatted a little bit more about our families and people we had known mutually at Klein. Almost two hours had passed. Our server had cleaned off our lunches, brought us coffee and dessert, and now Jack and I were just sitting and drinking our coffees. I felt so relaxed and comfortable here with him. I was still amazed at how much it felt like almost no time had passed between us. We'd had lots of lunch and coffee dates at Klein even though I never called them dates. We'd sit and stare at each other over a sandwich, both of us imagining the other naked, and then we'd practically run to his apartment when the sexual tension finally became unbearable.

I still felt that stirring of arousal I'd always felt around him, but it was different now. It felt deeper and more profound as if the years had morphed the feelings we had for each other. Morphed them into something tangible and meaningful.

I couldn't act on the attraction I still felt for him. I knew that. I knew it would just destroy us both. That didn't stop me from savoring and enjoying the low hum of attraction that simmered just beneath the surface.

Jack had just taken a drink of his coffee when I asked him about law school. I watched his entire body tense up the exact way it had when I'd asked about where he was working. I pushed anyway because I was desperate to hear about his life in the six years he and I hadn't seen each other. And since law school had been three years of that, I was dying to know how it was.

"Did you enjoy it?"

Jack shrugged. "Sure. I liked the classes. Most of my classmates were cool."

"But?"

"But what?"

I shook my head. "Jack, the 'but' is so obvious in those sentences. What didn't you like about law school?"

Jack regarded me. "You still know me really well."

I wanted to take the time to be flattered and excited by his words, but I was more interested in hearing about him so I said, "And I know there's something about law school that you don't want to talk about or that you didn't like."

"I just..." He sighed. "It's not really about school. I just never saw myself as a corporate lawyer, you know? I wasn't like most of my classmates that way. I've been working for my dad's firm for the past year and not a day has gone by that I don't wake up dreading the day ahead. I just can't stand the type of people and companies we represent. I've wanted to be a lawyer since I was little. I thought my dad was a superhero, but I was naïve. I wanted to help people. I still want to help people, and every day I get further and further away from that."

"You don't have to stay away from that, though," I said, wishing I could do or say more to make him feel better. "You don't have to work for him."

"Yeah, that would not go over well," Jack said with an unamused laugh. "First, I break off an engagement that he had championed from day one, and then I quit my job? He'd probably have a brain aneurism."

Jack must have seen the look on my face and realized what he said because a second later his expression fell.

"Fuck, Talia." He leaned forward. "Fuck, fuck, I didn't want to bring that up. I'm sorry."

"Don't be sorry," I barely managed to say. My throat felt like it was about the size of a sewing needle. "You don't owe me an apology for being engaged." It's not like he and I were a couple or even heading in that direction. It's not like we ever were a couple despite how much Jack had said he wanted to be when we were sleeping together in college. He didn't owe me an explanation or an apology. He didn't owe me anything.

"Not anymore," Jack reiterated.

I must have been a masochist because I knew it would kill me to hear about him being engaged to someone, but I asked the question anyway. "What happened?"

Jack hesitated for several moments until he finally huffed out a breath. "Look, Rachel was fine. I mean, she was basically my mother thirty years younger. Her dad is richer than god—works as an investment banker—and the entire Saltzman family is deep in the New York social scene. Rachel was a caretaker and wanted to be there for me. She was at Harvard Law with me, and it was nice to have her companionship. But she was..." Jack glanced at me, most likely seeing the pain and anxiety written all over my face at hearing him talk about his ex, even if it wasn't all good things. But I had no right to be upset. Jack had always wanted more with me, and the only reason we didn't have it was because of me.

"She was what?" I asked him quietly.

Jack looked as pained as I felt as he spoke quickly. "She was cold. She rarely laughed. She didn't like to go out dancing or to street festivals or farmers markets. She wanted to go to art galleries and museums, and I may be a fucking Harding but I hate that pretentious bullshit."

I let out a short laugh, trying with all my might to ignore the fact that the things he'd said Rachel didn't like to do were all things he and I had done together.

"So, you two just didn't have much in common?" I asked after a moment.

Jack's eyes locked on mine for a long, charged moment before he spoke. I felt like I was trembling from head to toe with all the attraction and adrenaline coursing through me. I sent up a prayer of thanks that I was sitting because I knew if I hadn't been, my weakened knees would have betrayed how much Jack still affected me.

"It wasn't just that," Jack said, his voice gone rough and quiet. "I knew what it was like to be lit on fire with how I felt for someone. I knew what it was like to only want to be around that person—to miss them when they went away, to want every moment with them. And I knew I couldn't live my entire life with less than that. Not after I knew how alive it made me feel."

It felt like my heart had crumbled to ash in my chest. My stomach was in knots at his words. His words that he didn't have to say were about me. His words that reminded me of how much we'd meant to each other all those years ago. I'd never wanted to admit it, never wanted to see what was right fucking in front of me. But here he was. Dark hair and piercing green eyes that never hid, that never shuttered, that always showed me the truth.

The truth was that I wanted him. But so help me, I couldn't have him. I couldn't put him through that again. What I wanted still hadn't changed. I wasn't looking for commitments and two point five kids and weekends at the country club. I wanted fun and freedom.

But for the first time in my life, the promise of fun and freedom and independence felt empty and hollow.

Chapter 5

We strolled along Massachusetts Avenue until the sun started to set. After we'd finished up at Green Hornet, Jack had suggested we go for a walk since it was a beautiful autumn night. And since I was desperate for more time with him, I'd agreed.

We stopped in a book store that was a favorite of mine as well as a kitschy little thrift shop and a few other stores here and there. The thrift store had a long gold necklace with an emerald stone hanging from it that I vowed to come back for when I got paid from my next gig, and I bought a few used books from a store a few lots down.

I wanted Jack with a severity I had never known, and it was only made worse by the fact that I knew I couldn't be with him. I hadn't sent him that message to rekindle an old flame. I'd messaged him because he'd said he valued our friendship and wanted to catch up. I wanted that, too, because at the end of it all, Jack had been my friend long before we'd ever slept together. He made me laugh. He listened to what I said and genuinely cared about it. In his message he said he cared about me, and I cared about him too. I cared about him way too much to fuck this up by complicating things with sex. Despite that fact that when we were at the book store, he'd been looking at a book and had pulled a pair of glasses out of his back pocket to read, and I almost fainted because he looked so sexy. I didn't want to complicate things even though when we'd been in that tiny thrift store, he'd brushed against me so many times that I could swear he was going to be able to feel the heat of arousal flaring off my skin.

That wasn't what today was about. Today was, in a way, about making amends. It was about reconnecting and catching up, and it wasn't about how hot Jack looked in reading glasses or that Henley or how his jeans hugged every curve in his ass and powerful thighs.

Relax, Talia. Get a damn grip.

"So, um."

Jack's voice interrupted the voice in my head that was practically yelling not to throw myself at him.

I looked up at him and he looked shy and vulnerable. *Shit.*

"This is actually my place," he said, gesturing up at the huge, gorgeous brownstone next to us. "Would you want to come inside for a bit? I could make you dinner."

When he said the words, I realized how late it had gotten and how I was pretty hungry again since we'd been walking around for a few hours. But I knew—I *knew* this would end badly. When he asked the question, it sounded innocent enough. It was just dinner.

Yeah, right, the annoying voice in my head piped in. Just *dinner. In Jack's apartment. Alone. At night. Please.*

There were about five seconds when I listened to that voice and planned to turn Jack down and just hop on the train and head back home. But then he smiled—that sweet, genuine, open and honest smile—and I knew I couldn't stay away.

"Sure," I said, pushing all my worries to the back of my mind and telling that voice in my head to fuck off. "Dinner sounds awesome."

◆ ◆ ◆

No man had ever cooked for me before.

This had all been a miscalculation on my part because I had no idea what a man standing in front of stove stirring sauce could do to me.

I was sitting on his center island, one leg crossed over the other, holding the glass of white wine Jack had poured for me, while I admired how strong his forearms looked as he mixed the pasta in the pot in front of him.

"Here, try this," Jack said, turning toward me with a spoon in his hand.

I took a bite of the creamy white sauce, and as I wrapped my lips around the spoon, Jack's eyes bore into me, making the simmering arousal in my gut flare to life. And just because I could—just because I wanted to—I licked my bottom lip slowly as I pulled away. Jack's eyes darkened as he stared at my mouth, and he cursed under his breath as he turned back to the stove.

"Good?" he asked, back to me as he stirred.

"Mm," I replied. "Garlicky. Yum."

"Glad you like it."

His voice sounded rough. I stared at his back, watching the muscles ripple under his shirt as he made small movements. He'd pushed his sleeves up to his biceps again after rolling them down as we walked in the cool air, and his arms looked thick and strong. His forearms were veined and sure as they worked the different utensils and appliances. I wanted those arms around me, squeezing me, holding me down as he—

27

My thoughts came to an abrupt halt as the large metal spoon Jack was using to stir clattered on top of the stove. Jack let out an exasperated sigh and braced his arms on the counter.

"You okay?" I asked his back.

He didn't say anything for several moments. I was going to get off the counter and go to him, but instead he turned and walked out of the room. I gaped after him, slightly stunned, until a few moments later he walked back in holding a small brown paper bag. He handed it to me wordlessly and then backed up so he was leaning on the counter next to the oven, watching me with an unreadable expression.

I looked at the bag and back at him, confused.

"What's this?"

"Open it," he said with a nod toward the bag in my hand.

I frowned at him and looked down at the bag right before I pulled it open and looked inside. I gasped when I saw what it was, and when I reached in and pulled out the gold chain, my mouth hung open as I stared at Jack.

"Jack, you shouldn't have—"

"It's not a big deal," he said with a shrug. He was trying to play it off but I could hear the anxiety and vulnerability in his voice. "I saw you looking at it earlier and I bought it when you were in the bathroom."

It was the necklace I'd vowed to come back for, the one with a real gold chain and a real emerald.

"It's too much." My voice was thick and faraway sounding.

"No, it isn't," he said immediately. "Just think of it as six years worth of birthday presents."

I looked down at the necklace and back up at him several times. It was so thoughtful and kind and too much, and he was *killing* me. I was trying so hard not to want him, not to let things go where I knew we both wanted, but he was making it so outrageously hard. How was I supposed to deny how I felt about him when he was giving me this necklace he knew I wanted and cooking me dinner and telling me all the parts of his life that I'd missed?

I wanted to keep fighting it, but I wanted him too much.

"Will you put it on me?" I asked him quietly.

Jack didn't hesitate. He closed the distance between us and took the necklace from my hands, his fingers brushing mine as he did, causing electricity to zing through me.

Our eyes were on each other as he reached up to wrap the necklace around my throat. He was so close. It would be so easy to just lean in and kiss him, but I didn't know if that's what he wanted. But the air was buzzing, thick with tension as our eyes stayed

28

locked and I felt the tips of his fingers brush the back of my neck as he clasped the chain. I shivered as he slid his hands down my neck and held me there for just a moment, eyes one mine, until he blinked slowly and turned away.

His back was to me as he started stirring his pasta again, seemingly unaware of the battle he had just caused to rage inside me. We sat in silence for several long minutes until he sighed loudly and ran a hand down his face as he slammed the lid onto the pot and turned the heat off.

I stared at his back, waiting, watching, fingers gently toying with the emerald, and when he spoke, his words almost made me come apart.

"I want you, Talia," he said. "I fucking want you just as much as I did then, and I'm trying not to. I'm trying to be respectful. I'm trying not to be a fucking caveman and shove you down on that island and fuck you until you can't breathe."

Jesus.

I'd forgotten. Forgotten how candid Jack always was, how candid he was about what he wanted, sexually and otherwise. I forgot how much it turned me on when he told me he wanted me. I forgot about how much every single thing about him turned me on.

"Stop trying," I whispered against my better judgment. Because right then I didn't care. I didn't care what it would mean. I didn't care how I would feel tomorrow. I just knew that right then, even with his back to me, Jack was everything I had ever wanted.

"What?" Jack finally turned around and the bareness of the emotion in his eyes was startling.

"Stop trying to be respectful."

Jack groaned. "Talia, don't say that to me."

"I mean it," I said. Then, I uncrossed my legs on the counter and spread them slightly.

"Jesus fucking Christ."

We held there for several moments, both of us staring at the other, lost in each other as the tension grew and grew around us. It surrounded us like a thick cloud, expanding and rippling throughout the room. My chest was heaving, taking in air difficult as I tried to breathe him in from this distance.

Finally, Jack moved. He stalked toward me across the small space between the stove and the counter, like I was his prey, like he could snare me so easily and never let me go.

And maybe he wouldn't.

As he approached, the tension grew to its apex, stretched tightly like the string of a violin. I spread my legs even more and braced my hands on either side of me on the counter. He was standing a breath away, almost in between my legs but not close enough to touch. His hands were clenched into fists at his sides and he looked even more big and imposing than he usually did. I could swear I saw a tremble in his broad shoulders as he stared long and hard at me.

He stepped closer so that he was in between my spread legs. The sides of his thighs brushed the inside of mine, and even through the tight jeans I was wearing it felt like his skin was on mine. I wanted to rip his clothes off. I wanted him to want me just like he did all those years ago. I wanted that look of hunger in his eyes to burn me up, to never leave his face. And I knew it was wrong. I knew it was selfish and cruel to take what I wanted even when I knew I still wouldn't be able to give him what *he* wanted, but I couldn't stop. Not now. Not when he was standing between my legs and one of his hands was moving until it was resting on my knee.

Jack squeezed gently and held my gaze as he slid his hand up my thigh. He stepped closer, bringing his other hand up to my other knee and moving his hand slowly once more. Up, up, *up*, until both of his big hands were gripping me low on my hips. He pulled me closer to the edge of the counter as he moved in, never breaking eye contact, every move and every look giving me permission to stop anytime I wanted while still letting me know how badly he wanted it. And Jesus did I want it, too.

When his hands left my hips and moved to my hands, I sighed at the feeling of skin against skin even if it was as innocent as his palms touching the backs of my hands. I was wearing a sort of Boho shirt with trumpet sleeves and a deep V in the front that showed off my cleavage. I could feel that my neck and chest were flushed but I didn't care. It was obvious how much I wanted him no matter what I was wearing.

His hands slid up my arms, slowly, dragging along my skin underneath the sleeves of my shirt until he had to move his hands over my shirt to continue his ascent. When his hands reached the skin of my shoulders, I shivered. Then he was cupping my neck and moving in closer, fingers brushing my necklace, and the only thing I had ever wanted was to feel his lips on mine. Would he taste the same? Kiss the same? Would his tongue wrap around me the same way it always had—like he was getting a sample of the most delectable thing he'd ever put in his mouth?

He didn't lean in immediately but instead kept staring at me, and I started to beg silently.

Do it, Jack. Kiss me. Put your mouth on mine. On my neck, on my body. Kiss me and never stop. I want it. I know you want it, too. Please, Jack. Please.

"Talia—"

"Kiss me, Jack," I whispered before he could ask for the permission he couldn't possibly think he needed.

I expected him to ravage me. I expected him to kiss me in a way that felt just like the fire that was brewing in between us. I expected him to suck and bite and claim. What he did was so much more devastating.

His lips brushed mine. Softly, gently. His tongue didn't even peek out of his mouth. It was just his lips. His soft, full, sculpted lips that had always known exactly what I wanted and needed. They were sensual and teasing and perfect. I wanted so much more, but I also wanted his sweet assault to never end.

I shifted imperceptibly, widening my knees ever so slightly, and for some reason that small movement and the huff of breath I let out when I felt his thighs rub against me again spurred him into action. He deepened the kiss, lips firm against mine, and when his tongue came out and brushed against mine I almost moaned.

Our tongues danced, battled, pushed and pulled and drank each other in desperately. I brought my hands up around his neck and pulled myself closer so our bodies were flush. He was hot and hard against me, and I couldn't wait to rip his shirt off and see all that rippling muscle underneath. The muscle I had always died for and could never get enough of. There'd been days at Klein, long after Jack had fucked me and fallen asleep that I would just lay next to him, running my hands all over his gorgeous body. When he was asleep, I wasn't afraid he would read into what I was doing, but I was still free to give into the urge to make him mine.

I wanted to see it, see if it was even better than I remembered, so as soon as Jack pulled his mouth away from mine, panting against my neck, I took that opportunity to lower my hands to the hem of his Henley and lift it over his head.

He was even more gorgeous than I remembered.

"You're so hot," I whispered, voice harsh and hardly recognizable to my own ears.

"You are," Jack responded roughly before reaching forward and pulling off my shirt in return.

I was wet. Wetter than I could ever remember being. I could feel it as I shifted my hips on the counter. I wanted him inside me. I wanted to feel him, hot and thick, rubbing against my walls, giving me exactly what I needed.

He didn't hesitate before reaching behind me to unclasp my bra, and I gasped and arched my back when the cool air of the kitchen met my nipples, causing them to perk up. He looked at my breasts for just a few moments, getting his fill, before he leaned forward and sucked one into his mouth.

31

My hands immediately came up to wrap around the back of his head, holding him to me as he sucked at me, ravaged me, claimed me for his own. I tilted my head back, moaning softly, a sound that might have been his name.

He worked on my other nipple for a bit before pressing kisses along my chest, up my neck, until his mouth met mine again.

He kissed me hard as I wrapped my legs tightly around him. When Jack began to slowly thrust his hips against me, I whimpered, feeling his hard cock through his jeans, feeling the evidence of how much he wanted this. Wanted me.

"Fuck," he murmured against my neck, moving against me.

I couldn't take it anymore. I slipped my hands between us and began fumbling with his belt, practically ripping it off as I made quick work of it. I was about to yank his jeans down, but he pulled back suddenly, taking my wrists in his hands and moving them so I was leaning back on my hands on the counter as he worked my jeans open. He kept his eyes on me as he slid them down my hips. I lifted to help him and his eyes darkened. He dragged my underwear down along with my jeans until I was completely naked on his countertop.

Braced on my hands, my chest was pushed out, and I could only imagine the sight I made. On display for him, flushed, wet, and ready for anything he was willing to give me.

"Look at you," he rasped out, taking one step back and just letting his gaze roam slowly up my body until his eyes landed on mine. The fire behind those green eyes gutted me. It turned me on even more, and when I spread my legs so wide he could see how wet I was, he looked down for a moment before his eyes shot up to mine. I didn't have a moment more before he yanked me off the counter. I fell against him briefly before he whirled me around and shoved me down against the counter so my front was completely flush with the cool marble.

I was panting heavily in anticipation. I heard him fumbling with his jeans before I saw him toss his wallet on the counter next to my head. I bit my lip when I heard the sound of a foil packet ripping a moment later. I turned my head to look at him and he was staring down between our bodies.

"Jack," I moaned, and his eyes snapped up to mine.

"You want this?" His voice was gruff and hoarse with need, and it made me clench in anticipation.

"So much," I managed. "Fuck me."

He grunted, and when he plunged inside me in one swift move, I almost screamed. He was even bigger than I remembered. Thick and impossibly hard, pressed against every inch of me, filling me up so

32

perfectly that it was like he was made just for me. He held there for a moment, and when I shifted against him, grinding myself on his cock, he gripped my hips tight to stop my movement.

"Jack, please."

"Don't fucking move, Talia," he growled. "I'm going to come if you move at all."

"Want you to," I said, trying to grind against him only to have his hands tighten on me so hard that I knew I'd have bruises. "Move, Jack, I need it."

I couldn't remember the last time I was this desperate for someone to fuck me. Couldn't remember the last time I wanted it rough, wanted someone so deep inside me that I wouldn't be able to breathe. Wanted someone to just fuck me, just take me and claim me and make me their own. But I wanted Jack to do all of that. I wanted him to make me forget everything but him. I wanted him to make me his.

Finally, he started to move, slowly pulling in and out of me, and I swore I could feel every single inch of his flesh on every inch of mine.

I moved my hands up, clutching the other end of the island and moving against him as much as I could despite his firm grip.

He took it slow, like he was savoring each glide, but I was so impatient. I wanted more. I wanted him and I wanted it now.

"Harder," I begged. "Faster, Jack, please."

"Yeah?" he grunted. "You want it hard?"

"Please!" I moaned loudly. "Please, please."

I felt him pull all the way out of me, leaving just the head of his cock inside me, and my walls trembled in anticipation.

"Tell me you want it."

I moaned, so turned on I couldn't think.

"I want it," I finally choked out.

"What do you want?"

My face reddened, and I was glad he couldn't see it. I knew what he wanted me to say, and I wanted to say the words. Was almost embarrassed about how much I would mean them.

"Say it, Talia," he growled.

I wanted it too desperately not to give him the words he wanted.

"I want your cock," I gasped.

Jack groaned loudly right before he slammed into me. Then he was really fucking me. Pounding in and out of me, holding my hips in his strong hands, and dragging me back and forth along his length as he plunged in and out of me. I couldn't take it, wanted more, wanted to come but never wanted this sweet torture to end.

He leaned forward, his front pressed to my back as he continued to tunnel in and out of me. He was releasing the sexiest, dirtiest sounds, little grunts and groans each time he slide deeper and deeper inside of me. Deeper than anyone had ever been, even him.

I closed my eyes, savoring the feel of him, moaning loudly and incoherently, and as I gripped that counter, I felt flooded with memories of him, of us. I was overwhelmed by the memories of us just like this, me bent over his bed, holding back the moans I wanted to release because his roommates were home, just on the other side of the door. And he would fuck me just like this, hard, fast, deep, but it had never been like this. Never this deep, never this desperate, and he'd never been this hard and thick.

"Fuck, Talia, you're going to make me come."

I moaned at his words, still going back and forth between the memories of us and the power of this moment right now.

I clenched around him and he groaned deeply before one of his hands left my hips. As soon as I felt his thick fingers circling my clit I knew I was a goner. I pushed back against him as he fucked into me. It felt like he was everywhere—behind me, on top of me, inside me, surrounding me—and I was so overwhelmed with the feelings that I was worried about what would happen when I finally reached the apex of my pleasure.

"Jack," I gasped. Then I was moaning his name over and over, and I felt him grow even thicker inside me, and as soon as he let out a shout and I knew he was coming, I went over right with him. The feeling of him hitting that spot inside me while his fingers worked me was the most exquisite torment.

It felt like the orgasm went on forever, like it would never stop, like I could die from how incredible it felt as each wave of pleasure continued to violently roll inside me.

When I finally came down, I relaxed against the counter, trying to catch my breath, and Jack was lying on top of me, his hot breath a short staccato in my ear.

He didn't speak as he pulled back and slid out of me. I couldn't move. I stayed there, blissed out on the counter as I heard him moving behind me. I saw him walk to the trashcan out of the corner of my eyes, and I assumed he was getting rid of the condom. When he came back, he cursed under his breath and smoothed his hands up and down my ass.

"You're even sexier than you were in college," he said, almost reverently. I bit my lip and looked at him over my shoulder. Then he leaned forward and his lips found mine. He'd pulled his jeans back up because I could feel them rubbing against the bare skin of my ass as he kissed me deeply.

Usually, after I had sex with someone, I didn't want to think about touching them again for a while. My body always felt overly sensitized and strung out, but right now, as I ground my hips back against Jack I realized I could easily take him inside me again. I wanted more.

He kept kissing me, still bent over my back while I moved my hips against him. And after several minutes, I felt him getting hard again through his jeans.

"Do you want to eat dinner?" he whispered against my mouth, his hungry eyes meeting mine.

With some of my senses returned, I could smell the sauce on the stove, but more than that I could smell the scent of us lingering in the air, and I knew exactly what I wanted.

"Fuck dinner," I huffed into his lips. "I want to eat you."

A moment later he was lifting me up, and I squealed when he put me in a fireman's hold as he walked in the direction I assumed was his bedroom. He smacked my ass and I giggled, and that's when I felt the first stirring of worry. It couldn't be this good. This easy. We'd spent the entire day together, talking and laughing and getting to know each other again. He'd fucked me better than anyone ever had. And I wanted more. Of all of it—of his stories, of his laugh, of his body. How was I ever going to walk away? How was I going to be able to tell him that I what I wanted hadn't changed?

But when I landed on my back on his bed, watching him strip his jeans off before he climbed over me, all I could think was that I wanted this moment right here, and tomorrow be damned. I wanted tonight.

Chapter 6

Jack was asleep, curled on his side in the bed, sheets tangled around him. It had been about an hour since he'd slid out of me and pulled me against him, holding me tight and telling me to stay.

If he hadn't said those words, if he hadn't whispered *"stay"* in my ear, maybe I would have been able to do just that. But I knew what was behind those words. I knew what Jack wanted because it was what he'd always wanted. With that word, he'd reminded me of exactly why I told myself I couldn't do this. He reminded me of why I hadn't seen him in six years.

I wasn't someone who stayed. No matter how much Jack wanted me to be, no matter how much he told me he wanted more, I knew I couldn't give it to him. He wanted me to stay, but that just wasn't who I was, and it was all anyone I'd known had ever done. I'd learned from the best.

I slid out of the bed as slowly and delicately as I could, not wanting to move the bed even a smidge for fear of waking him. I knew he'd be upset that I left, knew he'd remember all the times I'd done it before, and I couldn't do it. I couldn't see his face when I left, the disappointment that everything was the same as it had always been.

I shouldn't have slept with him. I knew that now, I'd known before, but seeing him in the kitchen, sexy and confident with every move he made, when I'd seen the struggle he had not to want me, when he put that chain around my neck, I threw caution to the fucking wind. Because I still wanted him just as badly as I always had, maybe even more than I ever did. He was different than he was before and yet the same. He was still sweet, sexy Jack, but age had matured him. He'd become sure of himself in a way he hadn't quite been before, but at the same time there was a new vulnerability in him he had never shown me.

When he spoke, he spoke with a sureness of someone who knew what he wanted while still revealing that there was more that he craved. He was still kind—truly, genuinely kind in a way so few people were—an attentive listener while still being able to carry on any conversation. He was intelligent, smarter now that he'd been through law school and six additional years of growth, and he had a strength of body and mind that I couldn't get enough of. I knew I'd have bruises where he'd held my hips. Maybe I'd have them around my wrists from when we'd moved things to his bed and he'd pinned my arms above my head, gliding into me deep and slow, holding my gaze the entire time. It had frightened me for a moment when he refused to look anywhere but me. It felt like he was telling me something, conveying something he couldn't with words as he held me with both his hands and his eyes.

You're mine, his eyes said. *You're still mine. You always were. You always will be. Even if you try to fight it, I won't let you go.*

I cursed under my breath as I found my clothes in the now dark apartment. The light above the stove was on, congealed food in the pots and pans. I wandered over to the kitchen island, the remnants of our earlier sex lingering in the air and strewn about the floor. My clothes were scattered everywhere on the tile. I pulled my jeans up quickly and yanked my shirt over my head, not bothering with the underwear or bra. I walked over to the front door where I'd kicked off my shoes and dropped my purse. I slipped on my shoes as I was shoving the underwear in my bag, and my hand was going for the door knob when I heard the voice that almost made me jump out of my skin.

"Leaving so soon?" Jack asked quietly. When I turned to him, he was leaning against the doorframe that led to his bedroom, a smirk on his face that didn't reach his eyes.

"Yeah," I said, voice trembling from the fright he'd given me and from seeing him, shirtless, so near. "I have band practice early tomorrow and thought I'd get out of your hair."

He didn't say anything for several seconds. I thought he wasn't going to reply, but when he did, the hurt in his voice and the disappointment on his face caused a flush of unbidden shame to creep up my neck before the anger set in.

"Same old fucking Talia," he murmured. He looked at me for another moment, and it looked like he was going to turn back into his room when I called out to him.

"What the fuck's that supposed to mean?"

He scoffed when he turned back.

"You know exactly what it means."

I dropped my bag on the ground and put my hands on my hips, anger and adrenaline coursing through my veins. I was anxious and furious at myself and at him, and I was itching for a fight.

"Why don't you enlighten me?" I practically hissed. I knew I was being shitty, knew he was right, knew what he was going to say, but I wanted to hear him say it anyway. Maybe that would make this easier on both of us. Maybe if he hated me it wouldn't hurt when I walked away.

Jack shook his head. "You take what you want, everyone else be damned, and when you get it, you fucking leave."

"Excuse me?"

Jack took several steps out of the room and toward me, and I held my ground.

"You fucking heard me," Jack growled. "You're selfish and cowardly. You don't even have the guts to tell me goodbye. You were just going to slink out of here, and I bet you planned on ignoring my calls and texts tomorrow, huh?"

I didn't respond because that's exactly what I'd planned to do.

"But I guess I should just blame myself," Jack went on. "I knew you hadn't changed. It's been six years and you haven't dated anyone seriously." The truth of his words stung, but I was too angry and upset to reply right away so he kept on. "You're still terrified of letting someone in, of opening yourself up to hurt. And it's my own fucking fault for sleeping with you when I knew—god, I fucking *knew*—things wouldn't be different. That's why I didn't want to want you. I didn't want to let you in again. Not like that."

"First of all," I said, finally finding my voice. "You reached out to me. You sent me a message wanting to get together. You invited me into your apartment when you *knew I hadn't changed*. You told me you wanted me. You fucked me. So don't put this all on me, Jack. I never made any promises. I never fucking have."

"Of course not," Jack interjected angrily. "Making a promise to someone implies that you give a shit."

It felt like the bottom had dropped out of my stomach at his words. "That's not fair," I said, voice hoarse, even though I knew it was. I knew I'd hurt him—*was* hurting him—I knew I shouldn't have opened this door again, but I wanted him too badly not to. I knew I shouldn't do this to him, but I couldn't stop myself because even after all these years he was still the only man who made me even think about wanting more.

Jack sighed and put his hands low on his hips, looking at the floor. He shook his head.

When he didn't say anything after a while, I said, "I'm going to go." I bent down and picked up my bag.

"Let me take you home," he said quietly, not meeting my eyes.

"No," I said, the tears threatening to fall because even when I'd hurt him—again—he was still thinking of me. "I'll call an Uber." I reached up, my bag slipping to my elbow as I grabbed for the clasp on the necklace he'd given me.

"Keep it," he murmured, still not looking at my face, his eyes on the necklace. "Please."

I turned toward the door before he could see the tear escape. I heard his footsteps as he closed the distance between us. I couldn't turn back, couldn't look at him or I knew I'd fall apart.

"It was good to see you again, Talia."

His words tore at something inside me because I knew they were goodbye. And this time I knew it was going to be forever.

"I hope you find what you're looking for."

It was such a fucking cliché. And it still destroyed me.

"Goodbye, Jack."

He watched me as I walked down the stairs, and even though I didn't look back I could feel his eyes on me. When I got out into the chilly New England evening, I could barely see the screen of my phone as I requested my car, the tears blurring the night.

◆ ◆ ◆

"Why did you sleep with him, Tal?"

Catrina's words made me feel even shittier than I already felt.

When I'd gotten home after leaving Jack's place, I couldn't sleep. I tossed and turned all night, stupidly refusing to shower because I wanted to smell his scent that lingered on my skin. Finally, I'd glanced at the clock on my phone and saw that it was six in the morning, so I gave up and pushed myself out of bed, sad and exhausted and regretting my life choices.

I'd sat in the windowsill of my tiny apartment, watching the sunrise and drinking coffee. I couldn't stomach eating anything. When I'd tried to eat a piece of toast, I'd run to the bathroom a few minutes later and thrown up. Then I'd called Catrina because I knew she'd be getting ready to go to rehearsal.

"Because I'm a fucking idiot," I said.

"I mean, the stuff he said was out of line," Catrina said slowly.

"It wasn't, Cat," I whispered. "I hurt him. Again. I wish I could stop hurting him."

Cat didn't say anything at first. She went so long without talking that I said "hello" to see if she was still there.

"I'm here," she said quietly. There was another long pause until Catrina said, "Look, Talia, I need to say something to you because I love you and you're my best friend in the entire world, okay?"

I braced myself. I didn't reply to Cat but my heart was pounding. I should've told her I didn't want to hear what she had to say. That if she was going to scold me about how vile I was to Jack—how vile I had always been to him—I didn't need the reminding. I knew all of it.

I knew I kept treating him like shit, but I wanted him so badly even though I knew I couldn't have him. Didn't deserve him.

So I stayed silent as Cat spoke.

"I know you have feelings for Jack. I know you've had feelings for Jack since college. If you want to be his friend, I think that's really awesome. But if you want to keep doing this—sleeping with him when you feel like it, when you know he wants more and you don't— just... Talia, just please don't. Jack is a nice guy. And he's been in love with you for years." I wanted to protest and tell her that couldn't be true because he was engaged only a few months ago, but my heart was still beating too hard for me to form a sentence. "You can't keep doing this to him or to yourself."

"I know," I finally managed, voice thick.

"I just want to know something, Tal."

"What?" I croaked.

Cat took a deep breath. "It's been ten years," she said, and blood started rushing in my ears. "How much longer are you going to keep pushing men away? They aren't all him. They aren't all either of them. Jack isn't—"

"Cat, I have to go," I interrupted quickly. "Rehearsal starts in a few hours and Isaac has been a hard ass lately about being on time. So, look—"

"Talia—"

"I'll talk to you later, okay?" And before my friend could even respond, I hit the end button on my phone and tossed it across my couch, unwilling to take another moment to think about both of the men who had taught me to guard my heart.

Chapter 7

Trying to play music with my band when all I could think about was Jack was an exercise in futility.

And it wasn't just Jack that I was thinking about.

"It's been ten years..."

God, was Catrina right? Had it been ten years already?

It felt so fresh and vivid in my mind that somedays it felt like it was still happening. Other times it felt like a memory of a time eons ago. Almost like a dream that I could only vaguely remember.

Today, it was the former. I could see his face smiling at me. I could see my eighteen-year-old self—stars in her eyes—looking at this guy and thinking he could have anyone he wanted and yet for some reason he'd chosen me. *I'm so lucky*, I would think while I stared at him as he talked.

It wasn't luck that had brought us together.

No, that wasn't what it was at all. It was the selfish desires of a boy who fancied himself a man, who felt himself invincible. It was the reckless pursuit of a girl who was so desperate for a man to love her that she couldn't see all the signs.

My girl, he would call me. *"There's my girl,"* he would say, or *"How's my girl today?"* Being his girl made me giddy with happiness. It made me crave him—his presence, his touch, his eyes on me. When he asked me how I was, if he listened for even a moment I felt honored. Even when he would look at his phone a few minutes later while I was still talking, even that small bit of attention would carry me on a cloud for days. When he touched my hair and told me it would look good shorter, I'd gone to the salon the next week. I kept that bob haircut for years because I thought it was the only way a man would find me attractive.

I'd let him take my virginity. When he moved over me, I ignored the pain because he told me I was beautiful. It didn't even bother me that it only lasted a few minutes and as soon as he was done, he rolled off me and grabbed his phone off his nightstand and didn't talk to me for another hour. He let me lay my head on his chest, though, and I kept replaying that moment when he said I was beautiful over and over. I'd given an enormous piece of myself to him and he didn't even ask if I was okay after. But he told me I was beautiful and that's what I'd clung to.

The day he left for New York after graduation, I'd sobbed into his chest. He rubbed my back, told me it would be okay, that we would see each other soon, that absence made the heart grow fonder. I swore I would come visit, and I regretted that I'd taken an internship at the Boston Conservatory instead of going back home to Queens for the summer, despite what an amazing opportunity it had been. I just wanted to be with him.

When he didn't answer his phone for the first two days, I attributed it to him being busy after just moving. Catching up with friends, having dinner with family, unpacking all of his stuff. He'd call me the second he got a free moment.

After a week I started to worry. My calls started going straight to voicemail so I started texting him frantically asking if he was okay. I called his friend Stephen who sounded taken aback when he heard my voice on the other end. He sputtered out a reply, saying something about having Vince call me if he heard from him.

It was two Saturdays after he left Klein that I got his text.

Hi. I can't see you anymore. Distance is too hard. Wish you all the best.

Seven fucking months. He and I were dating for seven fucking months and he had the nerve to send me a break up text that ended with *wish you all the best.*

And what I'd found out later had destroyed any remaining trust I had for men.

It was ten years later and it still hurt like hell.

"Jesus! Talia! I called your name like four times."

I looked up from the keyboard and saw Chuck, the guitarist of Flora and Fauna, watching me with annoyance clear on his face. Isaac was giving me a sympathetic look.

"Sorry."

"You've been distracted all day," Chuck said angrily. "Do you want to get this song perfected or not? Because you seem you like you couldn't give a shit."

Chuck and I had been friends once. Back when we started the group, Chuck and I were both doing open mic nights with nothing much to show for it. He was funny and charming and cute in a nerdy jock type of way. He was still a talented guitarist, but he was also a complete asshole who was addicted to cocaine and pills. When he was high he was manic—wanted to write a million songs and exude all of his energy—and when he wasn't, he was pissed off that he wasn't and that made him a jerk.

"Cool it, Chuck," Isaac said from behind the drums. "We all have our off days."

"Whatever," Chuck said, putting down his guitar on its stand. "I'm gonna take a break."

"I.e. get high," Isaac murmured as soon Chuck walked through the studio doors and out of earshot. He put his drumsticks in their holder and walked over to where I was still sitting at my keyboard, absently playing a random string of notes.

"That sounds nice," he said from behind me. "What is it?"

I looked up at him and stopped playing. "It's not anything," I said with a shrug. "Just messing around."

"Scooch."

Isaac sat next to me on the bench and began playing a harmony with the notes I'd just been playing. I wasn't lying to him when I said it wasn't anything. Chuck was right. I was distracted. I couldn't stop thinking about my past that I wanted to keep buried and the look of hurt and anger in Jack's eyes the night before. I was exhausted from not sleeping, and my entire body felt like an exposed nerve—raw and stretched too thin.

We played together for a few minutes. Eventually I started humming a melody and Isaac responded by humming an answering tune. He occasionally sang harmony on some of our songs, but I always forgot how nice his voice was. We sat like that, playing and humming together until the chords started to flow in a way that made sense, until we'd basically sat together and written a song.

I didn't know how much time had passed, but we kept playing as Isaac glanced over at me.

"You okay?"

This was the Isaac I adored—the guy who cared more about me, his friend, than he did about hooking up or flirting.

I sighed. "Been better."

He nodded. "Do you want to talk about it?"

"I'd rather just play this song with you," I said after a moment.

"That I can do," he said with another nod.

When Chuck came back in, his eyes were glassy and he was jittery and bouncy. Isaac and I exchanged a look, and Isaac went over to talk to him while I drifted over to my bag to check my phone. I shouldn't have even hoped for it, but I was desperate to hear something from Jack. But he'd said everything last night, and I was sure he never wanted to see me again after that. That didn't stop me from opening my text and Messenger app to see if he wrote anything.

When I opened my text app, I had texts from Catrina and Carver.

Catrina's text was apologizing for what she said on the phone earlier, so I shot off a quick response. *No need to apologize, Kitty Cat. I'm just tired and fucked up and I don't want to think about it anymore. Still love you.* She was at rehearsal so probably wouldn't respond for a while, so I moved to look at my friend Carver's text.

Carver Hicks was one of my best friends from Klein, along with Catrina and Callum Jeffries. He worked for Boston Public Radio and lived in an adorable townhouse in the suburbs and also had a shitty boyfriend that I despised.

Wanna get drinks tonight? Michael's being a fucking ass.

Of course he was. Carver and Michael had been on again/off again dating since college. Carver was a year older than Catrina and I, and Michael was four years older than Carver. They'd met at a bar Carver's sophomore year and had been seeing each other pretty much ever since. In college they would always date for a few months until Michael decided to break things off for some ridiculous reason—he needed to focus on work, he needed to help his family, his cat died and he needed to reevaluate a few things. A few months after Catrina and I left Klein, Carver had been the one to break things off. I'd thought it was the real thing this time, and it was for about a year. And then one night Carver met up with me, Catrina, and Callum for drinks, and when I saw Michael trailing behind him, I almost got up and left.

That was the longest span of time they dated—almost a year and a half—until Michael said he wanted to be with someone more serious. Someone who was going somewhere with their life. I thought that was Carver's final straw because I could see how hurt he was when he told me what Michael had said. As far as I knew, they didn't speak at all for almost three years. And then three months ago, Carver dropped the bomb on us that he and Michael were giving it another go.

As much as I wanted to let loose tonight and stop thinking about Jack, I didn't think I had it in me to pretend to care about whatever shitty thing Michael had done this time.

Can't tonight. Maybe Thursday or Friday? I replied to Carver. By then, though, he and Michael would've probably already resolved this current fight and moved on to the next one.

◆ ◆ ◆

A few weeks later, I was right. Carver and Michael were sitting across a high-top table from me, arguing quietly with each other. I had no idea what they were arguing about, but I kept exchanging glances with Cat and Callum who were sitting on either side of me.

The three of us were squished around a round table with Carver, Michael, and Brody. I had just finished playing a set and we were taking a break. Isaac was flirting with an emo looking guy at the bar, and Chuck was nowhere to be seen, even though I knew exactly where he was and what he was doing.

I knew that eventually Isaac and I were going to have to have a conversation with Chuck, but tonight I didn't want to think about that. I'd finally gotten my afternoon and evening with Jack Harding out of my head, and I was prepared to focus on making music.

The song Isaac and I had played together was really coming together as well as a few others he and I had been working on over the past few weeks. Over the years, we had released several EPs and one full length album. Because studio space was so expensive, we spent most of our time playing at different venues rather than spending time recording, but I was excited about what Isaac and I had done together and hoped to have a conversation soon about getting in the studio again for the first time in two years. Isaac may have been a total sleaze when it came to people he slept with, but he was a talented musician and I loved making music with him.

"And he's a complete ass, right?" Callum was saying. He was telling Catrina, Brody, and I about a student in one of his classes. "Every time he comes to my office hours, he swaggers in and plops down like he'd rather be anywhere else in the world. I'm not even sure why he bothers to come because I don't give them any credit for coming to see me, but he does. Every week. And here's the thing. The stuff he writes is really good. Like really, *really* good. When we were covering Hardy, he wrote this poem that gave me chills."

"Well, I know it seems like he doesn't care, but he obviously does," Brody said. Brody was a writer and Callum was an English Literature professor at Klein, so they often ended up swapping stories or talking about different books they were reading.

"Why would he show up to office hours if he didn't care?" Cat added.

"What do you usually discuss when he meets with you?" I asked.

"That's the thing!" Callum said, leaning forward on the table. "We hardly ever discuss the class or his assignments. He usually points out something he's read that week, asks my opinion on it, and then leaves after about fifteen minutes."

Cat and I exchanged a glance and Brody just shook his head.

"Weird, man," Brody said. "Maybe he doesn't care about the class then."

"He doesn't," Cat and I said at the same time.

Brody and Callum looked at us, and I looked at Catrina. "Do you want to tell him, or do you want me to?"

Catrina looked like she was trying to contain a smile when she turned to Callum.

"What is it?" Callum asked, frowning.

Catrina did grin then. "Cal, the kid's got a crush on you."

When Brody laughed, it finally got Carver and Michael's attention. Michael continued to pout, but Carver turned to us while I tried not to roll my eyes at the two of them.

"Who has a crush on Cal?" Carver asked.

"A kid in his intro class," I said.

Callum was shaking his head furiously. "That—well, that's not— you guys, that's not true. He doesn't—"

"Really?" I said exasperatedly. "He seems like he has no interest in the class. He barely pays attention and when he comes to office hours he doesn't actually want to discuss the class. He wants your opinion about the stuff he reads because he thinks you're smart and interesting. It helps that you obviously enjoy his work and I'm sure he knows it because you probably leave praising comments on his stuff."

"Oh, my god, that—" Callum sputtered. "No. He doesn't—no."

"He totally does," Carver said with a grin. "Oooh, I'm excited! A boy's got a crush on you."

At Carver's show of excitement, Michael got up from the table and walked in the direction of the bathrooms. Carver—to my delight— ignored him completely and scooted his chair closer to Callum.

"Tell me everything about him." Carver rested his chin in his hand and looked at Callum with wide, playful eyes.

"I refuse to get into this," Callum said. Even in the dark of the club I could see that his face was red.

"I think it's awesome," Brody said with a shrug. "The kid clearly admires you and values your opinion."

"And he's hot for teacher," Catrina said.

"Totally hot for teacher," I agreed.

"Is he cute?" Carver asked.

"I don't like men. And he's fucking nineteen," Callum said through clenched teeth.

"So?" Carver said. "I thought one of our interns this summer was hot and he was twenty."

Catrina and I laughed and Brody shook his head while Callum stayed silent.

"Anyway, I think he cares about the class even if it's only because he has a harmless crush," Brody said.

"Whatever," Callum said right as Michael rejoined the table. Out of the corner of my eye, I saw him put a hand on Carver's thigh. I looked at Carver to see how he would react since the two were clearly still pissed off at each other, and I noticed the smallest shift in him. The acceptance of Michael's olive branch. God, it enraged me seeing my friend settle for this guy when he could do so much better.

"What about you, Talia?" Carver looked at me. "Any new groupies lately?"

As if on cue, as if the universe was designed to be as cruel to me as possible, I looked at Carver, and over his shoulder, standing at the front entrance of the club, was Jack fucking Harding.

Chapter 8

F*uck. Fuck fuck fuck.*
Why was Jack here? And why did he look so damn good? He was lingering near the entrance, scanning the bar, and he looked downright edible. He looked like he'd come straight from work in a perfectly tailored gray suit that fit tightly over his arms and thighs making him look impossibly bigger. He'd taken off his tie and unbuttoned a few buttons, and the casual millionaire look was totally doing it for him. And for me.

When his eyes landed on me he gave me this small, nervous smile that made my heart flutter in my chest.

"Talia?"

When I looked up, Catrina was giving me a worried look as she glanced between me and Jack.

"I'm okay," I said before scooting off my chair. "I'll be right back."

I walked over to Jack, my eyes on him the entire time, and when I got close enough, he gave me another smile, this one more open.

"If you want me to leave, I will," was the first thing he said.

God, he was so considerate. Even after what I'd done to him, he was still thinking of me. Part of me wanted to tell him to go. I didn't trust myself around him, especially not when he looked this good. I didn't trust myself to not throw myself all over him and beg him to take me home. Not only that, but being on stage, having him watch me with that intense green stare, was going to be a huge distraction.

The bigger part of me, though, the one that still desperately wanted him and wanted him to want me, wanted nothing more than for him to stay and watch the rest of my set. I wanted him to see me with my band, to tell me I was talented, to look at me with that honest gaze and tell me he enjoyed seeing me in my element. And it was that part of me that replied to him.

"No, I don't want you to leave."

Jack's features softened a bit, and then he took another step closer to me, which forced me to tilt my head back slightly to keep his gaze.

"I'm sorry for what I said a few weeks ago," Jack said. "I... you were right. I was the one who wanted to see you. You didn't force me to do anything, and you're right. You didn't make me any promises. You never have."

"I shouldn't have left like I did," I replied, hands shaking. "I just..." I trailed off because I didn't know what to say, and I shrugged like a dope.

"I meant what I said. I missed our friendship, and, despite everything, I'd like to go back to that," Jack said. "We shouldn't have slept together, and we... we can't again. I get that. I get that it's what's best for both of us. But I still want to know you, Talia. I'd like to be your friend if you'd let me."

His words made my stomach clench painfully. Because as much as he might have been right that we shouldn't have slept together, it still hurt to hear the words come out of his mouth. I knew he was right, knew it was a mistake when we would never want the same things, but the last thing I wanted was for Jack to regret being with me. I was such an idiot.

"I'd like that," I said in spite of myself. Even if it hurt, I didn't think I was ready to let Jack go again just yet. Being his friend may drive me to madness, but I wanted to be around him so much that I just didn't care about the consequences. I'd take whatever scraps he was willing to give me. I just wanted to be near him.

When I brought him over to where my friends were all sitting, Brody was the first one up and pulled Jack into an embrace. I knew Brody and Jack were still friends, but I didn't know how much of our relationship he'd heard from either Jack or Catrina. If he knew anything, he never let on, but it still made me wonder. It still made me question if he somehow saw me in a different light knowing how things had gone down with his friend.

"Jack, you remember Callum and Carver, right?" I asked. Jack nodded and reached out his hand to shake each of theirs.

"Good to see you guys again."

"Likewise," Carver said with a broad smile.

"Good to see you," Callum said.

"This is Michael, Carver's boyfriend," I said gesturing to Michael who was sitting as far away from everyone as he could at a round table, not interacting with anyone. He nodded in Jack's direction, and I withheld an eyeroll. "And you know Catrina of course."

Jack smiled brightly as Cat walked around the table.

"It's so good to see you, Cat," Jack said as he and Catrina hugged. My stomach knotted painfully at seeing how happy they were to see each other, at how they embraced like old friends. Cat said something to Jack that I couldn't hear that caused him to smile again when they pulled away from each other. Sudden and overwhelming jealousy came over me in that moment. Not because I thought Cat and Jack meant something romantically to each other, but at the realization that the two had probably been in some form of communication with each other over the years. I was jealous over the idea that Catrina had possibly gotten to experience all those years that I'd missed out on.

It was crazy that I hadn't thought it before. I knew Jack and Brody were good friends. Of course they'd probably had him over for dinner in the six years since college had ended. When the thought came over me that they may have had both Jack and his fiancée over, I almost doubled over in pain.

"Talia?"

I jumped at the sound of Catrina's voice, and she shot me a small frown.

"Carver wants to do a round of shots. You in?"

"God yes," I said, not looking at either her or Jack.

A few minutes later, Carver brought back six shots—one for everyone except Catrina who was her and Brody's designated driver for the evening—and I still didn't look in Jack's direction as I threw back the shot and immediately went to the bar for another.

"What'll it be, babycakes?" Eric asked when I slid onto a bar stool.

"Tequila," I replied.

"You got it. Lime?"

I nodded, and when I looked over my shoulder and saw Jack, Catrina, and Brody all talking, I turned back to the bar and called out, "Actually, make it a double."

♦ ♦ ♦

By the time we finished our set for the evening, I was so wired that I was practically bouncing on my toes.

I had another shot of tequila before going on stage and a shot and two drinks while I was on. I was beyond buzzed, but the adrenaline from the show and from Jack's presence was almost having a sobering effect on me.

Which was why I was at the bar watching Eric pour me another shot of tequila.

"You're letting loose tonight, huh mama?" Eric said as he set the shot glass and the lime in front of me.

I giggled a bit when he winked at me, unable to get rid of my stupid crush on him no matter how hard I tried. He looked good tonight like he did every damn time I saw him, so of course I took notice—I'd have to be blind not to—but that didn't stop the thoughts of Jack from invading my mind.

During the show, I tried with all my might to keep my eyes off Jack. But when we got to the ballads, especially "In All Things"—a song I had written just a few weeks after I'd seen him the last time right after college when I was trying to pretend like I wasn't heartbroken even though I totally was—it was impossible for my eyes not to drift in his direction. I could feel his eyes on me the entire time, feel him watching me, studying me in that intent way he was so good at. The way that made it seem like I was the only person who existed in the entire world.

His eyes had only strayed once, and it was right near the end of the set when we played our second to last song—a funky, bluesy tune that was up tempo and almost had some bluegrass vibes to it. It was always a crowd favorite, and when my eyes had wandered to Jack, for the first time in the five years since we'd formed Flora and Fauna, I almost lost the beat of the song.

I'd seen Jack standing off to the side from the table where my friends were—all enjoying the heck out of my song and singing along—with a tall, beautiful woman with long black hair who basically looked like a gorgeous young version of Cher. She was stunning, and she kept looking at him and smiling, casually touching his arm as they talked. He gave her one of his smiles that made my heart stutter.

In that moment I wanted to take my drink and hurl it across the room at both of them, but I forced myself to look away and sing my heart out for the last two songs. When I'd gone off stage, my friends had tried to congratulate me and tell me what a good job we did, but I made a beeline for the bar, where I was currently sitting, sucking on a lime after downing my fourth tequila shot of the evening.

Five if you counted the double before I went back on stage.

Eric was right. I was definitely letting loose.

"Hey."

My heart lurched when I heard Jack's voice right before he slid into the bar stool next to me.

"Hey."

"You're incredible up there, you know that?"

They were the words I'd wanted to hear all night from him, but for some reason all they did was piss me off.

"Thanks."

"Do you—"

"What can I get for you?"

Jack looked up at Eric. "Just a water. Thanks, man."

Eric nodded and looked at me. "You good, babe? Need anything else?"

I blushed. *Of course* I blushed. And the bar area was lit enough for either Jack or Eric to see. Eric had to know how much he affected me, but he never let on, just smiling gamely when I went all school girl on him.

51

"Tequila," I told him.

Eric shook his head. "Tal, I cannot give you anymore tequila. You weigh a hundred pounds and I've already given you more than I probably should."

I laughed. "A hundred pounds?" I grabbed my ass and lifted a little off my stool. "You've seen my ass, right?"

I ignored Jack's intake of breath next to me when Eric just shook his head again. "Obviously I've seen it. The point still stands."

"Oooh," I slurred. "Checking me out? Aren't you married?"

Eric chuckled. "Babe, if I was checking you out, you'd know it."

When Eric set two waters in front of us and turned to go, I heard Jack laughing next to me.

I glared at him. "What?"

He shrugged. "Nothing. You just totally have a crush on that guy."

I opened my mouth and closed it a few times, caught unawares by Jack's completely correct observation and stunned that he would say it so casually. Did he care at all that I found another man attractive? He apparently really was only interested in friendship with me because even seeing him talk to another woman made me see red.

"No, I don't."

Jack scoffed. "You blush every single time he looks at you. When he said that thing about you knowing it if he checked you out I thought you were going to faint."

"Whatever," I murmured, taking a huge swig of the water Eric had left in front of me.

"I get it," Jack said. "He's a good looking guy."

"Sounds like you're the one with the crush."

Jack lifted one shoulder. "Maybe."

In spite of myself, I giggled.

Jack opened his mouth to say something, but right then Catrina and Brody came over.

"How you getting home, girl?" Brody asked.

"Um, *dad*, I live six blocks away."

"Um, *daughter*, it's midnight and you're a little girl," Brody replied.

"Don't tell her that," Jack said. "When the bartender hinted at it, she grabbed her own ass."

I shrugged. "I'm not little."

Catrina raised her eyebrows in my direction and I shoved a hand at her shoulder. "Hello? You're supposed to be on my side? Best friends? Hello?"

"I am on your side in all things except this."

52

I huffed and took another drink of water.

"I'll walk her home."

I choked on my water when Jack spoke.

"No, you won't," I said hoarsely.

Jack ignored me. "It was great to see you, Cat." Jack and Catrina hugged as I, again, tried to protest Jack walking me home and was, again, ignored.

I'd had too much tequila to be trusted if Jack walked me home.

"We're still on for Xbox and chill this weekend, right?" Brody asked as he and Jack embraced in a manly hug.

"Of course," Jack said with a grin.

"Bye," Catrina said as she wrapped her arms around me. "I love you, and don't do anything stupid."

When she pulled back, she gave me a pointed look, and I gave her one right back.

"Bye, Tally girl," Brody said as he hugged me.

After Brody and Catrina left, I stood up. "I can walk myself, thank you."

"Whatever."

Before I could reach for my back pocket, Jack threw a one hundred dollar bill on the counter and turned to go. I gaped after him.

When he made it a few feet away he turned back. "You coming, or what?"

Damn, I wish.

Chapter 9

The walk to my apartment was excruciating. It was only six blocks, but it felt like six hundred miles because of how desperately I needed to get home and away from Jack before I let the tequila take over.

We didn't speak the entire walk. I didn't know if I was the only one feeling the tension, but it was surrounding me like a fog.

I still wanted him. We couldn't be together. We wanted completely and utterly different things. Jack wanted a relationship and a future and love and commitment, and those were all things I had no interest in. Relationships ended in heartbreak, and who the hell would want to willingly subject themselves to pain? I wasn't a masochist.

Or maybe I was.

Because walking next to Jack, feeling his arm occasionally brush mine felt like the most painful thing in the world, but I still craved it. Every jolt of awareness set my heart racing and my hands shaking, made me feel like I was coming out of my skin, like one more light touch was going to set me ablaze.

When we got to my building, I stopped and Jack shoved his hands in his pockets and looked at the ground. His face was shadowed by the light coming from one of the street lamps, but he looked much more relaxed than I felt.

He didn't say anything for a while, and I wasn't really sure what I was supposed to do—hug him and thank him for coming to the show, for walking me home? Is that a thing that *just friends* would do? What I knew was that I wanted his arms around me, and that was a dangerous thing to want because if I felt his strong arms around me, I'd die from the want, from the need that had taken over my entire body.

I was just about to turn to go without so much as a word or acknowledgement since he'd made no move to do either.

"You're really talented," he said suddenly, still not looking at me.

I gaped like a fish, opening and closing my mouth because I was so surprised and flattered and pleased by his words that I'd stopped functioning like a normal human being who could just take a compliment and not think there was anything behind it other than that.

"Thanks," I finally managed.

"I never really got to see you perform in college," he said, studying his shoes. It was such a strange and insecure gesture from someone who was typically so sure of himself, from someone who just a half hour ago was teasing me about a crush I had on a bartender. "I mean, I knew you could sing," he added. "You used to sing in the shower and... yeah, I knew you could sing."

The reminder of us, of a past that felt like a lifetime ago and yet so vivid and present in my mind that it could have been yesterday, made my stomach flip. There had been nights over the years that I would lay awake and remember our time together—his hands on me, his mouth on mine, the way he smelled, the way he laughed, the sounds he made when he came—and I would ache for him. I'd gone years missing him, craving him, sleeping with other men and closing my eyes and trying to imagine it was Jack, trying desperately to cling to memories that had never faded over time, not even a little.

Sometimes it felt like a movie replaying in my mind incessantly, like a song I couldn't get out of my head no matter how many songs I listened to in an effort to just get that song out that was driving me mad. Sometimes it felt like I remembered every single moment together, every night we spent in his bed or in mine, all the times he came over smelling like beer and sweat and slid under my sheets and into my heart and into my body while we were forced to be quiet since Catrina's room and mine shared a wall. He'd put his hand over my mouth as he braced himself behind me, the sounds of his body slamming against mine louder than any sound I could have made even though neither of us cared even a little bit when we were lost to each other.

I remembered those other moments, too. Hearing him on the phone with his sister, who it was obvious he adored, dancing with him at clubs, the day he asked me to his sister's wedding and I lost it. And knowing that he might have remembered those different times, too—that he remembered me singing in the shower—made me feel an overwhelming affection for him.

"Everyone sounds good in the shower," I said, trying to deflect his compliment because it felt like if I let that compliment in, there was no telling how much it would blur the lines.

He finally looked at me. His eyes were dark and intense. "Not like that. Not the way you sounded. You're really good, and it was amazing to see you perform up there. You looked so at home on that stage."

I felt my face warm with pleasure. "Thank you," I said quietly. "I love being up there."

"Everyone can feel that," he said with a nod.

We looked at each other, unspoken words flowing out of us and between us—*I don't know if I can just be your friend*, his eyes seemed to say. *I don't know how to stop the way I feel about you*, my eyes answered back. *I want you, I want this, I don't want to see you with anyone else, and we need to get off this sidewalk before we do something that we aren't ready to face the consequences of.* Those were words from both of us.

"I need to go," were the words that actually came out of Jack's mouth.

"Okay." Regret washed over me, and I realized I didn't want him to go. I wasn't ready to say goodnight. It felt like my tequila buzz had worn off completely because there was no room for tequila when I was intoxicated by Jack's presence.

He didn't move despite his words.

"What if I don't want you to go?" I couldn't stop the words before they came tumbling out.

Jack's eyes flicked to my mouth, and then he shook his head.

"If I don't go, I'm going to kiss you."

His words made my heart surge. My god, did I want him to kiss me.

"I wouldn't mind if you did."

He looked at my mouth again, and I licked my lips.

"We still want different things," he said, eyes still on my mouth. "I don't want to do anything that either of us might regret in the morning." He stepped closer, and I tilted my head back slightly to look at his face. "Because if I kiss you, I won't be able to stop. And tomorrow, I'll still want more, and it'll kill me to see you walk away again."

His words gutted me. My throat and chest felt tight at the words he spoke so honestly and so bluntly. But he was right, no matter how badly I didn't want him to be, no matter how much it made me wonder if I was making a horrible mistake.

"So, I'm going to watch you walk up those stairs and go inside, and tomorrow we'll be friends."

I nodded even though everything in my mind and body was screaming at me to protest. "Tomorrow we'll be friends," I repeated.

This time it was him who walked away.

◆ ◆ ◆

"So, you got home safe and—"

"Did you and Brody have Jack and Rachel over for dinner?"

The question had been lingering in my mind ever since Jack had left me standing at my door while I was wishing things could be different. I wasn't going to be able to sleep until I knew the answer even though I knew I didn't truly want to know.

"Wh-what?"

"Just tell me, Cat. I have to know or it's gonna drive me nuts. Did you meet her?"

"Talia—"

"Catrina, please."

She sighed, and I knew the answer from that small noise.

"Shit," I whispered. "When?"

"Look, Tal, you always said Jack wasn't your boyfriend. And as untrue as I think that is, that's what it was. He was engaged to her, and he's Brody's friend. It could've—" Cat abruptly stopped. "Well, it didn't have to be that way, but that's how it was."

It could've been you. I knew that's what she wanted to say. *It could've been me.*

"Why didn't you tell me before?"

"What good would that have done? All it would've done was hurt you. Because even though you act like you guys were just sex friends, it was more than that. And knowing we had them over for dinner would've killed you, and I like you alive."

I huffed a laugh and then groaned miserably. "What was she like?"

Catrina paused before answering. "Uptight but nice."

I nodded because I knew I would get nothing else from her, and despite knowing she wouldn't answer my next question, I asked it anyway.

"What were they like together?"

"Talia."

I sighed and rubbed a hand down my face. This was all a mess. I was a mess. "He said he wants to be friends."

Cat scoffed. "Well, I don't think either of you are capable of that, but how did you respond?"

"I *thought* what you just said but told him I'd give it a go anyway."

"Tal," Catrina groaned.

"I don't know what else to do!" I laid back on my couch and propped my legs up on the back while holding my phone to my ear. "I... I'm not ready to let him go yet." When Catrina didn't say anything, I said, "What are you thinking?"

"That you're both idiots and that this is going to end in disaster," Cat responded immediately. "I love you, but you're being so stupid, Talia. I know what I'm about to say is going to sound really harsh, but how long do you think it's going to take for someone else to come along? How long do you think he's going to be your single buddy that you're in love with even though you don't want to be with him for real?"

"I'm not in love with him," I said stubbornly despite how true all her other words rang. "God, why can't you just be like normal friends and enable me?"

I could practically hear Catrina's eye roll. "Because I love you way too much not to tell you when you're screwing stuff up majorly."

"Fuck."

"Just think about that, Talia. Think about what it's going to feel like to eventually see your *friend* with someone else."

◆ ◆ ◆

How's work?

When Jack's text came through I grinned like an idiot.

The day after my show, I heard nothing from Jack, and I let myself revel in that moment when he told me had to go, when he essentially told me he couldn't control himself around me, that if he stayed he wouldn't be able to stop. I was anxious, though, because I wanted to at least try being friends with him, but since I hadn't heard from him I was worried he'd changed his mind, that he'd realized I wasn't worth the trouble, that even having me around was enough of a temptation and more trouble than it was worth.

But he'd texted me the following day with a funny gif from a show that we'd watched together back in school. We'd spent that entire day texting after that, even when I'd gone to Gia's to work. Every free moment I got, I checked my phone and found a new text for him either continuing our conversation or starting a new one.

I still wanted him. When our texts occasionally slipped into being flirty when we couldn't stop ourselves, I still felt that simmer of attraction to him that I would probably never be able to turn off no matter how long we remained friends. But as the days went on and we kept at it, everything felt natural and real, and even if we flirted, I just let it happen and let the worry about what it might mean just slowly drift away. One night he'd called me while I walked home from work around midnight, and we stayed on the phone for almost three hours before either of us realized how much time had passed. We talked about everything and nothing, and when the hours passed by and his voice started to become heavier and raspier with tiredness, I didn't let it bother me when I started to get turned on by the sound. I just let it happen because I wanted it, and we were still in relatively safe territory. I didn't know how long that would continue to be the case, but while it was, I was just going to enjoy being able to talk to him and get to know him all over again.

Soooooo slow, I responded to Jack's text. *I've been here since 11 and I've had one freaking table. Bored. Omg so bored.*

Lol... same here. I've been doing document review for the past four hours and my brain is about to leak out of my ears.

That sounds way worse than just sitting on a bar stool and drinking a glass of wine with Gia.

Yeah, you think? I wish I was having wine with an old Italian woman right now.

Oh yeah? I didn't know you were into older women.

Gia was currently arguing with her grandson—who was also the busboy and had just called in sick—on the phone in rapid Italian, and I almost audibly giggled at the image of Jack trying to flirt with her. I knew she'd been pretty in her youth, but now she looked... well, she looked like an old, Italian grandma who would whack you with a spatula if you said the wrong thing.

Especially the ones that perpetually smell like garlic and pasta.

I snorted. *Sounds sexy.*

We should go on a double date. Me and Gia with you and Gia's husband. What's his name again?

I sucked in my lips to stop myself from laughing. I'd told Jack days ago about Gia and Giuseppe, who bickered like younger siblings, rather than husband and wife, and how he would swat her with a towel and she would smack him over the head and swear at him in Italian.

Giuseppe. Yeah, I'd be into that double date. Giuseppe's hot. I'd definitely let him take me home.

He looked like the male version of his wife—short, round, with dark gray hair that was only about an inch shorter than his wife's short, severe cut.

Wow. It would be an honor to be Eskimo brothers with him.

I'd never even think about you again after I let him have me.

I find that VERY hard to believe.

This was the tricky territory that Jack and I often fell into. Where the conversation changed from just talking to mild flirting to maybe even beyond flirting when I started to wonder where to go next.

Part of me wanted to push him—see how far we could both go before one of us went over that invisible line. *I fuck you so good; yes, you make me scream.* I wanted to see how we would go back and forth, if I could push him so far that he threw away this "just friends" experiment and realized we had a chemistry that was so off the charts that nothing could stop us from wanting each other.

But just like all the other times when we teetered on the edge, I forced myself to remember that morning years ago when I told him I couldn't give him what he wanted, and when I remembered the look on his face, I knew I couldn't put either of us through that again. He wanted more, and *more* wasn't something in the cards for me. Not anymore.

Yeah, yeah, I ended up saying. *How are things at the office?*

Safe. Easy. Heart still intact.

We texted back and forth for another ten minutes before Maria, one of my coworkers and Gia's great niece, came to tell me I had a table.

I slipped my phone in my back pocket when Maria said, "He's cute, too."

But I knew it wouldn't matter to me if the customer was the cutest guy on earth. Unless he was Jake Gyllenhaal, I wasn't going to be interested in flirting with a cute customer, although it wouldn't be the first time. I'd gotten numbers from, had drinks with, and hooked up with customers more times than I wanted to admit, and even if this guy at my table was only looking for a good time, same as me, unless it was Jack, I couldn't imagine wanting him right now.

But want him, I did.

Because when I looked into the green eyes on the gorgeous face of the guy sitting casually at my table in the corner of the restaurant, I became a puddle on the floor at his feet.

Chapter 10

**W**hat are you doing here?" I knew I was grinning like a complete goof, but I couldn't stop it for the life of me.

"You said you were bored, and I wanted to see you."

Those words were dangerous, but I reveled in them anyway.

Jack looked incredible in his work suit. It was dark gray with very subtle pinstripes with a crisp, white shirt underneath, and a vibrant teal tie that brought out his eyes. He looked delectable, and as I stood in front of him, my knee on the chair opposite him at his table, I couldn't stop myself from imagining what it would feel like to run my hands under his jacket, feel his hard muscles there, rub my body all over his.

"Well, I'm glad you're here," I said with a smile. He beamed, and my knees shook.

I took his drink and food order—an iced tea and a roast beef sandwich—and since I had no other tables, I sat across from him and tried to ignore every time when his eyes briefly fell to my bare, crossed legs.

Gia didn't care what we wore as long as we wore all black, so I had a couple outfits I cycled through on each of my shifts. Today I was wearing a tight, knee-length, long sleeved black dress that rode up when I sat down, allowing Jack to catch a peek. And he took full advantage. When I'd walked over to put his order in, I could feel his eyes on me, and it took every ounce of my strength not to give him a sultry look over my shoulder.

"So, work sucks?"

"You have no idea," Jack replied.

He stretched in his chair, and I stared at his bulging biceps. My mouth may have watered.

"And to top off this *amazing* week, I've been *requested* for dinner at my parents' house on Saturday evening."

"What does that mean?" I asked with a laugh. "'Requested'?"

"That's the socialites' way of saying 'be there or suffer the consequences.'"

"Wow," I said. "That sounds lovely."

"Yeah," he said. "It's not."

I brought him some bread and when I sat back down I watched him rip a piece, dip it in a pool of olive oil and then bring it to his mouth. It shouldn't have been as sexy as it was, but then when a spare drop of olive oil dripped past his lip, I watched his tongue sweep it away and felt hot all over at the movement.

When he looked back up at me, I pretended to study a really interesting pattern on the wooden table.

"How is it working for your dad? Bet that makes things awkward at family dinners," I said.

Jack shrugged. "Yeah, not really. My dad basically thinks I'm the world's biggest fuck up, so his expectations are super low."

"Fuck up? You went to Klein and Harvard Law School. How can you possibly be a fuck up?"

When Jack didn't immediately respond, I suddenly remembered our conversation from back at the Green Hornet weeks ago.

"Oh. Breaking off the engagement."

"Yeah. My mother has barely even spoken to me since then, she was so furious when she found out."

"Do they care at all that you weren't happy?"

Jack looked at me like I was insane as he chewed and swallowed another piece of bread.

"Um, no. That's..." He scoffed. "No."

"That sucks." I felt awful for him in that moment. It was sad to think that he had parents who cared so little for him that they were more worried about their social position and how a broken engagement would look than the happiness of their own son.

"Well, I'm hoping Julianna will come," he said. "But she can't stand them even more than me, so it's going to be like pulling teeth to get her to come and bring the kids, too." Before I could respond he said, "Anyway. Enough about my dysfunctional family. Tell me how Flora and Fauna is doing. Any new music coming out? Your fans, like me, are dying to know."

I felt all puffed up with pride at his question. It felt so good to know that he liked my music and was interested in hearing about it.

"The band itself is okay. The music is getting there."

I saw his sandwich come up in the window, and I told him I would be right back with it. When I came back, I watched him watch me cross one leg over the other, and then he took a huge bite out of his sandwich and looked at me.

"What's going on with the band?" he asked with a mouth full of food.

I shook my head. "A lot of the same old. Chuck has a serious drug problem and doesn't really want to acknowledge it. Isaac and I have pretty much put up with it all this time, but now it's getting to the point where it's causing distractions. He'll show up an hour late to rehearsal, and it's frustrating because we pay for that space. And we can't do too much without a guitarist, you know?"

"Have you guys tried talking to him?"

"Isaac did once last year, and things got way better," I explained. "But now it's back to how it was before, possibly even worse." I'd put so much work—blood, sweat, and tears—into this band that it terrified me to think about what would happen if we fell apart because of Chuck's issues with drugs and alcohol. But I loved Chuck. He had been like a brother to me for five years, and if there was a way to salvage the band and also get Chuck the help he needed, then I would do everything I could to make that happen.

"Sounds like you all need to have another talk then," Jack said, looking like he was thinking about something. "You know, if you need a neutral third-party to be present or something, I could do that. I'm a good mediator."

I arched an eyebrow. "I don't think we could afford you."

He laughed. "No charge for friends."

Friends. Right.

We talked for the rest of his meal, and even after he'd finished. I cleared his plate, refilled his water, and when he made no move to leave I asked if he wanted coffee and dessert. After he said yes with that gorgeous smile, I brought him a cannoli and some coffee. One other party had come in since Jack, but Maria took that table so I was free to continue sitting with Jack. Maria and Gia kept giving us knowing glances, but I ignored them. And when I'd gone to get Jack's coffee, they'd both tried to bombard me with questions about who he was, but I said he was a friend and quickly got out from their clutches.

Jack was halfway done with his cannoli when he raised up a piece and gestured to me as if asking if I wanted some. I nodded, and he moved his hand to indicate that I come closer. When I did, I opened my mouth, and he popped the piece of pastry in my mouth, his fingers brushing my lips as he did so. His eyes stared at my mouth as I licked my lips and made a small hum of satisfaction, and then he looked up so his eyes were on mine.

Desire and lust arced between us, our eyes like pools of fire and need, and I didn't dare look away. I still wanted him, and I wasn't trying to hide that fact even if we were *friends*.

The door to the restaurant flew open and a group of people in professional clothes walked in laughing and talking. Jack had been here for almost two hours and had me all to himself during that time, but he still looked like he was sad when he saw the group come in, knowing I'd have to wait on them.

"I need to go anyway," he said after Maria sat them, and I nodded at her that I'd be right there. I saw her filling up water glasses and turned back to Jack.

"Thank you for coming in," I said gently. "It's been the best part of my day." I couldn't even stop myself from being honest about that.

Maria brought the table waters as I printed Jack's bill with my employee discount. When I dropped it on his table, he stood. He looked at me for a moment before he leaned in and wrapped his arms around my waist. I froze for a moment, and then reached up to wrap my arms tightly around his shoulders to return the hug. It went on for way longer than a hug between friends should have, but I wasn't at all eager for it to end.

When he pulled back finally, I walked toward my table to see if they were ready to order, and I looked over my shoulder at Jack to find him watching me with such a soft expression in his eyes that it made my chest ache.

The group of seven ordered some appetizers, and when I turned back to pick up Jack's check, I saw that he was gone. Disappointment lanced through me, but when I picked up the billfold and saw the obscene amount of money he left for me, I went to put in the appetizer order and send him a text.

That's ridiculous, Jack. I can't take that.

Superior service deserves recognition.

I tried to argue with him more, but he just ignored all my protests and told me to text him when I got some free time later.

I knew I was on shaky ground with him, but, god help me, I'd take whatever I could get.

◆ ◆ ◆

I was riding the blissful wave of lunch with Jack for the rest of the day even if my job suffered because of it. I got two orders wrong during the dinner rush because while I was putting the orders in the computer I was thinking about the way Jack hugged me when he left, the way his strong arms felt around my much smaller body, the way he seemed to swallow me into him making me feel so safe and warm and protected.

Around nine, the place had died down. I was scheduled to stay until after we closed at eleven, but Gia was so annoyed by how far in the clouds I was that she told me to get lost as soon as my last table left. I practically skipped home, and when I saw I had yet another text from Jack, I texted him back to tell him I was on my way home. A second later, I felt my phone vibrate, and I wanted to jump with glee when I saw *Jack Harding* on my phone screen.

"Hey you," I said, unable to hide the smile in my voice.

"Hey yourself," he said, and I knew he was smiling, too. "Don't tell me you're walking."

"It's a twenty minute walk." I tried to ignore how the concern in his voice sent a jolt of pleasure through me, knowing he was worried about me and cared for me. "Helps me clear my head."

"It's after nine."

The firmness in his voice was starting to turn me on.

"It's a Tuesday night, Jack."

"Oh, you think rapists and muggers take Tuesdays off?"

"Aww, you're worried about me."

I could practically hear his eye roll.

"Well. Yeah. The idea of my *female* friend walking home in the middle of the night by herself looking the way you do worries me."

I ignored the pang in my chest when he called me his friend and instead focused on his comment about how I looked.

"And how do I look?"

He scoffed. "You know how you look." When I didn't immediately respond, he sighed. "You know you're hot Talia. And I saw that dress you were wearing at work."

I knew he saw it. I'd caught him checking out my body way more than once when he'd been there for lunch, and I'd enjoyed the heated pulse that his perusal sent through me.

"Don't worry about it," I said. "I have mace, and I don't think they're concerned with how I look." I was trying to play it off despite how much it felt like a conversation between a boyfriend and a girlfriend rather than just friends. I doubted any of my *friends*, especially the men, would be this worried about me walking home. Cat often mentioned it, which was why she'd gotten me a can of mace for my birthday in June.

We talked for the rest of my walk home, and by the time I got home my face hurt from smiling so much. When I told him I was home I expected him to get off the phone, but he just kept up the conversation. I got inside, set my stuff inside the door, and kicked off my shoes as he told me how much he was dreading the dinner with his parents on Saturday. I sat on my couch with a bowl of cottage cheese and my phone between my ear and my shoulder and we just kept on talking. Eventually, I stripped off my clothes, brushed my teeth, and climbed into bed while we were still on the phone. We talked for hours, and it wasn't until my eyes started to feel heavy that I checked the time on my phone.

"Whoa," I said. "It's after two. We've been on the phone for over five hours."

Jack's voice was sexy and raspy with sleep when he said, "I didn't even notice. I like talking to you."

My heart sped up and I curled onto my side in bed, pulling the covers closer and imagining they were his arms around me.

"Me, too," I murmured.

"Sometimes it feels like no time has passed at all, you know?"

I knew exactly what he meant. He and I had both changed a lot since college, but it still felt as easy as it did then, as simple as it always was—laughing, talking, and wild, *wild* attraction that made us addicted to each other even with all the bullshit hanging between us. Talking to him felt like I was talking to a new crush but also like talking to an old friend who knew all the intimate, gory details of my life from years ago. I'd known Jack since I was eighteen-years-old, since before I knew who I was or what I wanted to do with my life. I met him three weeks after I'd met Vincent, and there had been days—dark, lonely days when I was missing him and us—that I wondered how different my life would have been if I'd met Jack first. Even though I'd met him when I was with Vince, I had still been attracted to him, but I'd also had stars in my eyes over Vince. Everything could have been so different if only Jack had gotten inside my heart long before Vincent had been able to break it.

"Yeah," I whispered. "I know."

"I should go." His voice was hushed, and I could hear the need in it. Would I ever stop wanting him? Would we ever stop wanting each other? "I have to be up for work in less than five hours."

"Okay." I barely recognized the breathless sound of my voice. I didn't want to hang up. I wasn't ready to say goodbye. Between lunch, talking tonight, and texting throughout the day, I'd spent most of the day talking with Jack in some form or another, but it still wasn't enough. I just wanted to hear his voice, feel him close even though he was across the river.

"I don't want to."

"Me neither," I replied quietly.

"But we have to."

"I know."

"I'll talk to you later, babe."

"Bye, Jack."

Our last words to each other were so quiet it was almost as if we weren't speaking. I could barely hear him, and I knew he could barely hear me. With overwhelming regret and already missing him, I hit the end button on my phone. I'd plugged it into the cord behind my bed hours ago when I'd first laid down, so I just set it on the table beside my bed. I didn't fall asleep immediately because I was thinking about Jack, but eventually my eyes felt heavy and I couldn't keep from falling under.

I dreamt of him the entire night, and he was the first thing I thought about when I woke up. I wasn't working at Gia's that day, so instead I stayed in bed until my stomach and my bladder forced me up. I kept staring at my phone whenever I got a chance and even turned the volume up all the way when I got in the shower because I didn't want to miss a call or text from Jack.

When he still hadn't texted me by noon, I gathered up a bag full of clothes and a book and walked to the laundromat at the end of my block, determined to stop thinking about him.

Maybe we had crossed some kind of line last night, and he was worried about pushing the boundaries between us. It had been him, after all, who'd wanted to just be friends, and I would have been fine continuing to casually sleep with him just like we'd done in college, even if it would've killed us both. But staying up all night talking might have been pushing it into a territory that felt like he was giving too much of himself when he knew I was still keeping so much of myself from him.

You can't have your cake and eat it, too, Talia. I tried to tell the voice in my head to fuck off, but it was insistent while I sat in the uncomfortable, hard, orange chair in the overly bright laundromat.

You have no idea what you want. You're fighting against something that you want to have without giving any bit of yourself to it. That's not fair to Jack, and he knows it, which is why he just wants to be friends.

As much as I hated it, that stupid voice was right, and so was Jack to decide that we would just be friends. Selfishly, I wanted to have Jack—my cake—but only on my terms. I wanted to guard my heart and protect myself even if that meant hurting Jack in the process for my own selfish desires. It wasn't fair to him, and I had to make more of an effort to be his friend instead of trying to get him to give up on being only friends—with actions or words—every time I saw him or talked to him. Because if I wanted him in my life, and I did, I would finally have to do it the way he wanted.

It wasn't until I was popping a frozen pizza in the oven for dinner later that night that Jack finally texted me asking how my day was. He told me he'd been crazy busy at work, and I felt a little better about not hearing from him until now while still acknowledging that this was normal. Most *friends* didn't text all day, every day.

I sat down with my pizza, put on a reality cooking show on Netflix, and looked at my phone to see that Jack had texted me again. And his text made all my resolve about respecting Jack's wish for us to be friends evaporate.

Wanna come over to my place for dinner Friday? I want to watch that movie we talked about.

I replied with *Sure, sounds good*, and a thumbs up emoji, but in reality, I was staring at my phone, grinning so hard I probably looked like a maniac.

Chapter 11

Movie night began with innocence and good intentions. Jack made an amazing meal—stuffed peppers and a simple salad with some kind of homemade lemon vinaigrette that knocked my socks off. My mom had always taught me to never show up to someone's home for a meal empty handed, so I'd brought a tray of cookies that we'd each had with coffee after dinner.

While we were having dessert, I played a demo of one of the new songs Flora and Fauna was working on. I didn't know if he was doing it just to be nice or to try and really show how interested he was, but when the song ended, he reached for my phone so that he could start it over. We listened to it all the way through again, and I just watched his face as he closed his eyes so he could just focus on the music and lyrics and nothing else.

It flattered and beguiled me how much he liked my music, how attentive he was, and it made me crave him in a way I knew I wasn't allowed to. It felt like no one had ever cared this much about something so important to me, like no one had ever cared so much about *me*, and I tipped further over the edge.

I didn't want to be just Jack's friend, and somehow I wanted to find a way to approach the topic of ending this farce of pretending we weren't attracted to each other and didn't each desire the other with a fierce desperation.

Or maybe he didn't want me like that anymore. Maybe he truly was only interested in being friends, and if that was the case, I would have to find it somewhere deep inside me to be okay with that.

Despite how full we both were after dinner and dessert, Jack had popped some popcorn and poured me a glass of wine while he got himself a beer before we sat down on his couch and he opened up the movie on his TV.

We sat close to each other, but not close enough to touch, and not closer than two friends would sit on the couch. He put the bowl of popcorn between us, and I tried to ignore the jolt of sensation that went through me every time his hand brushed mine in the bowl. I wasn't even hungry and didn't even particularly like popcorn, but I reached for more over and over just to chance having that moment where our hands might meet. I knew it was weird and pathetic and

69

something a fourteen-year-old girl with a crush would do, not a twenty-eight-year-old grown woman who already knew what the guy was like in bed, but I couldn't stop it. I just wanted to be near him and to touch him, and if a popcorn bowl was the only way to do it, then that would have to be fine with me.

I finished my wine about halfway through the movie, which was an incredibly intense psychological thriller, and the wine was making me feel warm and cozy. I took the throw off the back of the couch and curled my legs under me while Jack moved the popcorn bowl to the coffee table. When he leaned back and I draped the blanket over me, I realized we were much closer than we'd been before, my knees just lightly brushing the side of his muscular thigh while he draped his arm over the sofa back behind me.

I laid my head on the back of the couch, trying not to inhale too deeply because I knew if I caught his scent I'd be a goner.

I was trying my damnedest to pay attention to the movie. It was objectively a very good movie, and under any other circumstances I would have been hooked, but after a few more minutes, I noticed a light tugging on my hair. There was no possible way for me to pay attention anymore after I realized the tugging was Jack, his arm resting on the back of the couch lightly and absently running his fingers through my hair that was splayed on the couch back.

I reveled in the gentle touch even though I wasn't even entirely sure he knew he was doing it. But when he angled toward me, bending his knee up on the couch so that our knees were completely touching, my self-control began to fade rapidly.

My heart pound and my palms dampened as I tilted my head back slightly so I could glance over at him through my eyelashes. The glow of the TV in the dark room was illuminating all his features and causing shadows that made all the perfect angles of his face even more pronounced. Sometimes I forgot how beautiful he was. I got so wrapped up in how sexually attracted to him I was that I forgot about the simple beauty of all his features both inside and out. A nostalgic contentment came over me while I watched him, just ready and happy to enjoy this moment with a man who made me feel so many incredible things.

Without thinking of what it might mean or how he might react, I looked back at the TV and put my hand on his leg. I just wanted to touch him, wanted my hands on him even if it would lead nowhere, and when he didn't react or push me away, I actually started to focus on the movie again while carelessly rubbing my thumb back and forth at the spot where my hand rested dangerously close to his inner thigh. It felt so relaxed and comfortable here with him, where I could just be, that for a while my desire for him fell by the wayside. Just being here next to him was enough.

It went on like that for a while, me rubbing his thigh, him playing with my hair, and neither of us made any move to stop. I wanted to know if he noticed, if he cared, if it bothered him, but I was so worried about breaking the spell that I didn't do anything except what I'd already been doing.

Being with Jack

The movie was reaching its climax and I was on the edge of my seat, not because of the movie but because of how turned on and attuned I was to Jack. My head had slipped down from the couch onto his shoulder, I'd lifted one of my knees so it was sort of draped over his, and his arm was around me, holding me close while he kept on playing with my hair, his fingers going deeper and massaging more. My hand had slipped further in on his thigh and wickedly close to his groin. I wanted to look and see if he was as turned on as I was, but for some reason that felt like it would break some precious spell, like it would burst the bubble of peace we were in right then.

We were in full on cuddle mode, and all I wanted was for it to turn into naked cuddling on his bed rather than clothed cuddling on his couch. My mouth was dry for wanting it, my hands shaking, and all he had done was hold me to him and touch my hair. But that wasn't registering with my libido—that raging hormone didn't care that we were just innocently snuggling on the couch.

The credits rolled, and I was strung so tight I thought I was going to combust.

Fuck it.

The thought went through my mind just a second before I slid my hand even closer and turned so my face was in his neck, brushing my lips gently along his skin. He smelled like heaven, and I could have easily feasted on his neck and would have had he not curled his hand into a fist in my hair and pulled me back slightly.

If he was trying to stop me from wanting him, that action was not going to do it because all I could imagine was him holding me like that while he fucked me.

We held each other's eyes for a long time like that, unspoken words and wants and needs flowing in the space between us until finally he let out a shuddering breath and pressed his forehead to mine.

"I need to take you home."

NO! I screamed in my head. *Fuck what we said before, we both want this.*

I was going to protest but then he said, "But fuck I really don't want to."

I wanted to tell him not to, wanted him to throw caution to the wind, and I knew if I pushed even a little he would give in. But more than how badly I wanted him in his bed right that second, seeing his torment, I wanted to honor his wishes and respect his boundaries and save us both from a lot of heartache that I knew would come if we crossed this line.

"But you have to."

He sighed and pulled back, his eyes landing on my lips as he kept my hair clenched in his fist.

"I do." His voice was hoarse with need, and his mouth was slightly parted and all I desperately wanted to do was close the gap between us and take his lips with mine.

"Fuck," he said harshly before creating more space between us.

The car ride from Jack's place in Cambridge to mine in Back Bay was almost twenty minutes, and it was the tensest twenty minutes I'd ever experienced. Jack was gripping the steering wheel with one hand, the other braced on the window, and his left leg was bouncing while his other drove us. I couldn't stop fidgeting, trying with all my strength to find something to do with my hands so I wouldn't be tempted to touch him.

Jack parked in front of a fire hydrant near my apartment, a further sign that he wouldn't be staying, and I sat there for a moment before I got out, knowing he wouldn't walk me to the door like I knew he wanted because it would create too much temptation.

"Thank you for dinner," I said quietly.

"You're welcome. Anytime." His voice was tight like he was using every bit of his control.

"And the movie."

"I had fun," he replied shortly.

I knew we were in too dicey a position for me to do it, but I still leaned over and kissed his cheek, lingering there for longer than I should have, losing myself in the long sigh Jack released as I did it.

He stayed in his spot as I unlocked the front door of the small apartment building. I could feel his eyes on me, and right before I went in, I looked over my shoulder and waved, trying for friendly. I couldn't see if he waved back or not, so I walked in and climbed the stairs to my third-floor studio. I left the lights off and went to the window and saw that Jack's car was still parked in the same place.

I watched the vehicle even though I couldn't see him, wondering if all the thoughts that were racing through my head were in his as well.

How much longer can I just be his friend?

Why are we pretending we don't want each other?
Are we even pretending at this point?
What is stopping him? Me? Us?
I don't know if I can stop myself next time.
I don't even know if there will be a next time.
I want him. I need him. I want to be with him, but is there a way
for both of us to get the relationship that we want? Is there a way we
can do this and guarantee that neither of us gets hurt or has to do
something we don't like or give something up that we aren't ready to
give up?

Eventually, Jack sped off, and I got into bed, refusing to shower
and wash even the barest of his scent off me.

Jesus Christ, Talia, you're such a mess.

Chapter 12

"So Jack's here." Catrina gave me a knowing look, and I rolled my eyes at her, sipping my drink and seething.

"Yeah."

I glared at Catrina and she smirked. I was at Cat and Brody's huge apartment for their annual Halloween party, and I was slurping down my drink quickly in their kitchen, ignoring all the partygoers and opting instead to drown my sorrows. Cat was dressed as Ariel from *The Little Mermaid,* which didn't require many changes other than the costume itself because she had gorgeous long, red hair and already looked like a freaking Disney Princess. Brody was somewhere around in a black wig, dressed as Eric, and like Brody, I was also wearing a black wig, but mine was long and straight and parted down the middle into two braids, completing my Wednesday Addams costume.

"How's it going, being just friends?"

I hadn't heard a single word from Jack in the week since our ill-advised movie night. I'd gone to bed on edge and horny, dreaming of him, longing for him, and then as the days slipped on, it was clear that Jack had gone from wanting to be friends to wanting to be barely acquaintances. I knew he wanted to put boundaries between us for both our sakes, but that did not mean fucking *ghosting* me at the first sign of difficulty. Jack wanted things on his terms, so, fine. They would be on his fucking terms. And if that meant not speaking at all because we couldn't control ourselves around each other, then I was going to respect his wishes and give him exactly what he was giving me.

"Um, like fucking shit if you must know."

"Oh," was all Catrina said.

"Yeah."

"Do you want to talk about it?" she asked slowly.

"Not particularly, no."

"Tal—"

"We watched a movie together last weekend, we almost let things go too far. I wanted to. And I would have if he hadn't stopped it." I said everything in one long, angry breath.

"Oh, jeez, Tal..."

"I know, you don't have to say anything." I took another long swig from my gin and tonic. "I know this entire thing is a mess, but I really don't know what to do to fix it all. I want to be in his life. I know the casual sex thing is too hard—"

"On you or him?" Catrina interjected.

"What?"

"Is casual sex too hard for you or too hard for him?" She had this knowing glint in her eye that made me want to rage at her even though I knew she had the best intentions.

"Him, obviously," I said quickly. Too quickly.

Catrina rolled her eyes. "Oh, my god, can you please just admit you have feelings for him and having casual sex when you know those feelings are there is just as hard for you as it is for him?"

I stared at Catrina for a moment before I turned toward the counter I was leaning on that had all the booze and mixers sprawled across it. I yanked at a bottle of tequila and a tiny plastic shot glass, poured one, and swallowed it down in one gulp.

"Whatever."

"Whatever?" Cat repeated with a disgusted look. "Are you fifteen?"

"Can you stop laying truth bombs on me and be a pal and do a shot with me so I don't have to pathetically drink alone?"

"I..." She looked caught off guard for a moment. "I'm not drinking tonight."

I scoffed. "What do you mean you're not drinking? This is your apartment. You don't have to worry about driving, which is the best part of having parties at your own place." I reached for another plastic shot glass and poured two shots of tequila, sliding one over to Catrina and lifting mine up.

"I'm not drinking," she said again more firmly and like a light went off in my mind, everything clicked in place. "I have rehearsal tomorrow and—"

"Oh, my god."

"Talia."

"Oh, my fucking god, you're *pregnant*," I hissed.

"I—"

"Catrina!"

"What—"

"Why didn't you tell me?" I was almost shouting, and Catrina looked around, but there was no one in the kitchen but us.

"I..." She sighed. "We haven't told anyone yet," she whispered. "It's really early. I'm trying not to make a big deal about it. Like a fourth of pregnancies are miscarried or something like that, so I'm trying to—"

I cut her off by grabbing her and enveloping her in a tight hug. My best friend was pregnant, and it made all the stuff with Jack seem so ridiculously insignificant even if only for that moment right then.

"I'm so happy for you," I said into her hair.

"Thanks," she said when I pulled back to look at her. Then she reached for the napkins that were on the counter. "Fuck, I'm crying. All I've done for weeks is cry."

I laughed and grabbed her free hand as she dabbed her eyes with the other.

"I bet Brody is so happy," I said. "I know he's been wanting to pump a baby into that uterus for a long time."

Catrina huffed a watery laugh. "For sure. He's been hinting at it since we got back from Greece."

I gave her a deadpan stare. "You mean your honeymoon in Greece four years ago?"

Catrina nodded. "That's the one."

"Wow." I giggled. "Well, he finally got his wish."

"Who did?"

Catrina and I both looked up as Callum walked into the kitchen dressed as a *Harry Potter* character, which was basically just him in a white shirt, black pants, and a Slytherin tie I'd gotten him from a store in the mall when Catrina and I were sophomores and he was a junior.

"What are we talking about?" He grabbed one of the shots I'd poured, and he and I clanked the plastic together before we each downed the liquid.

"Catrina's pregnant." My throat was raspy from the burn of the tequila.

"Talia!"

"What? It's just Callum."

"I just said we weren't—"

"Seriously?" Callum's eyes widened with excitement, and Catrina couldn't help but smile.

"Okay, yes, seriously, just don't tell any—"

Callum grabbed her into a tight hug the exact same way I had.

"Wow, that's amazing," he said when he released her. "Congratulations."

I made mixed drinks for both Callum and I, and then the three of us went out to join the rest of the party. As soon as we got into the huge open living space, I spotted Jack across the room.

He was Clark Kent for the evening wearing a white shirt and pants that he was bulging out of, and the white shirt was open to reveal a Superman t-shirt underneath. He was wearing these incredibly sexy black framed glasses that made him look like a hot professor, and all I wanted was to rip all his clothes off and have him fuck me with nothing on but those glasses. But when I saw who he was talking to, I didn't want him to fuck me. I wanted to fucking kill him.

He was talking to—no, *flirting with*—Nia Silver, a tall, gorgeous black girl that Cat knew because they'd become friends when Nia was in the chorus of *Wicked* when Cat was playing Elphaba five years ago. She was stunning and looked like she was dressed as some kind of sexy, dead bride with a tiny white dress, five-inch white stilettos, and well done makeup that made her look dead but somehow even more beautiful.

When Callum saw the death stare I was aiming at them, he looked at me.

"What's going on there?"

"Don't ask," Cat murmured.

"I didn't know you guys were—"

"We aren't," I said, cutting Callum off.

Cat ignored my short, snarky tone. "They reconnected like six weeks ago or so. A few weeks before he came to the show. They had sex, she ran—"

"Like she does," Callum said.

"Fuck off," I said with a sarcastic smile.

"And now," Catrina continued. "They're trying to be friends."

Cal snorted. "How's that working out?"

Catrina laughed as I continued to seethe. "Yeah, not great."

When I looked up and saw Carver talking to Catrina's cousin Gabe, I practically stormed over to them.

"Hey, Talia," Gabe said. "How are—"

"Hey, Gabe," I said quickly before turning to Carver. "Let's dance."

Carver didn't hesitate before taking me up on the offer. Michael had bailed on the party, so Carver was Gerald without an Arnold from *Hey! Arnold*, and I knew he was just as pissed off and ready to dance and drink it off as I was.

I yelled at Brody to turn up the music, and he gave me a thumbs up before doing just that. The bass pumped through Cat and Brody's sound system, and I lost myself to the music, throwing myself around, grinding on Carver, taking shots that anyone brought over to me while I tried to push away the insistent reminder in the back of my mind that Jack was nearby. I refused to look around the room and somehow seek him out because I knew there was a good chance I wasn't going to like what I saw.

I danced with Carver and eventually Callum, Cat, and Brody when they joined. At one point, a friend of Brody's from college whose name I forgot came over to dance with us, too. He was tall and trim and good looking in a boy-next-door kind of way, but he didn't dance like a boy-next-door. No, he danced close and dirty, and I let myself be guided where he led me, too buzzed and pissed off to care one way or another.

After a while, my bladder became insistent, so I shuffled off to the bathroom, practically barreling over there because I was so scared I might catch Jack making out with Nia, or, even worse, dancing with her closely or talking to her in her ear—something intimate that I wouldn't be able to bear.

I went to the bathroom, washed my hands, and when I swung open the door, Jack was standing right there, hands shoved into his pockets.

"Sorry," I said, trying to sound calm and cool even though my heart was almost pounding out of my chest. "I'm done."

"I don't have to go, I came to find you."

"Oh."

Neither of us said anything for several seconds.

"How was dinner with your parents last weekend?" I asked because I didn't know what else to say, but I also wanted to prove that I could be the bigger person, that I could do this friends thing even though seeing him talk to someone else ripped me to shreds.

"Fine." He fidgeted when he said it and wouldn't look at me. Then he ran a stressed hand through his hair, and I softened somewhat at his expression. I knew he didn't get along with his parents, and the part of me that cared about him more than I cared about my petty jealousy had me asking if he wanted to talk about it.

He shook his head. "No." He sighed. "It's just been a rough week. That dinner fucked up everything for me, and I haven't been able to relax since."

I wouldn't have even known he was that torn up over it by how he'd been smiling and chatting with Nia earlier, but now that we were alone it looked like he was ready to let his guard down and be honest about whatever was bothering him. He had dropped the pretense, just for me, and while I felt honored that he was obviously comfortable enough with me to share that part of himself, I was also worried by how strung out he suddenly looked.

"What happened?"

Jack looked at me and then looked at the floor again. He looked vulnerable—shoulders hunched, body tense—when he looked back at me.

"They invited Rachel."

It felt like he'd shoved a freezing cold ice pick into my gut. A chill settled through me and the pain that started in my stomach and radiated through my entire torso was overwhelming. Everything made sense suddenly—why he hadn't spoken to me all week, why he'd been avoiding me all night, why he looked so worried about talking to me now. He and Rachel were getting back together, and it had taken all week for him to build up his courage enough for him to tell me, knowing how it would destroy me even if I pretended it didn't.

Blood was rushing in my ears. My face felt hot despite the chill that had washed over me. I could feel my hands and feet start to sweat, and I knew I had to get out of here before I had a fucking panic attack. I couldn't stand here and watch him let me down gently, listen as he told me that it had been fun while it lasted but he needed to get serious again and that meant not spending time with a woman he used to fuck while he was getting back with his fiancée.

I wanted to scream. I wanted to hit him and tell him I hated him, but instead, my flight instincts kicked in.

I didn't know if I said anything to him, but before I realized what I was doing or how I'd even gotten there, I was on Catrina and Brody's balcony, hurling into a potted plant. Vaguely, I heard a voice behind me and felt someone rubbing my back, but I kept on spilling the contents of my stomach and dry heaving when there was nothing left.

After a short while, I was being wrapped in a hug, small arms holding me tightly and a quiet voice telling me that everything would be okay.

"What happened?" Catrina asked.

"J-Jack—" I choked. "H-he—I-I f-fucked it all u-up," I said through sobs. "You were r-right."

It was all I managed before I started crying too hard to speak, clutching the fabric at Catrina's back as I wept into her shoulder, praying that the music at the party was loud enough that no one would be able to hear my pathetic wails.

The sounds of the party got louder for a moment, and I thought my head was finally starting to clear, but then I heard a voice and realized someone had opened and closed the door.

"Talia."

I almost collapsed when I heard Jack say my name. I held onto Catrina harder and shook my head into her shoulder violently.

"I don't think now's a good time," Catrina said quietly, rubbing circles on my back.

"Talia, I'm sorry. I don't—"

"I don't want to hear it, okay?" Catrina kept a protective arm around me as I whirled around. I probably looked like a complete mess, dark eyeliner and mascara most likely streaked down my face. "Don't fucking apologize. You don't have anything to apologize f-for." My voice broke on the last word, and I took a deep breath so I could finish what I needed to say with as much of my dignity still intact as possible. "I know I have no claim over you. I know we're just friends, but I can't do this. I *won't*—I won't be your friend while you get back with someone you were miserable with just because you can't stand doing the casual thing. I know I'm not her. I know I'm not—"

Catrina was stiff as a board next to me when Jack said, "Talia, what are you talking about?"

"Rachel!" Catrina's arm tightened around me when I shouted Jack's fiancée's name. "You and her—"

"Me and her, *nothing*, Talia." Jack looked angry now, completely ignoring Catrina and zeroing in on me. "I wasn't going to say that her and I got back together. Jesus. No. Never. I just wanted to fucking talk to you about what happened because I missed talking to you all week, and I just needed to vent to you even though I know things are stupid and complicated between us right now."

"Then..." I opened my mouth and closed it, taking another deep breath as I started to take in what Jack was saying. "Then why didn't you talk to me all week?"

Jack sighed and ran a hand down his face. "Because I'm trying to give us both space to figure out what the fuck is going on. I want to be with you even though I know you and I want different things, and when you came over to my place last weekend, I felt all fucked up when I dropped you off because I knew we were crossing lines. That's why I didn't talk to you. I thought that's what you'd want—"

"No," I breathed quickly, choking back a stray sob. "I... I would never want that."

Jack stared at me, his gaze going from stressed to angry to heated back to stressed again in the span of about thirty seconds. Finally, Catrina broke the tension by turning to me and grabbing both my shoulders.

"Hold on, Jack," Catrina said to him, and he walked to the corner of the balcony, looking agonized, so Catrina could whisper to me. "Are you okay?" I sighed and then nodded. "If I go inside, can you have this conversation and still be okay?"

I swallowed. "Yeah, I think so."

Catrina's eyes searched my face and then she leaned in closer to whisper in my ear. "Don't walk away, Talia. Remember those feelings just now when you came out here. Remember how you felt at just the thought that he would be with someone else. Don't let him be with anyone else. You two belong together. If you have to take it slow, I know he'll be okay with that. I know you're scared." I wanted to protest, to tell her I wasn't scared, I just didn't do relationships, but even just thinking it I knew it was a fucking lie. I was scared shitless. Scared of being hurt, scared of giving my heart to Jack and scared of him breaking it.

"Just don't..." Catrina took a deep breath. "Don't walk away again. Not for his sake. For yours."

She hugged me, and I felt fresh tears sting my eyes that I tried to wipe away when she pulled back. After giving me one last, meaningful look, she raised her hands to swipe her thumbs under my eyes—most likely trying to wipe away my mascara—before she said, "Okay, Jack, I'm going inside." He turned around quickly, and I saw him chewing on his lower lip, his fingers nervously tugging at the tie hanging loosely around his neck to complete his costume, the other still deep in his pocket.

When Catrina went back inside, Jack and I just stared at each other across the balcony for a long time. I had my hands crossed over my chest protectively, and I was shaking as much from the chill outside as the emotions and adrenaline coursing through me.

"You thought I was getting back with Rachel?" Jack took a few steps toward me when he asked the question.

I shrugged helplessly. "I didn't know what to think. I haven't heard a-anything from you in a week, and then when you said she was at the dinner, I guess I... I just assumed the worst, I guess."

He was still slowly walking toward me, his eyes glued on my face, and when I hiccupped, he gave me the gentlest smile before turning serious again.

"I wouldn't be with Rachel." His voice was low and hoarse, and despite all the mix of confused emotions, heat flooded my core. "I wouldn't do that to her or to me. I couldn't be with her when all I can think about is someone else."

I was walking toward him now, and when we met in the middle, I dropped my hands to my sides.

"Me?" I whispered.

The corner of Jack's mouth lifted as he nodded. "Yeah, you."

He closed the gap between us and took my face in his hands. "I'm sorry I made you think I was getting back with her."

I shook my head as much as I could with him holding me. "I freaked."

He kept studying my face. "You're so beautiful."

I laughed breathlessly. "I probably have mascara and eyeliner all over my face."

"Only a little," he replied. "Doesn't take away from how stunning you are."

"Jack," I gasped.

"What?"

"Kiss me."

As soon as his mouth came down on mine, I opened against him so he could slide his tongue in. He tasted like beer and something sweet, like lust and desire and a need so profound that it stole my breath. We were both breathing heavily through our noses as we each deepened the kiss further while I wrapped my arms around his waist and he gripped my neck.

"Fuck, sorry."

Jack and I both jumped apart but stayed close when Carver walked out onto the balcony.

"Sorry," he said again, holding up his phone. "I was just trying to call Michael." He looked back and forth between us. "I'll go out in the hall."

When he walked back through the balcony doors, Jack turned to me and grabbed one of my hands.

"Come home with me."

I sighed. I wanted to more than anything, but I still didn't know if I was ready to go there with him, didn't know if I was prepared to set my fear aside and let us go where we both wanted to go. What I did know is that I didn't want to see him with anyone else, but I didn't think it was fair to just be with him because the thought of him with another woman made me sick to my stomach.

"I don't think that's a good idea," I said.

"It might not be," he said honestly. "But I don't give a fuck. I want you."

Chapter 13

"Jesus, fuck, you are so fucking hot." Jack slammed me against the front door of his apartment, bending so he could slide his knee between my legs, and making me gasp as he bit my neck.

Jack had driven us back to his place like a bat out of hell, and the situation wasn't helped by the fact that I had my hands on him the entire time. He zoomed down Beacon Street like it was a high-speed chase, and I prayed we wouldn't get pulled over, especially because I was nibbling on his neck and his ear with my hands down his pants, stroking his straining cock.

He'd tried to stop me at first, telling me to hold on, that he had to focus on the road, but I couldn't stop, the desperation for him after these weeks of sexual tension permeating every single one of my senses.

Jack ground against me at his door since I didn't even give him the opportunity to turn the key before I was trying to unbutton his pants. His button and belt were hanging loose around him as I jumped up his body to wrap my arms and legs around him, and he shoved me back against the door, his hands sliding up under my black dress and gripping my ass to hold me close while his mouth ravaged mine.

I couldn't get deep enough, close enough, and I was frenzied as I tugged at different parts of him, doing whatever I could to get at every bit of him.

Panting, Jack pulled back and said, "Okay, fuck, inside." He grabbed the keys out of his pocket as I licked a stripe up his neck, and he groaned as he shoved the key in the lock while I sucked at the spot where his neck connected with his jaw.

"Hurry," I breathed against his neck, and he growled as he moved both his hands back to me and kicked the door wide open.

He barreled through the door with me in his arms, kicking it shut after we went over the threshold and stomping in the direction of his bedroom.

Do not pass go. Do not collect $200.

I almost giggled at the thought, but then the wind was nearly knocked out of me as I was tossed on my back on his bed and he climbed over me, bracing his hands on either side of my head as he dipped low to kiss me again. I gripped the fabric at his waist and yanked him down so he was flush on top of me and spread my legs wide so he could fit there.

The kiss was wet and messy and frantic, both of us panting and moaning, nipping, biting, licking, sucking, desperate, aching, longing.

Jack pulled back so he could look down at me, and I laughed when he grunted and reached up to yank the Wednesday Addams wig off my head and threw it across the room. I was still smiling against his mouth when he dove back in, sinking his hands into my hair so he could move me how he wanted, get the angle that would allow him to go as deeply into my mouth as he could.

I was trembling with how badly I wanted him inside me, moaning into his mouth, and when he moved his hands from my head down and underneath my dress, I whimpered at the feel of him sliding my panties down my legs.

His eyes were heated and intense as he slid my shoes off my feet, methodical as he rolled down my thigh high stockings and tossed them over his shoulder. But we were both too impatient for him to keep slowly undressing me because all it took was another soft moan from me to make both of us start ripping at each other's clothes.

It felt like not even a second had passed before we were both naked, and I was lying on my back trying to catch my breath as he rolled a condom down his long, thick length. My mouth watered at the sight of his naked, fit body, muscles bulging and skin glistening with a fine sheen of sweat as his chest—spattered with dark hair—heaved while he looked down at me and soaked me in the same way I was doing to him. His dark brown hair on his head was disheveled, and I'm sure mine looked no less wild because of how both of us had gripped each other there at different times while we kissed. He looked gorgeous in the dim light of his bedroom, and in that moment, I didn't think I had ever wanted him or anyone more.

"You take my fucking breath away," he rumbled harshly before he leaned down to just brush his lips against mine.

Then he was sliding inside me, his mouth just a breath from mine and his eyes on me as he used one hand to guide himself to my entrance, his other arm braced next to me. I couldn't take my eyes off him, but as he filled me up so completely, I tilted my head back, my eyes fluttering shut on a breathless moan.

He started moving slowly and deeply in and out of me, but it wasn't enough. I wanted the ferocity of when we'd first gotten to his apartment, and even though the deep glides felt heavenly, I needed him to give me exactly what I craved.

"More," I moaned. "Please, Jack, harder."

He kept his eyes on me, and then he maneuvered so he could put his arms under my shoulders. I gasped when he rolled us so I was on top of him, straddling his wide form as he went as deep as he could go and released a strangled moan.

"*Yes*," I hissed, and Jack nodded.

"Take what you need, baby." His voice was gruff and hard and sexy as his eyes raked over my body above him. "Fuck yourself on my cock."

Jack grabbed my hips as I put my hands on his stomach between my legs and shifted so I could find the perfect angle. Then he slowly thrust his hips up and I bit my lip to hold back a loud moan as he slid against that perfect spot inside me that so few had ever found.

I rolled my hips to keep the friction on that spot, and he kept thrusting his hips until we found this incredible, perfect rhythm that had me moaning at every thrust, every shift of my hips and his.

"Look at me," Jack growled, and with all the strength I possessed, I forced my eyes open and looked at him beneath me, his eyes glued on me, stormy with arousal, his dark hair a shock against the white sheets. He was so unbelievably sexy, his stomach muscles flexing beneath my hands, and I cried out as he thrust up into me harder and I moved against him more frantically. I looked down to the spot where we were joined and saw wet streaks on the short thatch of hair above his cock and groaned loudly at the sight. It was so incredibly hot to see evidence of my arousal marking his gorgeous body.

I continued to ride Jack's cock with everything I had, rotating, moving back and forth, bouncing up and down, getting every bit of sensation that I could. He slid his hands up from my hips to my waist and slowly up to cup my breasts. When his fingers gently tweaked and pinched my nipples, my back arched violently and I almost came. He kept his fingers there, teasing me, until he growled and yanked me down so he could suck one of my nipples into his mouth.

It was heaven, ecstasy, an exquisite torture that was so perfect I felt like I might die from it. If I did—if the pleasure killed me—my life would end on the highest note, a note I could never hope to reach again, the shrill chords of a shocking and boundless melody that would carry me off with it into the abyss.

"Fuck," I moaned loudly. "Yes, Jack, *god yes*." He wrapped his arms around my sweaty back, thrusting up into me as he alternated between each of my nipples, sucking hard as I tried to keep myself balanced on my arms above his head so I wouldn't collapse completely on top of him and suffocate him. But my arms were shaking, and I didn't know how much longer I could hold myself up with all the sensations pulsing through me. Like he knew I wouldn't be able to keep myself there for much longer, Jack pushed me back up so I was riding him again. He grabbed one of my thighs with one hand as I ground down on him, my walls pulsing and clenching around him as I approached the peak, and with his other hand he reached between my legs.

As soon as his thumb brushed my clit, I screamed, letting it tear out of me and echo off the walls of his bedroom. It felt so impossibly good, his cock filling me up, his thumb brushing the most sensitive part of my entire body, and I knew I wouldn't last. I didn't want it to ever end, but the train was barreling down the tracks, and I could feel myself coming apart.

The things this man could do to me... I couldn't even put it in words what he had the ability to do. If I thought for one moment that I ever could've lived with this—without him—that I could've walked away from him forever, I was insane.

"Yeah," Jack encouraged, his eyes on me.

I moaned his name. "Only you do this to me," I said in a strangled voice. "No one makes me feel like you do."

At my words, I felt Jack's cock thicken inside me as he sped up both his thrusts and the movement of his thumb while I answered in kind, jerking my hips against him until I felt his warm heat flood the condom, his neck straining as he let out the sexiest moan I'd ever heard. I couldn't stop moaning and whimpering as I followed him a moment later, my climax setting off a powerful reaction inside me that had my blood pumping through my veins, causing my body to radiate heat as I kept on thrusting against him, trying to keep the sensations that felt incredible.

The chords reached their apex—the beautiful music we made together reached its peak—and it felt like a it would never end. The strings of the bow rattled and shook, trembling along with me, and when I reached that final note, it felt like the sky was opening up. Our harmony combined into a seamless melody as we floated along together on the waves of euphoria.

Finally, I collapsed on top of him, and we both breathed heavily, trying to calm down and return to ourselves after such an intense moment between us.

After a while, I rolled off Jack and kept on panting in the bed beside him, staring up at the ceiling, one arm above my head and the other between Jack and I, brushing his hip gently.

Without a word, Jack turned and sat up, his back to me. I heard him taking care of the condom and saw him lean over to toss it in the waste basket under his bedside table. I thought he was going to lay back in the bed next to me, but he stayed sitting there. I felt strange and vulnerable as I stared at his back, and it didn't take me long to realize why.

I wanted him to ask me to stay.

Jack had been the only man I'd ever stayed in bed with. Every other casual hookup I had since him, I either left or made him leave after. It had become so much the norm for me that it was almost like muscle memory to roll out of bed and put my clothes on when we finished.

I wasn't ready to leave this time. I felt like Jack and I had finally broken down an important barrier tonight. After he saw how I reacted to the thought that he would get back with Rachel, there was no use hiding how I felt about him anymore. I wanted to be with him, and I couldn't pretend I didn't. I knew I'd said earlier that I didn't know if I was ready to give him more, that I was too damn scared, but I knew I didn't want to be with anyone else, maybe ever again, and even though I wasn't eager to name what we were doing, I still wanted to do it.

And that's why Jack's quiet words almost shattered me.

"I won't get mad if you want to leave. If you want to go, I'll respect that." He paused. "I just don't want to watch it."

I sucked in a shaky breath as silence settled over us at his words. They turned me inside out with the pain I heard behind them, and in that moment I realized that I wasn't the only one who was afraid.

My stomach was churning when, finally, I whispered, "Would you be mad if I stayed?"

Jack whipped his head around to look at me. He looked wary but hopeful, and I wanted to drag him to me.

"No," he breathed, huffing a small laugh as he turned more toward me. "No, I wouldn't be mad if you stayed."

We both grinned stupidly at each other as Jack crawled back into the bed with me. I felt light and carefree in way I could never remember feeling, and I wanted to cling to that feeling. Jack pulled the covers over us as I draped myself over his chest and put my ear next to his heart so I could hear the slow, steady thump in my ears until we both let sleep claim us.

Chapter 14

T he sound of the toilet flushing woke me out of a deep, satisfying sleep.

Jack's bed was without question the most comfortable bed I'd ever laid in, and that alone should have been reason enough to stay in bed with Jack when we were together weeks ago. I'd missed out on having a chance at this beautiful white mass of fluff and relaxation, but luckily I was here now, thick blankets and sheets spread on top of me as I luxuriated in the soft fabric, writhing almost like I was making a snow angel in his sheets.

I heard the sound of the faucet and expected Jack to come through the bathroom door when he turned it off. It was early morning—probably around seven if the way the light streamed in was any indication—and Jack and I had only finally gone to bed about three hours ago.

After the first time last night, I'd fallen asleep draped over Jack, and I couldn't have been asleep long before I felt Jack's hand just gently caressing my ass. It wasn't even really a sexual gesture, but when he saw me waking up, he'd slipped his fingers into me from behind, toying with me until I was panting as I came and then flipping me on my stomach and fucking me until we both came again. We'd both adjusted in the bed with every intention of going to sleep, Jack spooning me from behind as I pulled his arms tightly around me, loving the way his thick, strong arms felt holding me close. But after a while, his breath on my neck made me shiver and I'd shimmied against him to get even closer. When his cock hardened and nudged my ass, I'd lifted my leg back and over his to spread myself out as he reached behind to the table next to his bed to grab a condom. We stayed in the spooning position as he slid inside me and thrust slowly in and out, over and over for a time indeterminable, kissing me over my shoulder the entire time, taking me to a height of pleasure I didn't know existed. It was like we were starving for each other, unable and unwilling to sleep until we got our fill because even though it had been less than six weeks since our lunch date and the sex that followed, it felt like the sexual tension had been building ever since, only to finally combust between Jack's sheets.

By the time Jack gave me my fourth orgasm of the night, I was completely exhausted, sore, and satiated, but it wasn't enough for Jack. He'd slid down my body and ate at me mercilessly for what felt like forever—increasing and decreasing the pressure to constantly keep me on edge—until I came with a scream that might have been heard all over Cambridge. I hadn't been able to stop shaking after that. Jack had held me in his arms and whispered soothing words in my ear, but I was a quivering, over-stimulated mess and it took me a long time to come down from the high.

I knew what he was doing. I knew because it was the same thing I was doing by offering myself to him as much as I could that night. He was staking a claim, but not for anyone else to see or recognize other than me. He wasn't claiming me in front of the world as a reminder to other men to stay away. He was claiming me *for me*, reminding me that he was the only person who had ever given me a pleasure as powerful as only he was able. He was telling me, without words, how much he could give to me, how good we could be together.

I didn't need reminding of that. If there was one thing I was certain of it was that no one before or since him had ever made me feel the way Jack Harding was capable of making me feel. We were perfect together, and what I was trying to accept was that it wasn't just a sexual perfection. Sure, there was the sexual part, that even six years later it was like we knew on instinct exactly what the other wanted, how to push each button to bring the maximum amount of pleasure. But Jack could read me like a book, in and out of his bed. He knew when to push and when to retreat, he knew my moods and what made me happy or angry or sad or excited. When we were just us, there was a mutual understanding and a connection and a respect that made me care so deeply for him and what we shared together. That was important and necessary, but, my god, in his bed he could play me like the ivory keys of a piano, and I wanted him to know that I could do the same to him.

When the shower started running, I slid out of the bed and didn't bother to put any clothes on. I glanced briefly around Jack's bedroom that looked like a tornado had come through. Our clothes were thrown around the room, and I almost laughed when I saw my Wednesday Addams wig resting on top of Jack's dresser from when he'd yanked it off my head and sank his fingers into my hair.

I opened the bathroom door and Jack peaked around the shower curtain.

"Sorry," he said. "Did I wake you?"

I shook my head and basked in his perusal as his eyes raked over my naked body, looking at me like he wanted to devour me. I held the heated look as I walked across the tiles, and I didn't even wait for an invitation before I climbed in with him.

"Good morning." My voice was hushed as I wrapped my arms around his neck and he pressed his firm, wet, hot body against mine while he slid his arms around my waist and held me tightly to him.

"Very good." His voice was hungry as I wriggled just slightly against him, just enough so he could feel my skin, warm and tight and just for him. When he said, "I'm glad you stayed," I buried my face in his neck so he didn't have to see how pleased those words made me. Jack had been so vulnerable last night when he'd told me he wouldn't be mad if I decided to leave. Even if it destroyed him, Jack had always been willing to respect my wishes. Sure, there had been a few times we fought about it, especially toward the end of the seven months we'd been sleeping together at Klein, but even at the end, he almost always told me he was fine with whatever I wanted to do.

I was glad I stayed last night, too. I didn't know where we would go from here, but last night I'd decided I wouldn't fight it anymore. I still didn't think I was interested in having a relationship or anything long term—not least of all because the idea of giving myself and my heart to someone that way again was terrifying—but I wasn't going to actively resist it anymore. I was just going to let go and enjoy my time with Jack, and whatever happened over our time together, I would try to embrace with an open heart and mind. I was tired of fighting my feelings for him, tired of hurting us both, so I was ready to go along for the ride, ready to be open to whatever naturally progressed between us even if it might kill me. I wasn't ready to give him up.

Jack ran soapy hands up and down my back, feeling every inch of the skin there, lighting me up with his touches—touches that could drive me wild, that had the ability to turn me on in ways no other man had. When he slid his hands down to cup my ass and lift me upward against him, my lips found his, and I didn't hesitate before I slipped my tongue into his sexy as sin mouth.

He was hard against my stomach, and when I shifted my hips to rub against him, he groaned into my mouth. After last night, I shouldn't have been this turned on, I shouldn't have wanted him this much, and I should've been embarrassed by how I threw myself at him, whimpering lustily, already wet with the need to have him buried so deep he might never find his way out.

But there was something I wanted even more than I wanted him inside me, something that I'd been thinking about for six weeks, maybe six years, something I'd missed like hell in the time we'd been apart.

I dropped my arms from around his neck and pushed out of his hold so I could sink easily down to my knees. His eyes widened a bit, and he stared down at me with desire and greed and lust written all over all of his features—his face flushed from his arousal and the heat of the water, his lips slightly parted, chest moving up and down as he watched me. I turned us so that he was under the spray and I could avoid getting water in my eyes. I could've stayed there, on my knees, just admiring how fucking hot and sexy he was forever, with the water streaming down his muscles, making his body glisten, showing off all the bulk he'd worked so hard for. But when his cock nudged my chin, I knew I couldn't just sit there and stare forever no matter how badly I wanted to.

I dropped my eyes from his, and they landed on the hard spike in front of me. Even after all this time, after all the casual hookups I had over the years, Jack still had the most gorgeous cock I'd ever seen. It was long and thick and cut, and the head changed colors depending on his level of arousal, letting me know now by its deep, angry, purple color that he was past the edge of just being turned on. It only turned that color when he was desperate to come, and my god I wanted my mouth to take him there. How either of us could be this desperate—he this hard and me as wet as I was—after all we done last night was just a testament to how much we'd held back our want in the time we'd decided to play at being just friends.

I licked my lips, and Jack groaned as a bead of pre-come burst from the tip, opaque as it slid down. It was about to drop to the shower floor when I leaned forward and flicked my tongue over Jack's swollen head to catch it.

"Fuck." Jack panted and slammed his hands against the tiled wall as if he didn't want to touch me for fear of pushing me too far. I appreciated his thoughtfulness, but I was going to change that very soon. I was going to tease him until he was desperate, and I wasn't going to give him a choice but to go as rough as he needed.

I rested my hands on his thighs and leaned forward to suck just his thick tip into my mouth. Jack continued to breathe heavily above me, and when I looked at him through my lashes and slid my mouth further down his length, he made a strangled sound, his eyes locked on mine.

He tasted just like I remembered, and affection flooded me at the thought. It was like being away from home for years and coming back to having your favorite meal cooked by your mom—the taste of home and comfort and love and everything perfect in the world. Jack's cock—his skin, his pre-come—tasted like all of the good things. It tasted like a memory, like something I thought I'd never have again, and those thoughts made me want more of it.

91

I brought one of my hands to the base as I slid further. Jack choked out my name, and I began to move more, back and forth on his delicious cock, savoring the taste, the heavy feel of it in my mouth as I jacked him while I sucked eagerly.

Losing myself in the moment, I went at him like I couldn't get enough, getting even wetter at the incredibly sexy sounds Jack was releasing. I knew he was holding back, and if the sounds were anything to go by, he was almost to the brink. I wanted him there. Right there. I wanted him to take what he wanted, to fuck my mouth like he couldn't help himself, so I slid my hands up to his hips and shifted my grip to urge him to move. Hesitantly, he started to thrust as I moved my mouth on his length, but when he went a bit too far, I gagged slightly, and he immediately pulled back, apologizing breathlessly.

"It's okay," I gasped. I looked up at him. "Take what you want."

"God, hearing you say that." He leaned his head against the wall, trying to catch his breath. "You can't say that to me. Not when I'm this fucking close."

"I want it," I said, sliding my fist up and down his length, making him groan. "Fuck my mouth, okay?"

"Talia." His voice was hoarse and raw. "I don't want to hurt you."

"You won't," I said as I leaned forward to lick his head. "You couldn't."

And then I leaned forward and took him as far back in my throat as I could, trying to relax that channel so he wouldn't have to worry about gagging me. He started off slowly at first, still worried about hurting me, but when I started to adjust more so I could take him deeper, he finally let go of some of his control over himself, moving his hips steadily and finally sinking his hands in my hair like I knew he wanted.

"Fuck, Talia," he moaned. "Fuck, you're gonna make me come."

I looked up and nodded, going faster, taking him deeper, squeezing the round mounds of his firm ass to encourage him.

"Yeah, you want it?" He groaned when I nodded again. "You want my come?"

I really fucking did.

His thrusts became more erratic and unmeasured as he started moaning a constant stream of curses and incoherent begging and other words that sounded vaguely like my name and "more" and "yes."

I felt him thicken in my mouth, and I hollowed my cheeks, sucking him hard, breathing heavily through my nose so I could give him everything we both needed.

"I'm gonna come," he gasped. "Fuck. Touch yourself."

I immediately obeyed, moving one of hands from his ass down to my clit. His eyes looked down so he could see what I was doing, and they flicked frantically between my mouth and my hand as he got even thicker in my mouth, moaning over and over like he was going to die if he didn't come soon. I was so turned on I thought I was going to combust. I probably could have come just from sucking him but touching between my wet lips was going to take me there and beyond.

I moaned around his cock, so aroused at the dirty thing we were doing. I'd given blow jobs to men before—I'd given *many* to Jack while at Klein—but I'd never been this close from it, this desperate and needy to have a man's come down my throat. But I wanted it. I wanted it more than anything, and as he watched me touch myself I felt myself getting closer, just as turned on by sucking him as I was by his eyes on me and my fingers on my clit.

"Coming," he said, voice strangled, clutching my head tightly. "Fuck, baby, I'm coming."

I jacked him through his release as it spilled onto my tongue. It was somehow both sweet and bitter and so uniquely him that I swallowed it down and savored it like it was a decadent treat, moaning as I sped up my fingers, while I continued to suck in every last drop of the fluid, moaning around his still shooting cock.

When I finally pulled off, Jack was leaning heavily against the wall, panting, and staring down at me in wonder.

Then, without another word, he bent and put his arms under mine to yank me up. He pushed me against the shower wall as I panted, eyes on him. He didn't waste time before he sank one hand in my hair and brought the other between my legs. I tilted my head back as he toyed with me, and I moaned nonstop, so incredibly turned on by what we'd just done that it only took about a minute before my orgasm washed over me so forcefully that my legs shook.

Both of us were panting as I came down, and Jack put his head against the shower tiles as I leaned forward to put my head on his heaving chest.

"That was the hottest thing I've ever experienced," he finally managed through heavy breaths.

I looked up at him after a moment, lust slicing through me anew when I saw the tender look in his eyes, and I wanted to kiss him badly but worried he wouldn't want to after what we'd just done. He removed any doubt when he bent and wrapped his arms around me, kissing me heatedly, tongue diving into my mouth to share in our combined flavors.

We made out under the stream of water for a long time until Jack pulled back so he could run a wash cloth all over my body. He cleaned me thoroughly, making my skin heat, making me want him again as he took such good care of me, making me feel cherished as he cleaned every inch of my body. He didn't take his eyes off me the entire time, and my heart started to race. I felt like we were sharing in a moment that was bigger than just cleaning off in the shower, like he was trying to convey something to me in his gazes, something I wasn't sure I was ready to see. But I did the same for him as I took my turn cleaning him, savoring his beautiful body, getting my fill with both my eyes and my hands if that was even possible.

We didn't speak as we got out. I felt suddenly shy as he wrapped me in a towel and gave me one of the soft smiles of his that I loved so much. He pulled the towel tightly around me and then kissed me tenderly, his tongue roving my mouth leisurely, like we had all the time in the world.

He told me he was going to make breakfast and that I was welcome to any of his clothes if I needed them. He showed me where he kept his t-shirts and athletic shorts, but I knew everything would be too big for me, so in a moment of inspiration when he left the room, I grabbed the white button down he'd worn for his Clark Kent costume and slipped it over my shoulders. It was long on me, and I didn't bother with anything underneath, buttoning it only from about the middle of my torso and down so a significant amount of my cleavage showed. I felt sexy and desirable, and when I brought the collar up to my nose to inhale Jack's scent, I felt hot all over.

When I walked out of his bedroom, Jack dropped the spatula he'd been holding. I smirked as it clattered to the floor, and his eyes followed me heatedly as I walked further into the kitchen. He kissed me silly when he finally got his hands on me, and then pushed me away, promising to get some food in me before I wasted away.

My stomach growled when he put the eggs, toast, and half a grapefruit in front of me. We chatted throughout breakfast, just enjoying each other's company and the low, constant undercurrent of sexual tension that thrummed between us.

After breakfast, I was in no rush, and Jack didn't seem to be in any hurry to see me go. Sunday was always the one day of the week I was off because Gia's was closed (she was a devout Catholic who did not believe at all in working on holy days and usually spent the entire day at mass) and we never had rehearsal. So, Jack and I snuggled on his couch, watching a Netflix series about a serial killer.

We spent the entire day cycling between eating, watching Netflix, and fucking. He took me against his kitchen counter while he was making lunch and on the couch a couple times, once with me straddling him, another with him on his knees behind me, pounding into me while I begged him for more.

It was incredible to spend the whole day with him with no worries and no pressure. I didn't let myself think about what might be in store for us or what anything might mean, and I just focused on letting myself enjoy my time with him in all the ways that I could.

Until the buzzer sounded at his door, letting us both know that someone was downstairs.

"Sir," the doorman said from several floors below when Jack answered the call, sexy and shirtless, sweatpants slung low on his hips. God, he was mouthwatering.

"Ms. Saltzman is here to see you."

I saw Jack's shoulders stiffen as I tried to figure out who that was and why it would cause that reaction. I racked my brain—Saltzman... I didn't know any Saltzmans, but the way Jack replied tightly let me know it was someone he didn't want to see.

"Can you let her know that I'm busy and that if she needs to contact me, it can be over the phone."

There was hesitancy on the other line.

"She's quite upset, sir."

"Fuck," Jack sighed to himself, running a hand down his face. He pressed the button on the intercom again and said, "I'll be down in a minute."

Jack didn't look at me as he strode to his bedroom, and when I walked after him and stood in his doorway, wearing nothing but his t-shirt, his voice was almost a growl as he dug angrily through one of his drawers.

"I'll be back in a few minutes," he said, still not looking at me as he shoved a shirt over his head. "Just stay up here, okay?"

"Is everything all right? Who's down there?"

Jack finally looked at me, and when he did, his features softened only slightly. He looked off in the distance for a moment, and then back at me, making my heart hammer with nerves. What the fuck was going on?

"It's Rachel," he said, sounding exasperated.

My heart thumped painfully. "Rachel?"

He nodded.

"What's she doing here?"

He shook his head. "I'm honestly not sure, but I'm just going to go down, make sure she's okay, and then I'll be right back."

I looked at the floor for just a moment. I felt anxious and flayed wide open, and I knew Jack probably understood how I might be feeling because he knew how insecure the topic of Rachel made me, no matter how much I hated that fact. I didn't want to let this affect me—it had only been a few months really. Just a few months ago he had broken their *engagement*, their almost three-year long

95

relationship and now he was with me. It wasn't out of the realm of possibility that he might still have to deal with his ex, but I still couldn't face it. I felt better about the direction Jack and I were heading in, but, fuck, this was hard. It was hard standing here, knowing that I couldn't possibly compare to this gorgeous woman that he'd had a real relationship with, compared to me, who didn't even want to call Jack my boyfriend.

I wouldn't let this break me. I wouldn't become that person who was like a scared rabbit when it came to exes and the past. So, instead of breaking down, begging him not to go down there and stay here with me, I squared my shoulders and looked back up at him.

"I'm going to go."

I moved to start gathering my things, and I felt him at my back.

"Please don't go."

I pulled Jack's shirt over my head and reached for the black dress I'd worn yesterday for my costume, yanking it on.

"You should invite her up," I said, despite the voice in my head screaming, *What in the hell are you talking about?!* "She's obviously upset." I slipped my feet into my black flats and walked into this living room to find my clutch. "You can't leave her standing down there, and you definitely won't be able to have a conversation in your lobby." I could hear how flat my voice sounded, but I couldn't change it. I couldn't let my true feelings show.

"There isn't going to be a conversation," Jack said from behind me. I bent to the floor in front of the door where I had tossed my clutch when we'd come in the night before. "I'm going to tell her there's nothing left to say and leave it at that."

"Jack—"

When I turned to face him, he crowded into my space. I backed up against the door, and he brought his hands to my face, his eyes searching. Almost reflexively, I brought my free hand up to his hip and left the other with my clutch hanging at my side.

"Talia, please don't go."

"I need to."

"Why?" he breathed.

I let my eyes flutter closed. "Because if I stay, I'm going to beg you not to go down there, not to talk to her, and that's not fair."

Jack rested his forehead against mine, and I inhaled deeply, breathing in the scent of his skin—soap and sex.

"I just want to make sure she's okay," he said quietly.

"I know," I said. I liked that about him—adored how caring and kind he was.

He kissed me then, just a brush of his lips against mine, but I felt it like electricity all over my skin. The past day with him had been nothing short of perfection, and even though I hated that it was ending like this, I knew that it had to, knew that I was already at the edge of something I didn't know if I could handle, the urge to flee like a brand on my skin.

"Let me call you a cab."

"I can coordinate it with Patrick."

After another kiss and a few more whispered words, Jack and I took the elevator down to the first floor of his building, his hand firmly in mine. When the doors dinged open, I tried to pull my hand out of his so Rachel wouldn't see, but he just held on tighter. We rounded the corner where the bank of elevators was, and I saw her immediately. Even with a tearstained face, she was stunning, and even though it was a Sunday evening, she was dressed for the boardroom, towering and almost as tall as Jack when she stood in her heels.

She looked back and forth between us. Jack met her eyes, and when I looked up at him, it was almost like he was glaring at her. I had no idea how their relationship had ended, but based on the way they were currently staring daggers at one another, I had to guess it hadn't ended well.

"Pat, can you call a cab for Talia?" Jack asked, turning to his doorman who sat behind a long wooden desk.

"Of course, sir," he replied in his Irish brogue.

"And please make sure it's charged to my account."

Patrick gave a curt nod and picked up the phone.

Jack turned to me. "I'll call you soon, okay? Text me when you make it home."

I nodded, and he reached for my other hand so he was holding both of mine in his, his eyes beseeching mine. "I had an incredible time with you last night and today." His voice was low, but there was no way that Rachel wouldn't be able to hear it from where she was standing.

I felt a blush stain my cheeks. "Me, too."

He turned us more so his back was to Rachel, and I glanced over his shoulder, seeing how furious she looked, before I looked back up into Jack's eyes, the most beautiful, green, clear, sincere eyes I had ever seen.

"I have no expectations," he whispered. "If you want to keep being friends, I'll take this weekend and savor it for what it was. I want more with you, but if you don't want that, I'll respect that and give you whatever you need."

I heard the sincerity in his voice and saw it all over his face, and I knew that if I told him I wasn't looking for anything more than friendship and occasional sex, he would abide by it just like he had for so long. I was done fighting the truth of what I wanted—what I had wanted for nearly as long as I could remember knowing him. I wanted to be with Jack and no one else, and I sure as hell didn't want him with anyone else, but how could I explain what the night before and this entire day had meant to me when I could feel his ex-fiancée's eyes boring holes into me? How in the world could I tell him I thought I wanted more when I could see her wipe away a tear?

"Call me when you're finished," I said by way of response. He frowned slightly but then nodded, leaning in to give me a soft, brief kiss before dropping my hands and guiding me with one of his big, warm hands on the small of my back over to where Patrick was sitting, obviously trying to pretend like he wasn't extremely uncomfortable with this entire scenario.

"Send me a text when Talia makes it into the cab, would you, Pat?"

Patrick nodded. "Will do."

I stood there, smiling tightly at Patrick while he picked up his phone and Jack walked over to Rachel.

"Who is she?"

I knew she was trying to be as discreet as possible, but the large room carried the sound of her hiss over to both Patrick and me. I closed my eyes.

"We can talk about this upstairs," Jack replied. Then to me he called out, "See you soon, Talia," as I heard the sound of angry heels clacking across the tile in the lobby.

I couldn't bring myself to look at him, so I just muttered, "See you," with my eyes still closed as I braced myself on the counter.

I heard the elevator ding, and just before they closed, I heard Rachel ask again, "Who the hell is she?"

Chapter 15

I waited for the cab for two agonizing minutes, imagining all the things Jack and Rachel were saying and doing, each worse than the last, before something came over me. Something intense and powerful that I couldn't let go of as it slowly began to consume me. My arms started to tingle with the weight of it, and I knew I couldn't just leave. I knew it was crazy; I knew it was jealous and insecure, and had I been in my right mind, I would have gotten in that cab and left.

Instead, I stood up from one of the plush chairs in the lobby and said to Patrick, "Could you cancel my cab? I left something up in Jack's apartment."

Patrick gave me a knowing look and looked like he was trying to contain a smile, but all he said was, "Sure thing, Ms. Emery. The elevator is ready for you."

I took a deep breath in and out as the elevator slid shut in front of me. I shouldn't be doing this—I knew I would only regret it, but I couldn't stop myself. It was like an invisible fish hook had latched into me, and it was slowly reeling me in the direction of Jack's apartment, making me powerless to stop it.

As the elevator door opened on his floor, I could hear the sounds of angry voices seeping out into the hallway, which was exactly what I'd been hoping for when I decided to stay. It wasn't until I approached the door, though, that I could hear what the voices were saying.

"—long have you been with her?"

"Rachel."

Jack sounded frustrated and annoyed, but Rachel sounded furious.

"I think I deserve to know, don't you?" The sound of her voice seemed to move as I pressed my ear against the door, which I assumed meant she must have been pacing the length of Jack's living room. "Were you with her when we were together? Is that why you ended it? Were you cheating?"

It was strange hearing her voice like this. Granted, I'd never heard her voice before today, but from what little both Jack and Catrina had told me about her, she was cold and indifferent, almost emotionless. That's what I expected to hear in her voice, not the vitriolic anger I heard drip from every single word.

"You know why I ended it," Jack snapped. "Jesus, you know I wouldn't cheat. Do you really think so little of me?"

"I know the reason you gave," Rachel snapped back, ignoring the second part of what Jack said. "Some ridiculously noble thing about how I needed to find someone who could give their whole heart to me. But, Jesus Christ, Jack, that was barely four months ago, and I come to your apartment—the apartment that you *never* let me move in no matter how many times I suggested it, the apartment that smells like *sex*, by the way—and you've got some woman—"

"She's not some woman," Jack interjected angrily, making my heart thump. "I've known Talia since college. We've been friends for ten fucking years, Ray, she's not just some woman. And I meant what I said. Would you really want to spend your life with a husband who didn't love you the way he should?"

"Yes! I wanted to spend my life with *you*."

"You wanted to spend your life with the idea of me," Jack said, sounding annoyed and exasperated. "You wanted us to have that perfect, storybook life on the outside that was nothing but coldness and resentment on the inside, just like our parents. We were not good for each other. My god, you hardly smiled when we were together. This is the most emotion I've seen you show about our relationship ever. You weren't even this upset the day I ended it. So why now?"

There was a long pause where neither of them spoke, giving me the chance to consider how ridiculous and psychotic I looked and probably was, my ear pressed to the door of my lover's apartment, listening to him argue with a woman who, up until four months ago, he was going to marry.

"I... Seeing you last weekend, it just..." Rachel's voice got quieter and I strained my ears so I could hear every word. "We worked, Jack. It was simple. We both knew what we wanted and what we expected from each other."

"We worked because neither of us was willing to give anything to the relationship," Jack said, his voice quieter than before. "We worked because we were both just existing in a relationship that neither of us was truly invested in."

"We were invested in the important things," Rachel countered. "We weren't worried about the frivolous things. We were worried about what was truly important."

"Like merging our families and creating a joint bank account?" I could almost see the incredulity on Jack's face. "That's not love Rachel. That's a business transaction."

"But it worked for us."

"Did we make each other happy?"

I sucked in a breath, and then immediately covered my mouth, fearful one of them would hear it through the door.

"What?" Rachel's voice was almost a whisper, shocked, and I pressed my ear harder.

"It was simple because there was no passion. There's no way you were happy being with me when both of us were passionless."

"You made me happy," Rachel said, and I could hear the tears in her voice. "It was in our way, and may not have been like everyone else, but I was happy."

Neither of them spoke for a while, but when Rachel finally did, I held my breath.

"Is she the reason you left me?"

"Rachel."

"Just tell me, Jack. Is she the reason?"

I didn't know which answer would be more devastating.

Which is why I didn't stick around to hear it.

I took the elevator down to the lobby, and I saw Patrick perk up when I rounded the corner.

I wanted to scream.

My skin felt tingly and too tight for my body, and I was jittery with nerves and adrenaline.

"Is she the reason you left me?"

On the one hand, the idea that Jack left Rachel because the feelings he had for me had lingered after all these years made me feel an overwhelming joy and a profound connection to Jack. I knew he wanted me, knew he wanted to be with me—he'd done nothing but show me that since our lunch date at the Green Hornet—but knowing that his feelings went so deep to cross time and other relationships made me feel... light. It made me want to throw myself into his arms and never let him let me go. But there was this bigger part of me that felt an unerring pressure knowing that that might be the case. How could I possibly live up to six years of expectations about what our relationship would be like? Would we finally be together for real, and he'd realize, over time, that I wasn't worth the hype—that he'd built me up in his mind to be this incredible person he'd longed for but who was really just a grown ass woman too terrified to even commit to a pet?

"Would you like me to call you another cab, Ms. Emery?"

I looked at Patrick and then back out at the street in front of the building.

He'd just asked a simple question, but it suddenly felt like the most important question anyone had ever asked.

Stay.

Or go.

I could go. I could let Jack finish is apparently unfinished business with his ex. I could ignore his calls, let him realize that I wasn't worth the trouble in the simplest way possible. By ignoring him. I could decide that my insecurity about Jack's relationship with his ex-fiancée far outweighed my trust in and care for Jack. I could end it with him before he got the chance to end it with me. I could protect my heart the way I had for a decade.

Or I could stay. I could trust Jack. I could let myself be open to a future with him, let myself be open to the hurt because whatever potential hurt there might be today or days, weeks, or years from now didn't matter in the face of how happy I was when I was just sitting in the same room with Jack. I could admit to myself that the pain of leaving right now would be so much worse than the delightful ache of staying. I could go back to the way things were—I could be Talia, musician, friend, and woman who never settled down with a partner because men would screw you over every single time. Or I could be with Jack. I could stop denying that he was who I'd wanted for years, and he made me happier than I'd ever been. I could stay.

"Ma'am?"

"No, Patrick," I said quietly. "I'm just going to wait down here for Jack to get done if that's okay?"

Patrick beamed. "That's fine by me, ma'am." His grin took up his entire face, and I couldn't help but return his smile. Patrick was totally Team Talia, and I adored him for it and wondered what Rachel had done when she'd come here in the past to make him root for me instead of her.

"Can I get you anything while you wait? We have water or coffee in our breakroom, and I'd be happy to bring you some."

"No, I'm all right." I sat down on one of the big, comfy lobby chairs, tucking my feet underneath me. I was going to take out my phone, but I realized it had died a while ago since I'd left it in my bag all night and day and hadn't charged it since before I'd left for Catrina and Brody's last night. So, instead I angled toward the concierge desk and spoke to Patrick.

"So, where's home for you?"

"Southie, Ms. Emery. My family's lived there for four generations. We came to Boston at the turn of the century and never left."

I rested my chin on my arms on the back of the chair and listened to Patrick tell me about his family. I guessed he was maybe five to ten years older than Jack and me, while he told me about his ex-wife, who was an elementary school teacher and who had remarried a year ago. Patrick said he liked his wife's new husband, which made no sense to me, especially when he told me it was his cousin.

"I didn't really know him growing up. There are lots of O'Shaughnessy's in Boston. It was a possibility she was going to marry another one of us."

He had three kids—two girls and a boy, seventeen, sixteen, and nine—and he was beside himself with excitement when I asked if he had any pictures. His seventeen-year-old daughter was in her senior year of high school and was going to be starting at Boston University next fall, and his sixteen-year-old daughter was basically a volleyball star at their high school. His nine-year-old son was the spitting image of him, and Patrick puffed up with pride when I told him so. He told me that he and Maureen—his ex-wife—shared custody since they lived in the same neighborhood and it wasn't too much of an adjustment for them to move from his house to their mom's each week since they lived in the same school district.

We'd been talking for probably twenty or so minutes, and Patrick had just blushed when I'd asked him if he had a new woman in his life when the ding of the elevator interrupted his answer. Patrick slipped back into his professional demeanor, and I turned my head to see the tall, elegant, beautiful form of Rachel round the corner. She'd obviously been crying but still looked stunning, but when she saw me leaning against the counter that Patrick occupied, her face twisted into a nasty sneer and she scoffed.

She didn't respond when Patrick told her to have a nice day, and she glided out of the lobby, her chin in the air without sparing either of us a second glance.

As soon as she was out of the building, Patrick turned to me and lifted one eyebrow but said nothing. I just shrugged and was about to ask him again about lady friends when there was a second ding.

It was like the heavens opened up when I saw him.

Jack looked harried and hadn't even bothered to change out of his sweats and t-shirt. His hair was disheveled liked he'd run his hand through it several times, but when he saw me standing there and his face instantly lit up, he'd never looked more beautiful.

He closed the distance between us in an instant, and without a thought about the man standing just a few feet from us, he grabbed my face in his hands and brought his lips down to mine. I grabbed his forearms to steady myself, and even though the kiss barely lasted a second—just one hard press of lips—I felt dizzy when he pulled back.

Out of the corner of my eye, I saw Patrick put up a sign that said, "Back in fifteen minutes, please ring the bell for assistance," before he quietly turned into a door directly behind the desk to where I assumed the breakroom was.

"You're here."

Jack sounded happy but shocked, and I smiled at him through my nerves.

"I'm here."

His eyes searched my face. "I thought I would have to hunt you down and convince you that Rachel and I are over."

"I thought so, too, for a while."

"But you stayed."

I sighed and wrapped my arms around his neck as he slid his arms around my waist and pulled me close. We just held each other, in the lobby of his apartment building, breathing each other in for so long that I thought Patrick was going to come back. I wouldn't have cared if he did. Being in Jack's arms made me forget everything else in the world.

"Why?" I heard Jack whisper into my hair.

I could've brushed it off so easily, and I knew he would have let me. There was too much to explain, too much to make him understand, so instead I settled for the simple truth.

"I trust you."

A small noise escaped the back of his throat, and he squeezed me tighter.

Finally, I pulled back, and he studied me intently though neither of us spoke.

I wasn't trying to put a label on what we were or what we were going to be, and I didn't want there to be any pressure. I just knew I wanted him, was tired of pretending I didn't. I wanted more with him than friends with benefits or casual sex if that's what he wanted, too.

"I want more," I said quietly.

His face went slack with mix of shock and elation.

"You do?"

With our arms still around each other, I nodded.

"I don't want there to be any pressure or expectations for either of us, but I know I want something more." I swallowed. "With you."

"Come back upstairs," he murmured, his voice raspy, his intentions clear.

God, I wanted to, but there were... logistical things that needed to be taken care of.

"I have to shower and get into different clothes," I said with a small laugh.

"Shower here." His eyes darkened. "Wear my clothes."

I bit the corner of my lip. How could I resist when he was looking at me like that?

"Okay."

His smile could've lit the lobby that was darkened like the sky outside and nearly did.

Without a care for who might see, he kissed me then, deeply, making my toes curl and my fingertips tingle as he held my face in his hands and dipped his tongue in and out of my mouth, caressing every single curve and crevice as if the world around us didn't exist. I felt a peace wash over me as we kissed, and then he pulled away finally, called out a loud thank you to Patrick, and took my hand to guide me back toward the bank of elevators, grinning down at me the entire time. I didn't know what was going to happen between us, didn't know what the future held for Jack and me, but I was ready for whatever was in store.

Chapter 16

"**I** can't believe you're taking me to Vermont. To hang out with your *mom*," Jack quipped from the passenger seat. "You know that's like totally something you would do with your boyfriend, right?"

"Shut up." I squeezed the steering wheel, simultaneously annoyed with him and fighting back a smile.

"I know that's a dirty word for you, but I think it's true. I think I'm your *boyfriend*."

"Can it, Harding."

"When you introduce me to people around town, are you going to say, 'this is Jack, my boyfriend' or are you going to say 'this is some dude I know'?" I could hear the smirk in his voice.

"Probably that."

"Hm. Interesting." I glanced over at him and saw him rubbing his chin like he was contemplating something. "I wonder if there are pretty girls in Vermont. Since I'm apparently a free agent and all."

I punched him in the arm and he laughed.

"You better not be looking at or talking to any pretty girls."

"I won't," he said, feigning sincerity. "I wouldn't do that to my *girlfriend*."

It had been almost two weeks since Halloween night.

Two weeks since I had finally stopped pretending that I was cool with just being Jack's friend. Two weeks of dates almost every night, of spending at least some portion of every day together. Two weeks of showing up to our rehearsals with a stupid grin on my face and ignoring Chuck and Isaac when they asked what the hell was up with me. Two weeks of Jack. Two weeks of being the happiest I could ever remember being.

It had also been two weeks since the encounter with Rachel. Since then, something had come over me. It was like I had finally stepped back and was able to see all the ways that Jack had proved that I was it for him, that no matter what got thrown at him or at me or at us, we were able to keep finding our way back to each other.

Escucha.

Listen.

That's what abuela would have said. That was always her way of telling us not to ignore what was around us, not to ignore the signs and everything that God was trying to tell us.

I was trying my damnedest to listen and accept everything for what it was, and the thing that I kept on hearing over and over was that Jack chose me. He had six years ago, he had a month ago, and he kept on doing it even when I tried to push him away. He chose me. He chose us.

Listen.

I'd asked him to come with me to Vermont on a whim, on a day that I was trying especially hard to listen. Before I could think about what it might mean, what he might think, or the fact that he might say no, I'd just said it. It was three nights ago while we were eating pizza in my apartment and watching reruns of *Law & Order.* I'd been planning on taking the week off for months, and when Jack asked me if I wanted to go to a concert with him on Saturday, I told him I couldn't because I was going to Vermont to visit my mom for the week.

"Bummer," he said, giving me a smile even though I could see in his eyes that he was disappointed. "I hope you have fun, though."

"Wanna come?" I blurted.

I almost wanted to take it back a second after I said it, but the smile he gave me made all my fears and doubts just dissipate into the air. He looked so genuinely pleased that I'd just thrown myself in his arms and kissed him through yeses.

Jack and I hadn't had a conversation about what we were.

Well, that wasn't exactly true. The truth was that Jack had subtly attempted the conversation probably half a dozen times over the past twelve days, and every single time I shut him down. I didn't know what we were, and I didn't know what I wanted us to be. The only thing I knew was that I wanted to be with him. That he made me happy. I'd even taken to ignoring Catrina's calls (something I had never, ever done) because I knew she was going to make me answer questions I wasn't even prepared to hear, let alone answer.

Talia Elizabeth Gonzalez Emery, I know you're ignoring me, and I'm going to let you do it because I know you and I know you're probably freaking out but probably fucking Jack like a teenager. But when you get back from Vermont, WE ARE TALKING. I don't care if I have to break into your apartment.

I'd responded to Catrina with a winking face and a thumbs up emoji, but inside I'd been practically trembling with nerves thinking about how that conversation was going to go.

I just didn't even understand why we had to *call* it something. Couldn't we just be together and not worry about *what we were*? I wanted to tell Jack to fuck off, but I knew that this wasn't just his way of teasing me. He told me he had no expectations, and I wanted to remind him of that, though I didn't because I knew his questions arose out of his fears—fears I had put inside him. I knew he was worried I was going to do exactly what I'd done to him the last time we were together and freak out if he so much as thought the word "relationship." I wanted things to be different this time, but I also just wanted to take things slow and see where it went without the pressure of a label like girlfriend or boyfriend.

He had also tried to have a conversation with me about Rachel, yet another conversation I had shut down. My reasoning for not wanting to have that conversation was different, though, because it wasn't about my fears or insecurities. Seeing Jack that night come down to the lobby, knowing that as soon as he was finished with his conversation with Rachel, he was going to leave his apartment and come find me immediately made me realize that we didn't need to talk about it. I knew where I stood, and it was so abundantly clear where Jack stood that I didn't feel the need to have him explain himself or tell me all the reasons I should be okay with everything because, surprisingly, I was.

So, instead, I invited him to Vermont where I hoped we didn't have to worry about Rachel or *us* for at least a week.

The drive to East Alburgh was four hours. I'd told my mom I was bringing a guy I was seeing, and she was elated. I'd almost called him my friend, and even though he couldn't hear me at the time, it felt like I would be betraying him somehow by calling him that. Because I didn't know what the hell we were, but I knew he wasn't just my friend. And it felt like lying to my mom to say that that's all he was.

The trip there went by quicker than any of the other times I'd driven to see my mom. Jack and I talked and flirted the entire time, except when he was teasing me about being my boyfriend. We stopped in Burlington because I knew I wasn't going to be able to hold my pee in for another hour, and when we were coming out of the gas station, Jack had grabbed my hand and yanked me to him. He'd just looked at me for a few seconds before he smiled and gave me the sweetest kiss. My heart had pounded in my chest, and when he pulled away and gave me a playful smack on my rear, I wanted to jump him.

I loved how playful and goofy Jack could be while also being smart and serious and genuine at other times. It was the perfect juxtaposition of characteristics and they each made up so much of what I adored about him.

We were about fifteen minutes away when Jack started to fidget.

"Oh my god, will you sit still?" I finally said. "You're stressing me out."

"Shit." He ran a hand through his hair and huffed out a small laugh. "I think I'm nervous."

I looked at him from the driver's seat, and my heart bloomed in my chest. Sometimes even the simplest things he said gutted me. He never held back how he felt, gave himself all of me, even if it was something like this.

"Really?" I grinned.

"Don't make fun," Jack said. "I'm not good with meeting parents."

"I don't believe that for a second," I said. "And anyway, my mom is so nice and welcoming, so don't even worry."

"Is she going to be suspicious of me?" he asked. He sounded like he was only half joking. "Ask me what my intentions are?"

"Doubt it," I said with an eye roll. "Okay, she's definitely going to greet you with a hug, so hug her back and don't be weird about it."

"Try to sneak a feel of your mom's boobs. Got it."

I swatted at him, but he grabbed my hand with a laugh and brought his mouth to my hand. My heart fluttered. I moved my hand to put it back on the steering wheel, but he kept his hand on my thigh. The small show of intimacy made me want to lean over and kiss him.

"Give her a hug and don't be weird, creep," I said, and he laughed again. "She'll probably have dinner and dessert made. Don't put more on your plate than you can eat because she hates that and expects you to clean your plate. Don't tell her you like something if you don't like it because she has this uncanny way of being able to tell when people like her food or not, and she hates when people say they do when they don't. So just be honest."

"Jesus," Jack muttered. "I feel like I need to take notes."

"Um, are you not? Because, yeah, you should be." I was teasing him, but when he took out his phone and started typing, it was so adorable that I didn't even tell him I was kidding.

"Remember that her last name is one of my middle names, so do not call her Ms. Emery. Call her Ms. Gonzalez. She'll tell you to call her Monica, but she still likes the show of respect to begin with. When Brody met her, he jokingly called her 'Mon,' and she didn't forgive him for like six months."

Jack howled next to me. "Wow, I love that. Can't wait to remind him of how much your mom hates him the next time I see him."

"She doesn't hate him! She's just... she tries to be a modern woman but she's secretly super traditional."

"Noted," Jack said. "What else?"

"She likes to talk politics, but not at the dinner table," I explained. "But we never discuss the forty-fifth president, so don't even hint at it."

"Perfect," Jack said with a snort. "I wouldn't want to hurl up my dinner anyway."

"I knew I liked you," I said, glancing at him just as I turned the corner that led down a long road that led to my mom's restaurant and her little home.

My mom's house was a little white cottage with brown roof shingles and a chimney stack. It had a porch in the front with two rocking chairs and lots of plants that my mom took meticulous care of, and in front of the porch there were asters in full bloom.

"This place is beautiful, Talia," Jack said as we pulled down the driveway and parked right behind my mom's blue sedan.

"Oh, tell my mom that," I said as I opened the door. "She'll love you immediately."

My mom's diner was next to her house about a thousand feet down the road. It was separated from her house by two tall oak trees, and it matched my mom's house in color and shape, though it was a bit bigger. It was just after eight, so the diner had been closed for a little over an hour and it looked sleepy and quiet down the road.

Jack slung both of our bags over his shoulder and grabbed my hand with one of his while he shut the trunk with the other. I savored the feeling of holding his hand as we walked across the large green yard. I looked up at him and smiled right when I heard a squeal.

"Talia, mi amor!"

"Mama!"

She ran down the porch stairs, and I dropped Jack's hand so I could throw my arms around my mother.

It had been over five months since I'd seen her. I hadn't been able to take a trip to Vermont since Mothers' Day, and she'd been so busy with the diner that she hadn't been able to come to Boston at all either. I hadn't realized until this moment how much I had missed this woman.

My mother was gorgeous. She was petit, like me, and even more curvaceous in her tiny body. She had long black hair that went past her butt and that she took great care of. She had stunning deep brown eyes and a heart-shaped face that made her look much younger than her forty-eight years.

My mom grew up in San Juan, Puerto Rico to Puerto Rican parents. She'd moved to New York when she was thirteen and had been there until she'd moved to Vermont five years ago. My abuela still lived in Queens, my abuelo died when I was ten, and we had lots of family in Queens and in San Juan and other parts of the Caribbean still.

"Look at your hair, mija, que bonita."

"Thanks, Ma." I was still in her arms when I reached up and touched my shoulder length light brown locks. Then she looked over my shoulder.

"And who's this young man?"

Jack flashed a huge white smile as he stepped forward and held out his hand. "Jack Harding, ma'am. It's a pleasure to meet you."

"Muy amable," she murmured to me before she released me and walked to Jack, ignoring his hand and wrapping him in a hug. I gave him a thumbs-up behind her back and reminded myself to tell him later that my mom liked how polite he was. Then she looked over her shoulder and mouthed, *y guapo*, and I stifled a giggle.

"Nice to meet you, Jack," My mom said when she pulled back. Then she turned to me and pulled me against her to walk me into the house. "I made a lot of food," she said to me. "I hope you're both hungry."

I looked over my shoulder at Jack. He winked, and I melted.

Chapter 17

I climbed into the kayak carefully, limbs shaking as I tried not to tip the damn thing over.

"You doing okay there, Tal?"

"Fuck off, Harding."

I heard Jack laugh from where he was already comfortably seated in the back of the kayak and cursed myself for pushing him away from me earlier and telling him I didn't need any help getting in.

The small boat wobbled precariously, and I froze.

"Come on, Emery," Jack said. "I'm heavy enough. It won't tip."

I flipped him the bird before finally managing to get into the boat without incident. I grabbed the paddle that was strapped to the front when I felt his hand on my shoulder.

"You did good," he said. "You survived."

"I've never kayaked before, rich boy," I groused as I tightened my life jacket. "So, give me a break."

"Baby, I tried to help you, but you chose that moment to pull out the feminist card."

"Whatever," I muttered as I gripped my oar.

"It's going to be fun, I promise."

Even if I didn't have any fun and I was terrified the entire time, I was definitely going to enjoy the incredible view.

Lake Champlain was stunning. The water was crisp and blue, and the backdrop of mountains covered with fall foliage was so picturesque and perfect.

That view didn't even compare to the view behind me.

It was cold, so Jack and I were both pretty bundled up. We were both wearing dry suits, and while I looked like a blob of material since I was also wearing several layers over my suit, Jack had opted for just the suit, a beanie, and nothing else since the sun was shining brightly. The black material was tight across his entire body, showing off the thick muscles of his legs and arms, as well as the broadness of his shoulders. He looked like a superhero, and when he'd walked out of the bathroom this morning, I'd almost had to wipe the drool off my chin.

"Okay." Jack adjusted in the kayak, causing it to wobble a bit, and I gripped the edge of the boat with one hand, trying not to drop my oar with the other. "Have you ever done any paddling or anything before?"

I shook my head and told him no but didn't look at him over my shoulder because I was still too scared to move. The absolute last thing I wanted was to fall into the freezing cold lake, even if having Jack warm me up might not have been so bad.

"It's not too hard once you get the hang of it," Jack explained. Something about having him talk to me in that cool, calm teacher's voice was making me heat up despite the weather. "You're in front, so you're in charge of our speed. I'll steer from back here and help with the speed as well. We alternate on the paddling for the most part—left, right, left, right—but the main thing you need to know is that we need to paddle in sync, so if you want to sort of look over your shoulder a bit to see how I'm doing it, you can. But I'll make sure to match your strokes, so don't worry too much about it. Got it?"

I actually felt a small frisson of excitement. I was stressed the hell out about falling into the water, but I was still thrilled to share in this experience with Jack. Having this first with him made me feel like we were taking a step forward, like it was something a real couple would do, and in this moment, that didn't even freak me out.

"Got it."

"Baby?"

He'd started calling me that a lot over the past few weeks, and I couldn't even pretend that the endearment didn't make me feel all kinds of ooey gooey inside. He said it so simply, so casually, as if we'd been together forever, like it was the most natural thing in the world. It made me feel special and wanted even if it was just a generic term that a ton of people called their significant others. The way Jack said it to *me* made it feel like it was just for us. And I loved it.

"Yeah?" I chanced looking at him over my shoulder, and Jack leaned forward to rub a hand down my back.

"I swear on my life that I'm not going to let anything bad happen to you." The look in his eyes was earnest and sincere but still playful. "You trust me, right?"

I nodded instantly. "Of course." I laughed nervously. "Just don't let me drown, okay?"

"I wouldn't," Jack said as he started to paddle us slowly away from the shore. "Your mom would kill me if I did."

It didn't take long for me to get the hang of rowing. Once we got further into the lake it actually started to feel really good and natural. The moves became almost instinctive as my muscles started to remember each movement and stroke. We paddled easily as I got the hang of it, and Jack talked to me about his summers on Long Island, kayaking near Riverhead with his sister.

I loved hearing about Jack's childhood. Our lives had been so vastly different, and it was fascinating to hear about someone with a summer house, someone who spent the summer on the beach or traveling the world. It made me want all of those things with him, to have those experiences that we could share. Because even though Jack spoke of happy memories, there was this sad lilt to his voice, and I didn't really know what was behind it. He rarely spoke about spending time with his parents on those summers, and I wondered if that's what was behind it. Jack's sister was older, and it almost seemed like she'd stepped in as another parent. It was clear he adored her, and when he spoke about his nieces, he glowed with joy and pride.

When Jack started talking about rowing crew while he was in high school, I couldn't help but mercilessly tease him.

"That is so preppy, Jack," I interrupted. "I can't stand it."

He laughed. "Well, that was the thing to do, you know? Some people have football or basketball teams they root for at their high schools, but we had crew."

"Do you still do it ever?"

We'd stopped for a bit and were just floating around in the water. I angled myself so I could see him, feeling much more secure in the boat now that we'd been out for a while. He'd taken off his beanie, and the sun was glinting off his chocolate brown hair. He had his sunglasses pushed up on his head so I could see his bright green eyes, and, god, I could eat him alive if given the opportunity.

"I go on the rowing machines at the gym all the time," he said with a shrug. "But I don't get out on the water as much as I'd like to."

"How come?"

He shrugged again and looked out at the water away from me so I could only see his face in profile. He looked oddly contemplative.

"I don't know," he replied.

Since I'd inherited my mother's ability to read people really well, I knew he wasn't being totally truthful, and his body language had shifted drastically in the past minute or so. Jack was always so open with me, and I knew if he was keeping his real reasoning from me it had to be for something that felt too major to share.

"You can tell me, you know," I told him. I wanted him to feel like he could be honest with me. I wanted him to feel like he could lean on me in a way I knew I could lean on him. I wanted to be someone he could rely on instead of the girl who always walked away.

I wanted to be the person who stayed.

Ever since the day Rachel came to his apartment, I realized I didn't want to walk away this time. I wanted to be with Jack. For real. And while he was sitting across from me thinking about crew, I was silently having a life changing moment realizing for the first time since Vincent that I wanted a real, actual relationship with someone. Even if I feared he would leave me, even if everything went down in flames, I wanted to be with him. I wanted to try and build something with him even if I could only have it for a short time. I would give both of us what we'd wanted from the beginning—what we had both wanted and I had denied since the beginning of our senior year. I would do that for him, but more than that, I would do it for me.

Jack looked back at me, and he looked vulnerable in a way I'd rarely seen him. He opened his mouth and shut it, and then he shook his head briefly like he was trying to shake out the thoughts.

"The last time I rowed on the water was right after Klein," he said quietly. "The week after things ended between us."

I could feel my mouth hanging open slightly and my heart pounding in my ears. It was what I wanted—for him to open up to me about this—but it still fucking hurt knowing I'd hurt him that badly. I'd never wanted that. I'd never wanted for either of us to get hurt, which is why I'd been so adamant about not being in a serious relationship with him. But I'd blurred the lines all those years ago, and so had he. Despite how much I'd wanted to save us both from the hurt, I'd put us both through it anyway.

"Why?" I managed to ask.

Jack sighed. "Look, I don't want to make you feel bad or anything. It was a long time ago. I was twenty-two and I'd had my heart broken for the first time."

"And then didn't row again until today," I added.

"I..." Jack started. "Yeah."

"So tell me why," I said softly. "I know you aren't trying to make me feel bad. I wouldn't ask if I didn't want to know."

"After I left that day, I was just a mess. Went out with some friends that night. Got wasted. Told them all how much I hated you even though it wasn't even close to being true. The next morning I was sick to my stomach from the booze and from missing you." He was looking out at the water again, but I was staring at him, mesmerized by how willing he was to bare his soul and amazed at how much his own experience reflected mine. I'd been the one to call things off, but I'd been a mess for a long time, too, lying in bed crying and missing him until Catrina forced me to get up and go with her to the mall just to get out of the house. I knew she wanted to call me out for my behavior because I was the one getting in my own way, but she didn't. Instead, she took me to the movies, let me

115

lay my head on her shoulder while I cried silently, and when Brody called her, I'd heard her whispering that they couldn't see each other that night because her best friend needed her, which had only made me cry harder. I knew breaking things off with Jack was what was best for both of us, but I couldn't stop wanting him. I couldn't turn it off. So instead I cried.

"Being on the water always made me feel better," he continued. "So I went out that afternoon and rowed until my arms gave out. I... well, I wasn't in a good place that day. Did a lot of sad and unmanly things that I don't need to recount." There was a small lift to the corner of his mouth, but he still didn't meet my eyes. Imagining him out on the water, hurting, possibly crying, made me want to crawl across the small kayak and hold him even if it meant I might fall to my watery death.

"I tried going back out on the water a few days later, but just standing on shore reminded me of that day. Of how much pain I'd been in, and even looking at the water made me sick. I told myself I would go a few more times after that, but I just couldn't do it. So I stopped trying."

I didn't know what to say. *Sorry* seemed woefully inadequate, and it wouldn't express how much I truly regretted hurting him. Nothing I said would erase the pain I'd caused us both, so instead I chose to focus on now. This moment here between us.

"Thank you," I said, making him finally meet my eyes again. "For telling me that, and for bringing me out here today. I'm glad I could be here for your first time out on the water again. I'm honored."

Jack smiled—a soft, open, pure smile—and reached forward. I angled even more toward him so I was almost completely turned around and grabbed his proffered hand.

"Now," he said, his smile transforming into a mischievous grin, clearly trying to lighten the heavy mood. "Tell me you're my girlfriend."

I didn't roll my eyes at him. I knew he was mostly ribbing me, but my stomach was roiling with nerves. I was tired of pretending that my feelings for Jack weren't enormous—that they hadn't consumed me already. I was still petrified of what all of this would mean. For me. For us. But I'd denied us both for long enough. I wanted the real deal, and I wasn't going to let my fear of being hurt again stop me from getting what I wanted. Not anymore.

"I'm your girlfriend," I whispered, my throat and mouth drier than they'd ever been.

Jack's face went from amused to slack with shock in an instant. He squeezed my hand and pulled me closer despite the boat we were in.

"Are you serious?" I felt as raw and exposed as he looked. I nodded.

And after a few more moments of shocked silence, Jack shoved a fist in the air, clutching his oar, and whooped. The boat rocked precariously, and I glared at Jack.

"I swear to god, if this boat tips—"

Uncaring, he leaned over and pulled me to him. It was a stretch but he was able to bring us close enough so he could put his lips to mine.

"This boat can tip for all I care," he whispered against my mouth, his eyes on mine. "It only took ten years, but I finally convinced you to be my girlfriend. Let the boat tip. Because I'm happier than I've ever been."

He grabbed my face with one of his hands, holding onto his oar with the other, and kissed me deeply. On a cold November day in the middle of Lake Champlain, birds chirping, trees rustling around us as the wind whipped our hair, this moment became one of the best of my entire life.

We paddled for a little while longer after that until I felt and saw the kayak begin to veer off toward a tiny little island to our right. I looked at Jack over my shoulder and he nodded in the direction of the island.

"The kayak company owner told me about this place," he said as he paddled us toward it. "I thought we could check it out."

When he got us close enough to shore, Jack hopped out, his feet splashing in the cool water, and dragged the boat up to anchor us to the shore. Feminism be damned, I let him help me out, and as soon as I was on my feet, he yanked me against him. His mouth was on mine in an instant, and he was kissing me like he couldn't get enough. I kissed him right back, meeting his intensity, wrapping my arms tightly around his middle while he held my face in his hands and moved me exactly how he wanted.

"I love kissing you," he breathed against my lips when he pulled back just enough to rest his forehead against mine.

"I love when you kiss me," I said breathlessly. "Do it again."

He was gentler this time, more teasing with little nips and sucks. His tongue gently brushed against mine and I held him tighter, wanting more. The temperature couldn't have been more than forty degrees on the water, but I suddenly felt hot all over. He pulled back only slightly so he could sink his teeth into my lower lip, and I whimpered. Then he took a step back and I chased his mouth with mine, but he put his hands on my shoulders, grinning down at me.

He unzipped my life jacket and tossed it into the kayak along with his, and I kept my eyes on him the whole time, begging him silently to kiss me again.

"Come on," he said, taking my hand in his and pulling me along. I didn't even try not to stare at his ass in his dry suit.

Chapter 18

The island was small, maybe a little bit more than two thousand square feet, but the vegetation was spectacular. The island was covered in maple trees that were close to losing all their leaves but hadn't yet. Some were yellow and orange, but others were this vibrant red that I couldn't take my eyes off of. I was staring at several bushes of yellow flowers when Jack glanced back at me.

"These are witch hazel," he said, gently running his fingers along one. "Apparently there used to be a house on this island, but the owner died and had no family at all so it went back to the state. Most people don't know this is here, though."

We walked a little further, and when we walked around the row of bushes, I gasped. Behind the bushes, there was a big blue blanket with a wicker picnic basket on top. Above it, there was a maple tree with white Japanese style lanterns hanging from it right above the blanket.

I whipped around to Jack and gaped at him.

"You did this?"

When all he did was nod, I stared back and forth between him and the blanket and lights.

"This is amazing," I breathed. I turned back to him. "Thank you."

He pulled me along a few more steps and then sat on the blanket, tugging me down next to him.

"Your mom made empanadas and fried plantains for us," he said as he started pulling stuff out.

"She knew about this?"

"I told her my idea the other night after I called to make the kayak reservation and the owner told me about this place," he said. "I didn't even think about asking her to cook, but she offered."

"Wow, you must be special," I said, watching as Jack pulled out two plates.

Jack shrugged and looked at me out of the side of his eyes as he continued unpacking different items from the basket. "Well, she does think I'm polite and handsome."

I jerked my head up and gaped at him. "You understood that?"

He nodded, smirking. "I know a lot of Spanish. Studied abroad in Costa Rica in college, and when I took a year off between college and

119

law school, I spent most of that town in different parts of South America."

I narrowed my eyes at him. "What else don't I know about you?"

His smirk turned into a full-on grin. "Guess you'll have to find out."

"Oh my—holy shit, is that flan?" Whatever I'd planned to snark back to Jack quickly fled my mind when he pulled out two small tins that each appeared to have the mini caramel cakes inside.

"Wow, I'm not leaving Vermont," Jack said as he glanced at the containers. "I need to stay here and let your mom fatten me up."

"Don't joke about that in front of her," I said. "She might try to keep us here."

"I could live with that." I looked up at him, and before I could take in the soft look on his face he pressed his lips to mine in a quick kiss.

We feasted on all the food my mom made for us, and Jack popped a bottle of champagne. My mom had packed a thermos of her amazing coffee that we drank when we ate the flan. When we finished, Jack pulled another blanket out of the bottom of the picnic basket, and we laid back on the blanket on the ground as he wrapped us in the other one and cuddled close to me. I was buzzed on the food and champagne, and beyond content in this moment with Jack as I burrowed even closer to him. He rubbed his hand in circles on my back while I laid one of my hands on his stomach. I couldn't get to any bare skin with his dry suit on, which was the only thing that I wanted to change about this absolutely perfect moment.

I was so full of happiness and contentment that I thought I might burst. My feelings for Jack were so beyond anything I'd ever felt, and I didn't know what to do with them. There was this small part of me that was itching to flee from the feelings he caused, to deny they even existed, but the bigger part of me just wanted to sink into them, to let them draw me in like quicksand and never let me go.

"Thank you," I told him again. "This has been... It's been like the best day ever."

"Same here," he said into my hair.

"And thank you for telling me all that earlier," I murmured. "About rowing and all that."

"I don't want there to be this cloud hanging over us about our pasts," Jack replied quietly.

"I don't either," I said. "But I still want to know those things about you." My voice was hushed when I said, "I want to know everything."

"Me, too." Jack squeezed me to him tighter. "I know we still have five more days here, but I already never want to leave."

I couldn't agree more. Boston felt like another world away. A world I was not eager to return to. I loved my life there. Loved my friends and my job and my music, but I'd really needed this time away. I hadn't realized it until we'd gotten here the other night, but now that I had, I wasn't ready for it to come to an end. I wanted to have more moments like this with Jack. I wanted to just *be* with him, to just enjoy our time together in a way we'd never quite been able to. God, I wanted him so much. Every single piece that he was willing to give me.

After a while, my slow caresses on his stomach started traveling lower and lower. His hand on my back had traveled up to the bare skin of my neck. He was petting gently while occasionally squeezing and massaging. It was making me shiver while simultaneously making me incredibly hot.

"Talia," Jack said, his voice a warning.

"No one's around," I murmured as I pushed myself so I was more draped over him, practically humping his leg. I could feel his hard length against my stomach, and I knew he wanted me as badly as I wanted him.

I kissed him like I was starving for it. I dug my hands in his hair as our tongues met in a wet, heated embrace. The sun was beating down on my back, but I still shivered in the cool air and burrowed closer to Jack's warmth. It was such a perfect moment and I was completely lost in it. I craved him with a fierce desperation. He tasted like champagne and caramel and Jack, and I was so turned on I was trembling. I knew, logically, that we were way too clothed and it was way too cold for us to take this any further, but I didn't care. I moved against him, my mouth so intensely attached to his that I didn't even know whose mouth was whose, whose tongue belonged in which mouth. I just wanted him. Needed him. Wanted to show him every single thing he made me feel even if I didn't have the guts to tell him.

I was overwhelmed with sensation. The dry suit I wore rubbed against my sensitized skin, and that, combined with the feelings and emotions swirling inside me, were making me whimper against his mouth.

Jack moaned my name as we broke apart. I immediately moved my mouth to his neck, and he slid his hands down my back until he was gripping my ass in his big hands and shifting me so that I was straddling his waist.

I wanted to feast on his skin, but I wanted his mouth more. I kissed him, grinding on his erection as I did, and Jack let out a choked groan and grabbed my hips to stop me.

"Talia, we can't do this here."

I bit his ear lobe, and he sucked in a breath.

"Why not?" I gasped against his neck when he moved his hands down again so that they were wrapped around the backs of my thighs. Even through the layers I could feel his thumbs right beneath my mound. I was wet under all those layers, and I didn't want to stop.

"It's freezing, and we can't take off these clothes," he panted as I licked a stripe down his neck. "And this is a public place. No one's here now, but anyone could come."

"Who cares?"

Our mouths met again, and our kiss intensified as he lifted his head to meet me lip for lip, tongue for tongue. He slid his hand up and down between my spread legs, and when I moaned loudly, he plopped his head down on the blanket.

I was about to lean down and kiss him again, but he put his hands on my shoulders. He was panting, and his eyes were bright with desire when they met mine.

"We have to stop," he huffed.

I looked at him for a few moments before I realized he definitely wasn't going to let this happen. I knew he was right. I knew this wasn't the place, but my lust-addled mind wasn't really interested in reason.

I pressed my forehead to the place where his neck met his shoulder. We laid there, both trying to calm our breathing and relax our libidos. Finally, Jack sat up and I climbed off him. He leaned back on his hands as I plopped on my back. He looked down at me with that intensity still in his eyes, and I bit my lip.

"Why did I stop us again?"

I sighed. "Because you're trying to be practical."

Jack looked at his watch. "It's only one o'clock. If we leave now we could make it back to your mom's place while she's still working."

We raced back to the beach. I used every bit of rowing skill Jack had taught me, and he obviously used his years of crew to get us back to the docking point in record time. But to both of our huge dismay, there was construction traffic on the highway that went back to my mom's house. When we were about a half hour out, I was still convinced we would have time before my mom got home, but when she texted me, I groaned miserably.

"'Things are dead at the diner. Rosie's going to close up. What do you say we go to North Hero for an early dinner?'" I read my mom's text to Jack.

He slammed his head against the headrest. "Fuck."

I laughed and leaned over to kiss his cheek.

"Maybe next time, lover boy."

Since we were only about five or so minutes from North Hero, I told my mom to head down and we would meet her there since we were so close.

A few minutes later, we were pulling into the gravel drive of a gorgeous little inn that was right on the water. Jack and I made out in the car for a few minutes before finally forcing ourselves out. Neither of us had changed back at the kayak place in our desperation to get home, so we went into the bathrooms at the inn and changed into normal clothes so we wouldn't be at dinner looking crazy in dry suits.

Jack wore jeans and a green Henley, and my heart pounded when I saw him. It was the same one he'd worn in the photo I'd seen of him and Rachel at Christmas a year ago. I wanted to rub myself all over it, mark my territory, so when he walked up to me, I wrapped him in a hug and snuggled close as we stood in the lobby waiting for my mom.

"You look amazing," he said into my hair. "You smell even better. Like sun and water and you."

It was the most romantic thing he could've said right then. My knees shook as I looked up at him. I was dressed pretty simply in a long turtleneck gray sweater, black leggings, and black ankle boots, but I loved that he liked the way I looked.

Dinner with my mom and Jack was wonderful. I watched the two of them talk and laugh and get to know each other, and I savored the moment with two of my favorite people in the world. I was so unbelievably happy. I wanted to bottle up that evening, hold it close and never, ever forget it. It was as close to perfect as my life had ever been.

After dinner at the inn, we all came back and watched a movie before going to sleep shortly after. I hadn't realized how exhausted I would be from rowing all day, and that was the only thing that stopped me from wanting to fool around with Jack. The next morning, he'd massaged my sore arms, and since my mom was already at the diner, I tried to convince him to fuck me, but he kissed me hard before pushing up off the bed and telling me he'd promised my mom we'd come down for breakfast before he wanted to take me down to a petting zoo near South Hero.

My mom's house was tiny, and when Jack and I had been making out pretty heavily the next night, I'd heard my mom close one of her drawers from her bedroom and immediately pushed him off me. I hadn't realized how thin the walls were until that moment, and I absolutely refused to let my mom hear me have sex.

It was our fifth day in Vermont, and I'd wanted to stay in bed with Jack this morning so we could finally at least do *something*. But of course, I'd told my mom I'd help her down in the diner before she opened, and since we only had about a day and a half left before we headed back to the city, I wanted to make sure I spent as much of that time as I could with her.

I loved helping my mom prepare to open up her diner in the morning when I came to visit. She started before the sun came up, and even though I was always tired, it was peaceful. It felt so right being here with her, helping her prep the place that had been her dream since I was little.

She was checking the salt and pepper shakers while I filled a few of the syrup containers when she said, "I really like Jack, mija. He's so sweet and funny. I love the way he looks at you."

I could feel my face heat and my heart rate speed up. These past few days with Jack and my mom had been like a dream. I felt like I was in this cocoon of love and warmth. I loved seeing my mom and Jack talk and laugh and get to know each other. They would occasionally chat in Spanish, since he was much better than he'd originally let on when we were having our picnic, and one night after dinner, I overheard him talking to my mom in Spanish in the kitchen when they both thought I was still in the bathroom. He told her his dream was to start his own immigration law firm and help families make a better life for themselves in the states, and I lost a little bit more of myself to him.

Jack fit in with me and my mom so seamlessly it was like he'd been around for years. And in the quiet moments when I would catch him looking at me, giving me that soft look that I'd only ever seen him give to me, I could almost imagine our lives in the future. Holidays visiting my mom, taking long walks and going for scenic drives, camping by Lake Champlain, but still excited to go back to the hustle and bustle of the city. For the first time since Vincent, I was imagining all those things I'd always secretly wanted. A friend, a companion, a lover, a partner. Someone to share everything with. Part of me was terrified to want those things because I knew how fragile this was. How fragile a relationship could be, how it could end on a dime when you least expected. But every day as Jack and I grew closer, I found myself imagining more and more. I wanted so much from him, with him, and it scared the hell out of me.

"You're quiet, mija."

"I know, ma."

"What's wrong? Jack isn't as great as he seems? He snores, doesn't he?"

I laughed and then sighed. "No, he's probably even greater than he seems. I just... god, I really like him. I can see a future with him." It was the first time I'd ever said that out loud.

"Then what's wrong?" When I didn't answer my mom came to the counter where I was sitting and faced me while I stared at the syrup. "Is it about that boy?"

I hated that she was right, hated that he still had an effect on me. "A little," I said quietly.

"That boy was a selfish prick who didn't care about you at all," my mom said firmly, putting her hand on my arm and squeezing gently. "Not all men are like that, mi amor. Many are kind and giving and loving, and any one of *those* men are the only ones who deserve you. Don't you think Jack is one of those?"

No. I didn't *think* he was.

I knew he was.

"I see the way you look at him, too," my mom said softly. "I see the love in your eyes. And baby, I've never seen you more happy."

I turned to her, my eyes welling with tears, and she opened her arms. I went into them willingly and she hugged me tightly.

"Just let him in," she whispered in my ear. "Let him love you."

Let him love you. What would it be like? To have Jack Harding love me? To give him the space to do so? Would things be different? Would I? I'd loved Vincent. As much as I wanted to pretend like I hadn't, I did love him. It had been the love of a girl, the love of someone who had never loved anyone before, the love of someone who didn't truly know what it was like to love someone and have them love you, but it was love all the same. I would've done anything for him, would've been anything he wanted me to be if only I could hold onto him. If only he would hold onto me. But now I knew, even if it had taken years, that love wasn't about being who someone else wanted you to be. Love was about that other person bringing out the best in you. It was about their love amplifying all the good parts of you.

I wanted to be that person for Jack, and I wanted him to be that person for me. It scared me to death that he might already be.

When my mom and I pulled out of the hug, both of us were crying, and she laughed and wiped the tears off my face.

"Look at us."

I let out a watery laugh just as the bell of the diner door tinkled. My mom turned—most likely to tell whoever it was that we weren't open quite yet—just as I looked up.

"What the fuck are you doing here?"

"Talia."

"No, mom, what is he doing here?" I leapt up from my chair at the counter and took two steps toward him. "What are you doing here, Kenny?"

"Talia, it's so good to see you."

The man standing just inside the door was tall and broad-shouldered, a quarterback in his youth and someone who clearly worked out in his later years. He had dark hair peppered with gray at his temples and hazel eyes. He was wearing a flannel shirt and blue jeans, and I didn't care what he was wearing because I wanted him gone.

"Yeah, can't say the same," I spat.

"Talia," my mother hissed. She pulled me by my arm across the restaurant and around a corner where the storage closet was.

"Mom, what the fuck is going on?"

"Will you watch your mouth?" my mom breathed. "Sometimes he comes to visit when he's traveling from New Haven to Montreal. We—"

"So, what, you guys are like *friends*?" I could feel myself vibrating with anger, feeling this odd sense of betrayal from my mother while also desperately wanting to protect her.

"Well—"

"Oh, my god, mom, please tell me you aren't seeing him?"

"No," she whispered forcefully. "Of course not. But he is a friend, yes."

"I'm going back to the house."

"Why don't you say hi?" my mother beseeched. Her eyes were wide and searching my face. She looked like a deer caught in headlights. Like someone who had been caught in a lie but was trying to remedy it as quickly as possible. "I'm sure he'd love to talk to you after all these years."

"I'm sure he fucking would," I said as I pushed past my mom and back out onto the floor. Kenny was still standing in the same spot, and at least he had the grace to look nervous, his hands shoved in his pockets.

"Talia," he said, looking up when he saw me approach.

"I don't know what your fucking end game is here, but I don't want anything to do with it," I said angrily. "And I want nothing to do with you, so excuse me."

"Talia, please. I'd really like to—"

The door behind him opened again, and I was relieved but also terrified to see Jack pulling the door open. He looked gorgeous, his hair wet like he'd just gotten out of the shower and come down. I didn't want him to know this part of my life.

"Hey," he said, looking confusedly between the three of us, the tension thick and obvious.

"Come back to the house with me," I said quickly, pushing past Kenny and putting my hand in Jack's to pull him away. He looked at my mom briefly before he let me drag him out into the crisp autumn air.

"Who was that guy?" he asked when we got back inside my mom's little cottage.

"That," I said, pouring a cup of coffee and taking a huge swig before slamming the mug on the counter. "Was Kenneth Emery. My fucking father."

Chapter 19

Jack sat on my mother's plush couch as I paced the living room. He'd started a fire while I paced silently and then sat down and watched me.

God, why was Kenny here? It had been such a nice week until he showed up and ruined it, just like he always did.

I felt like I was thirteen again, waiting for him to come when he never did. And when he would actually come, all I could think about was that I had no clue when I would see him again. Because that's what Kenny did. He'd spent my entire childhood flitting in and out of my and my mother's life. He was the first person who'd taught me that men didn't stay. Not when something better came along, not when they just couldn't be bothered anymore. And like an idiot, I'd thought Vince was different. Vince. The second man who'd broken my heart.

Kenny was the first.

I thought Vince would be the one who showed me that men could be different. Instead, all he did was show me more of the same.

He'd done to me exactly what Kenny had done to my mother.

"Talia."

I stopped pacing and looked at Jack. He looked calm, but I could see the faint nervousness in his eyes. I knew he didn't know what to say, but I also knew he wanted to know what the hell was going on.

I stood there, staring at him, and he stared back at me, unwavering. In that moment, all I wanted in the entire world was to go to him. To be in his arms while he held me and I told him about Kenny. But seeing my father after more than a decade had made my skin itchy. It reminded me exactly why I couldn't give myself to Jack the way I knew I wanted to.

What would it be like to let him love me? What would it be like to watch him walk away?

"Fuck, I can't do this."

"Talia, talk to me, please."

"I…" I looked around frantically, not even sure what I was looking for. "I have to go."

I started walking toward the guest room to grab the keys to the rental car, my hands trembling as I did.

I couldn't find them when I got into the room, and I could feel my heart rate picking up. *Get out, get out, get out.* It was all I could think as I searched. When I saw Jack standing in the doorway, my voice was almost a yell when I said, "Where are the keys to the rental?"

I yanked back the covers on the bed—the bed that still smelled like him, like us—and I was about to ask him again when I heard the jangle. I whipped around, and Jack was still standing in the same place, holding the keys in the palm of his upturned hand.

When I walked toward him, he closed his fingers around the keys, and I glared at him.

"Give me the keys."

"I'll drive you," he responded simply.

I wanted to scream in frustration. "Jack, give me the fucking keys."

"Talia, I'm not letting you drive when you're like this, and I don't care how mad that makes you. I'll drive you wherever you need to go. I won't even say a single word if you don't want me to, but I'm not letting you go alone." He had a hard, determined look on his face as we glared at each other. And a few moments later, he softened a bit. "Talia."

I kept looking at him until he reached out and grabbed one of my hands. I looked down at our hands and then back up at him.

"Let me help you." No matter what we'd been through, no matter the time, the years, the distance, I knew Jack was as honest as they came. I didn't know if he wouldn't hurt me years from now, but I knew that right now he genuinely wanted to be there for me.

I felt like this was some kind of test. Sure, I told him I was his girlfriend, and I wanted to be, was happy to be. This, however, was about more than that. It was how I would prove I was serious about it. About us. I felt like he was asking me, *"where will we go from here? Will you let me in?"* Everything in me was screaming to run like hell, to get as far away from Kenny and Jack and my mother as I possibly could. If I could outrun the memories, outrun the past, I wouldn't have to face the feelings swirling inside. I would run like the wind. But Jack was looking at me with his green eyes, and I knew he was asking for so much more than just to let him drive.

Let him love you.

I threw up my hands in frustration.

"Fine."

When we got in the car, we didn't speak. Jack drove for about ten minutes before stopping at a gas station to fill up. I sat in the passenger seat with my arms wrapped protectively around me, staring out the window. When he walked out of the station, he was wearing sunglasses and his hair was blowing in the wind and the way the sun landed on him, he looked like a movie star. When he saw me looking at him, he gave me a small smile—one that made my heart stutter—but when he got back in the car, he still didn't speak.

We drove down Route 2 with the windows down. It was a chilly day like all of our days here had been, but the cool air felt amazing on my heated skin. Jack kept the heat turned down low just so it wouldn't get too cold, and it was perfect. I stared at the water and the stunning foliage as we passed. Vermont really was beautiful. My mother had talked about it for years, and I remember being in our tiny apartment in Queens, above the restaurant she used to work at that the owner rented out to us for cheap, her pulling up pictures of Vermont in autumn.

"Isn't it beautiful, mija?"

"I guess," I shrugged. "I like Queens, though."

"I know." She smiled. "I like Queens, too. It's just nice to see what else is out there, yeah? A world that's so close to ours but looks different."

I remember I looked at the picture for a little bit longer, and after a while I thought I started to see what my mother could see. The beauty of the trees, of the forest, of the water. I never appreciated it before. Even when she'd moved here years ago, I'd never fully taken it in like I was doing now. Usually I groused about how long the drive was, but now, here, I was grateful for it.

I looked at Jack and studied his profile. He was so gorgeous, and like the beauty of Vermont, sometimes I didn't fully appreciate Jack. His hair was longer on top and buzzed on the sides. Usually he styled it, but since we'd been in Vermont, he'd let it lay naturally and it looked incredible. He'd taken off his pullover sweater from earlier and was just wearing a blue and green plaid shirt and tight jeans with the shirt tucked in just the front. Ray Bans covered his eyes, but I knew how much those eyes could unravel me. They were deep pools of sea green, stunning in their clarity. He had an arm propped up on the open window, one hand on the wheel, and I admired his corded arms that I knew he worked hard for. He went to the gym every day religiously, even if it was only for a half hour. He was so big and strong, but also so gentle. He was open and honest. He was kind. He was funny and charming and smart as hell.

Even after all we'd shared this weekend and before, I couldn't believe he wanted me. Couldn't imagine what he could see in me. I was a waitress and a struggling musician. I was crass and moody. He was wealthy, cultured, a world traveler, and the only place I'd been to besides Queens, Boston, and Alburgh was San Juan to visit my mom's family. I was short, and I needed to lay off Gia's pasta if I ever wanted to stop staring at my ass and thighs in the mirror with annoyance. But Jack always made it clear that he loved my body. In the time we'd been together since Halloween, he spent hours exploring me, every dip and curve, loved rubbing his hands on my ass, loved the way I looked in form fitting dresses that showed off just how curvy I was. He would often turn me over when we were fucking, and later confess that he loved seeing my ass when we were together.

The thing that got to me, though, wasn't just that Jack loved all the parts of me I was insecure about, but that he liked me *because* of them, not in spite of them. He liked my attitude, my crassness, my curves. He admired my music, listened to it even when he didn't go to my shows. He didn't care that I didn't know what the *Dow Industrial* was. He listened intently when I went on rants about things I was passionate about, like film studios remaking classic movies for no good reason. He cared about every story I told him. He loved everything I cooked for him even if it sucked. He just found me *interesting*, the same way I found him so. And as I gazed at him, I appreciated him—truly appreciated him—for the first time the same way I was appreciating Vermont for the very first time.

"Sorry I freaked out earlier."

He jumped. "Shit, Talia, you scared me." It had been quiet in the car for so long, it didn't surprise me.

I smiled. "Sorry. But yeah. And you were right. I shouldn't have been driving. Thanks for... thanks for taking me away. Thanks for being here. In Vermont. I'm really glad we did this."

Jack reached out and put his hand in mine. He intertwined our fingers and brought my hand up to his mouth to press his lips to my knuckles in a kiss.

"Thanks for inviting me." He turned his head toward me for a moment before looking back at the road. "I've had the best time I've had in a really long time."

We sat in silence for a few more minutes, holding hands, until Jack spoke again.

"Do you want to talk about what happened?"

I sighed. "Not really."

"You don't have to," he said. "Just thought I'd offer in case you needed that. You've never talked about your father before, so I know nothing about this. I didn't even know you knew him. But we don't have to talk about it," he added quickly.

I angled slightly toward him, sighing again as I adjusted. Jack glanced at me again and smiled before bringing our hands up and kissing my hand once more.

"You're beautiful."

131

My heart hammered in my chest as I stared back at him. The feelings I had for him were staggering. I'd never in my life felt like this. I felt like my heart was too big for my chest. I wanted to wrap myself in the warmth of his affection, of his presence.

I leaned my head against the headrest, watching him for a while before I got up the courage to talk about something I had never talked to anyone about. Not even Catrina, who only knew that my dad was a dick who was never around. It felt huge. Monumental. Like sharing this with him would mean more than anything we'd shared before. I felt like I would be becoming more than just his girlfriend.

Jack wasn't far off when he said he didn't know if I knew Kenny because I always pretended like he didn't exist. My friends from Queens knew he existed but even they knew it was off limits to discuss. And since I'd stopped speaking to him before I went to Klein, I never even brought him up while I was there. It was easier than explaining the truth. But for the first time, I wanted to open up about it. I wanted Jack to know everything about me, the good and the bad.

When that one nasty and unwelcome thought popped in my mind, I was almost powerless to stop it: Maybe if he knew the bad, it would make it easier when this inevitably came to an end.

"I didn't even know about Kenny until I was six," I finally said. "When I started school, you know kids ask questions. 'Where's your dad?' 'Did your dad die?' Stuff like that. One day I asked my mom and she said he loved me, but he couldn't be with us. I sort of just accepted that. Because I trusted my mom and she was all I needed. You know, we were definitely poor growing up, but I never felt like I wanted for anything. I didn't get lots of new clothes, and I wasn't one of those kids who got a ton of presents for Christmas, but I always felt loved. We had enough, even if it wasn't much."

"Your mom is awesome," Jack said.

I smiled softly. "She so is," I said, even though I was pissed at her. "So anyway, on my sixth birthday, my mom and I were having dinner with my abuela. My mom asked if I'd like to meet my dad, and I said sure. It didn't really mean much to me one way or another, but it seemed like my mom wanted me to meet him so I agreed."

"How'd that go?" Jack looked at me for a moment before looking back at the road.

"The first meeting was awkward. He apologized for not being in my life, said he wanted to get to know me. He seemed nice. I kept thinking he looked like Superman." I smiled at the childish memory.

He had. He'd had dark black hair back then and these piercing hazel eyes. Ones I'd inherited.

"So why was he out of the picture for so long?"

"It took me a while to figure that out," I told Jack. "I knew my mom didn't want me to know. She wanted me to have this idealized version of him. The same one she had. Probably still has." The anger surged through me at the memory of earlier—the hurt, the betrayal, and the utter confusion that she'd let him in again. "Kenny has another family." It was matter-of-fact, almost emotionless, when I said it. I'd stopped caring about it so long ago that I barely ever thought about it.

"My mom got pregnant when she was nineteen. Kenny was thirty. Already married, had two kids. When my mom found out she was pregnant with me, she didn't tell him. Didn't want to ruin his perfect little life. The only reason he found out is because he came to the restaurant looking for her one day and I was there, since I was always there after school."

"Wow," Jack said. "So did you get to know him?"

"At first. For the first few years, he was really, really good and present. He took me to the zoo, to Central Park. Even came on a few of my school field trips. My mom was so happy. I'd never seen her like that. She smiled all the time. When we'd come in the apartment from one of our outings, she'd glow." It had taken me years to realize what was going on with my mom and Kenny. He'd come back into our lives when he wanted to restart his relationship with my mom. When he was having trouble in his marriage, that's when we would see Kenny. And my mom idolized him despite the fact that she had always been and would always be second best in his life. I wasn't exaggerating to Jack when I told him she would glow. It was like light was shining off her skin she was so happy anytime he was around.

"But it went bad eventually?" Jack sounded hesitant when he asked the question.

"It always did." I hated how small my voice sounded. "I never knew how long he would be around. The first time was the longest it lasted. He didn't disappear until I was nine or so. Then he was gone for a year. He'd come back for a few months, then disappear, come back for a day and then leave. For a while, I didn't care. I loved it when he came around even if it was only for a month. I loved spending time with him. Loved seeing my parents together. Just loved having a dad, you know?"

My voice trembled on my last words and Jack squeezed my hand.

"So you haven't talked to him in a while?" Jack asked after a few minutes of silence.

I shook my head even though he wasn't looking at me.

"As I got older, the comings and goings just made me more and more angry. I didn't know about his other family then. My mom would say he was busy with work or whatever."

"When did you find out about them?"

This was the hardest part. It was the reason I hadn't talked to Kenny in ten years. It was the part I had never, ever talked about. The part that hurt the most.

"It was right after I found out about getting into Klein," I said. "I had applied to a few other schools, but Klein was the one I wanted the most. They have a great music program, you know, and I knew that's what I wanted to do. Kenny and I... he loved music, too. We bonded over that a lot. We would sit in his car and listen to Louis Armstrong or Ella Fitzgerald. He made me fall even more in love with music." I could feel the backs of my eyes burning, and I hated myself for it. Hated that after all these years he still had any power over my emotions.

"I was so excited. I just wanted him to know. I... it sounds so stupid, but I wanted him to be proud of me. And excited for me."

"That doesn't sound stupid at all," Jack said softly.

I let out a shaky breath. "I guess not. But it was stupid to try and find him. My mom told me he worked on Wall Street, and I thought it would be cool to go to his work and surprise him. When I was searching his name online to find out which firm he worked at, I was giddy. I didn't even think about what it would look like—some Boricua from Queens showing up at some huge investment banking firm and asking to see Kenny Emery. He was pissed. Told me I shouldn't be there, that I had to go." I held onto Jack's hand even tighter. "I went to this pizza shop around the corner and just cried. About twenty minutes later, some old man showed up. He asked what I wanted, how much money, and I was just confused. I told him I just wanted to talk to my dad, and the guy went so white I thought he was going to pass out."

"Who was he?"

I laughed humorlessly. "Kenny's dad. My good old granddad."

"Jesus."

"Yeah. When I went home, my mom was frantic. Kenny had called her apparently because she started yelling at me that I shouldn't have gone. She said I should've talked to her about it first. I asked her what the big fucking deal was, and that's when she told me everything." I huffed another unamused laugh. "The stupid part of me was excited when I found out I had two older brothers. I'd never had siblings, and I thought it would be so cool to know them. My mom told me it wasn't possible."

"Did you ever meet them?"

"No," I said quietly. "I don't think they even know about me."

"I'm so sorry, Tal."

I shrugged. "I guess it taught me a lot. About people, about the world."

"So did you just decide to stop talking to Kenny after that?" he asked.

"Not exactly," I scoffed. "He came by later that night. I heard him yelling at my mom, and I was furious. I stormed in the room and told him to leave. My mom got all mad at me, but then when Kenny started yelling at me, she told him to get out. Then he started apologizing, and I thought she was going to forgive him but she didn't. She told him to leave and not come back."

I could see a muscle in Jack's jaw ticking. I couldn't see his eyes, but I knew he was angry and upset on my behalf. On mine and my mom's. Kenny had put us through hell for years, and I knew that until that night, my mom had still wanted him through it all. But she chose me. She chose our little family. Or so I'd thought.

I hadn't thought about that night in years, but the memory was just as bad as it had been that night. The memory of him walking out the door was one of the worst I had in my life. My mom had had her arm wrapped around my shoulders while silent tears streamed down my face.

"I got into college," I whispered as his hand touched the knob. "That's why I wanted to see you."

He hadn't even turned back before he walked out.

"I can't believe his father did that," Jack said after a few minutes as I surreptitiously wiped away a stray tear that had escaped. "That's cruel."

I stared out at the water out Jack's window. I was looking past him when I said, "The Emery's are well known in Manhattan. Incredibly wealthy and present in the social scene. They have an image to uphold. Nothing would tarnish that image like their oldest son's mistress and love child."

Chapter 20

J ack was silent for a long time for the rest of the drive south. We sat there like that, still holding hands, until I saw the sign for Burlington in ten miles. He asked if I wanted to stop for breakfast, and even though I had no appetite, I agreed. We stopped at this little vegan deli downtown, and Jack was still relatively quiet throughout our meal. I didn't mind. I was thinking about Kenny and remembering that day so long ago that I was lost in my own thoughts as well. After we ate, we went for a walk hand-in-hand past cute shops and cafés. I wondered if Kenny was still at the diner or if he had moved along. Like he always did. I wondered when was the last time my mom had seen him. When had they started being friends again? I wanted to ask her, but part of me didn't want to find out. When we got back in the car, Jack asked if I wanted to drive around more or if I wanted to head back. I said it was fine to head back even though I dreaded the possibility of needing to have a conversation with my mom. Luckily she was going to be working all day so I wouldn't have to worry about it for a while.

The drive was quiet. Jack turned on the radio and we listened to a podcast played from the Bluetooth of his phone. It ended when we were about twenty minutes away. I thought he was going to turn on some music, but he pushed the button to turn the radio off. I was about to ask him if he was okay when he spoke. His voice was rough, and he sounded so unlike I had ever heard him.

"You think I'm like him, don't you?"

Stupidly, I replied, "Who?"

"Kenny," he said quietly. "You think I'm like Kenny."

I didn't think Jack was anything like Kenny, but I couldn't deny at least the similarities between their families and backgrounds. I'd never thought of it in those explicit terms, but when Jack asked the question, it made me feel like something clicked into place. It felt like it had the ring of truth to it even if I'd never necessarily thought of it like that before.

Jack's family was rich and successful and classy and sophisticated. I'd always known that. And maybe there had always been this part of me that felt like he was slumming it with me the same way Kenny had been with my mother. His dirty little secret. And when someone else who was elegant and high-class came along, he would always choose that over me. Hadn't he, in a way? With Rachel?

"I don't…" I didn't want to tell him what I felt. I knew it would upset him. And at least a small part of me knew that it was an unfair comparison. "I don't know."

The rest of the short drive back to my mom's was silent. I could feel the waves of stress wafting off Jack like a fog, but I didn't know what to say. I just kept thinking about the question he asked and wondering if he was right, while knowing deep down that he was. That that's what I thought. That I worried what his family would say, what they would think about me, if they would tell him he could do better.

When we parked the car, Jack sat there, and I looked at him. I thought he was going to say something, but instead, he opened the car door and got out. I watched him walk inside, and I followed him because there was nothing else I could do.

He had his hands braced on my mom's small kitchen island when I walked in, his back to me. It reminded me of the first day we were together after we reconnected when we'd stood in his kitchen and he fought his feelings for me.

I stood in the doorway of the kitchen, not knowing what to say.

"I have no idea how to convince you of how much you mean to me."

"Jack—"

When he whirled toward me, I went silent.

"Do you really think that I'm—what?—*slumming it* with you? That you don't mean everything to me?"

Hearing my thoughts echoed back to me felt like a knife to the gut.

"How can you not be?" I could hear the quiver in my voice. I could hear every bit of fear and uncertainty folded into every syllable.

Jack gaped at me. "Talia, I've wanted you since the day I met you. Since before I knew where you were from or whatever the hell you think is important to me. I've never once thought that you weren't good enough. When you flirted with me at that party when we first met freshman year, I thought I was the luckiest guy in the room. It took me years to even try and pursue you because I thought I wasn't good enough. That you could have any guy you wanted. *I'm* the one who isn't good enough for *you*. I'll never deserve you, but I want to try."

A tear slipped down my face before I could stop it, and Jack closed the distance between us, wiping the tear away with his thumb.

"You are so much more than enough. You always have been."

I hated the sad, insecure words that came out of my mouth next, but I had to say them. Had to know how he would respond. "What about Rachel?"

Jack's face hardened. "What about her?"

"She was... Jack, she's the opposite of me. She's the type of person you should be with. Sophisticated. Gorgeous. Refined."

Jack growled and pushed against me until he had me pinned against the wall. "She is not the type of person I should be with. You are the type of person I should be with. You *are* who I should be with. You. You are gorgeous. You're passionate and talented and funny and *alive*." He slid his hands up my arms until they were cupping my neck, and I shivered. "I wasn't waiting for her to come along and replace you. I was with her when you didn't want to be with me. But Jesus fucking Christ, Talia, when are you going to get it?"

"What?" I breathed.

His eyes darted between mine. "You are all I've ever wanted."

It was me who closed the distance between us completely. I stood on my toes and threw my arms around his neck and pressed my lips to his.

He kissed me back with a ferocity he never had. Our teeth clanked and our tongues dueled. He tasted like the coffee he'd had for breakfast mixed with the sweet taste that was uniquely him. The taste that I could never get enough of. The same way he'd tasted six years ago. Jack.

"*Jack.*"

When I breathed his name, Jack grunted and bent his knees, wrapping his arms under my legs so he could lift me up. He spun us around and sat me down on the island. It was just like that first night, just like the day I'd remembered every single button of mine that only Jack Harding had been able to push.

We stood there kissing for I don't know how long. We each whispered each other's names several times as we broke apart. He feasted on my neck and I did the same to his. His hands were on my ass—his favorite spot—as he ground his dick against my center, driving me crazy with each slow thrust. My legs and arms were wrapped tightly around him. I clung to him desperately, unwilling and unable to let him go. I needed more than his words. He told me I was enough, that I was what he wanted, but I needed more. I needed him to show me. It didn't matter that he had already shown me so many times. I needed it right here, with his words as the backdrop and his actions as the proof I craved.

Show me, Jack. Show me how much you want me. Show me you need me as much as I need you.

"Please," I whispered against his lips.

My plea seemed to unleash something in him. He let out the sexiest, neediest groan I'd ever heard, and a moment later he was lifting me again.

We kissed fiercely as he walked us to our room. He kicked the door shut and walked over to the bed, and I was wild for him. I wanted him with an urgency I couldn't control. I hadn't had him since the morning we'd left for Vermont almost a week earlier. Except for that day on the lake, we hadn't even gotten close to this. We'd been spending so much time with my mom and exploring the area since then that by the time we got home every day my mom was home as well. My mom's little two-bedroom cottage was not at all big enough for Jack and I to have sex undetected. Not when I was incapable of being quiet.

This point was evidenced by the fact that I let out a soft moan as soon as we landed on the bed. In the week and half between Halloween and our trip to Vermont, I'd been with Jack every day, sometimes multiple times a day if I stayed at his apartment overnight. Being without him for so long was wreaking havoc with my system.

Once we were on the bed, Jack tried to pull back, but I couldn't let him go. I needed him close.

"Baby," he whispered against my neck as I clung to him. "Let me undress you."

I shook my head, holding him tighter. If I let him go he might disappear. This apparition of a man, the perfect, beautiful, wonderful man might cease to exist.

Jack murmured my name and pulled back enough so he could meet my eyes.

"Let me love you," he rumbled as he slowly pulled my arms from around his neck. My breath caught in my throat. I felt numb but in the most perfect way. Like Jack could do anything to me and all I could do was let him. His words—the exact words I'd been thinking all day—should have scared me. They should've caused me to seize up with panic and stop whatever was happening. But all they did was cause this slow hum to spread throughout my body. It was just this faint buzz of joy and contentment and peace that settled into my bones. I was still desperate for him, but his words gave me permission to let go and just feel.

"Let me," he whispered as he unbuttoned my jeans and slowly slid them down my legs. "Please," he breathed when he peeled my shirt off me. "Just let me."

His words were unraveling me, breaking me apart piece by piece and allowing him to seep into all the cracked parts of me.

I was writhing on top of the bed by the time I was fully naked and Jack hovered—clothed—above me. He stared down at me, taking in my body, a dark and hungry look in his eyes. I basked in the glow of his perusal, spreading my arms out on the bed as if to say, *"Yes, look. I'm all yours."*

"Fuck," he growled before he dove in to kiss me. I dug my hands in his hair and kissed him back with as much passion as he was showing me. I spread my legs and bent my knees so he could settle there, and when he slowly thrust his hips, the friction against my folds was delicious. I spread even further, wanting more of that feeling, but Jack pulled away only slightly. I wanted to protest, but then he was sliding down my body, leaving a trail of kisses on my neck and chest. When he sucked one hard nipple in his mouth, I moaned loudly and tightened my fingers in his hair.

Jack could do the most wicked things with his tongue. He sucked hard on my nipple, almost to the point of pain, but then he would pull back. The cool air would cause the nub to tighten even further and then he would take just the tip of his tongue and swirl it around, igniting every nerve ending. He repeated the move, alternating between my nipples while massaging my breasts until I was strung so tight I thought I was going to come just from his mouth there.

I'd never done it before, never thought it was possible, but the relaxed feeling that had settled over me along with his expert attention to every detail of my body was making me think it would be a first for me.

He sucked hard, and when his teeth came out to nip, I bowed off the bed.

"Jack, please."

I didn't know what I was asking for. More? Yes. Definitely more.

"You want more, baby?" His hot breath on my nipple made me shudder.

Had I spoken my last thought out loud?

"*Yes.*"

Jack slid down, placing kisses along my stomach, until his head was between my legs. I was panting as I watched him spread my thighs open. When he looked at my pussy and licked his lips, I bit back a moan. It was so dirty, having him look at me like that. But then he took it even further.

Jack slid one hand up the inside of my thigh. When he was right at the juncture of my ass and my thigh, he moved his hand and raised one finger. He looked up at me, then back down, and slid that finger, slowly and gently, just right on the inside of my folds. I inhaled a shaky breath and then exhaled heavily when he pulled back his finger and I saw the glistening moisture on it. I knew I was wet for him, but seeing it right there, in between us, was something else entirely.

Then he brought his finger slowly to his mouth and licked every bit of my juices off. He made a soft noise in the back of his throat like it was the most delicious thing he'd ever tasted.

"Jack," I was frantic now. Seeing him savor the taste of me was too much. I needed him. I needed him inside me, pounding me, taking no mercy, and giving me everything he could. "Jack, oh my god, you have to fuck me."

"Not yet."

And then he dipped his head between my legs, and I almost screamed. He licked my mound first, just a tease, not nearly enough. His fingers spread my lips apart, and he continued his teasing. Just little flicks of the tip of his tongue, causing violent jolts of sensation to my clit interspersed with moments of nothing. The lack of constant pressure, that combination of intense pleasure and relief, was doing something strange to me. My whole body felt like it was on fire. I was clutching the sheets on the bed, grinding my pelvis against his face, desperate, more desperate than I had ever been. I wanted to moan, to cry out, but every sound was caught in my throat. My body was strung tighter than a bow, and all I wanted was for Jack to take me over the edge but also to never stop. Never, ever, ever stop.

After continuing with the teasing flicks for what felt like hours, Jack started doing to my clit what he'd been doing to my nipples, alternating between the flicking of his tongue and sucking hard. I was finally able to get noise out of my mouth, and I started moaning constantly, muttering incoherent begging and pleading. He was doing something to me. Unspooling something deep and hidden within me that I didn't know existed, bringing me to a brink of pleasure that I'd never known.

Without warning, without the usual build to the finish, my climax was on me in an instant. It was like the entire time had been one slow, gradual, powerful build, that my body didn't even need that final acknowledgement that the end was close. I just toppled over harshly, moaning Jack's name over and over, begging him not to stop, begging him for more, more, *more.*

"Fuck, Talia."

His mouth was on mine a moment later. I could taste our combined flavors, and I devoured his mouth. He rubbed his jeans against me, and even though he'd just given me the most powerful orgasm of my entire life, I wanted more.

He pulled back and started unbuttoning his shirt as I fumbled with the button and zipper on his pants. It felt like he was naked in record time. And then he was moving over me. I wrapped my legs around him and could feel his thick, long, hard cock rubbing in between my folds, sliding along my core.

"Jack, now," I moaned. "I need it."

His head slipped just inside my entrance and I moaned like I was coming because it felt so damn good. God, I wanted him. I wanted him inside and I wanted him to never leave. I wanted everything, anything, he was willing to give me. The buzz that had settled over me intensified, making my limbs shake with it. I wanted him so much I couldn't stand it.

He slid further in, and then cursed.

"Fuck." He pulled out. "Fuck, I need a condom."

"No!" I shook my head frantically. Somewhere—somewhere far, far away in the deep recesses of my mind, I knew I was in a fog of lust, and I knew it was the lust that was talking. I knew it was probably irresponsible and that we hadn't had the conversation about getting tested, but in that moment, I didn't care. And more than that, I *trusted* Jack. He had been my friend for ten years, my lover for almost a year total out of that time, considering our time at Klein and now. I knew he wouldn't put me at risk. I knew if he thought there was even any remote possibility of danger he would stop.

"Talia..."

"Please." I wrapped my legs around him and felt him slip in again. He groaned and I sucked in a breath. "I want it. I'm safe. I trust you."

At my last words, his eyes snapped up to mine. We held there for several moments, letting the meaning behind those words sink into us both. And then he was sliding all the way in and there was nothing else in the world but us—but this moment, this feeling.

"Fuck... Jesus fuck, Talia, you feel so good. I've never..."

He slid in and out of me, staring at the point where we were joined, and for a moment I clung to his words. Had he really never? Not even with...

No. I wouldn't think of her right now. I refused to bring anyone else into this bed but the two of us. So I closed my eyes and let myself feel.

He was hot and hard inside me. I felt like I could feel every bit of his flesh sliding along my walls—every inch, every movement, every twist. I clutched his arms that were on either side of me and lost myself in the feel of him pounding in and out of me. It was everything.

I could feel the climax building this time, and I was grateful that I would have some kind of warning before he sent me over. He was making the sexiest sounds, and I was moaning loudly in the silence of the guest room, not even caring if my mom came in from the diner. I didn't care if anyone heard us in that moment because there was no way I could contain the feelings that he was eliciting.

"Look at me."

My eyes flew open and he leaned down. We were close enough to kiss, our lips brushing occasionally, but we kept our eyes on one another. He slowed his movements and grabbed a hold of me under my ass. He tilted my hips up and moved me so I would meet each of his slow thrusts. He pulled out, so only the tip was still inside and then slowly but surely slid all the way back in. He held there, deep inside me, pulling me close while he pressed in. I didn't think he could get any deeper, and I thought he would pull out and repeat the move, but then he gripped me even tighter and twisted his hips, going impossibly deeper, never taking his eyes off me as he did it.

Let him love you.

My arms were wrapped around his shoulders, and when he rotated his hips again, going deeper than he'd ever been, I let out a soft whimper.

"Jack." My voice sounded desperate and frantic.

"I know, baby," he whispered. "I feel it, too."

Tears stung my eyes as I clung to him, but they never fell. I was overwhelmed with emotion, the pleasure making me feel raw and exposed. He moved his hips, slowly starting to move in and out, though staying deep each time, and I quaked. I trembled with need and held onto him, never looking away from his eyes, letting him see—for the first time, maybe the only—every single thing he made me feel. I held nothing back, hid nothing from him, and when I came, I held his gaze, falling over the edge with the sound of his name on my lips. He did the same only a few moments later, his hot release flooding my insides along with just a whisper.

"Talia."

We panted against each other for a long time after that. He slid his arms around my back and buried his face in my neck, and I held onto him just as tight as he held onto me. It felt like he was still hard inside me, and he proved that when he ground his hips against mine. I gasped, feeling and hearing both of our wet releases squish inside me. The sound was wicked and debauched and I twisted my hips to get more of it. Aftershocks were shooting through my channel as we held there. Our bodies were sticky with sweat, but I didn't care. I couldn't let him go, not just yet.

I had given so much of myself to Jack already, but there was still so much more to give. I'd revealed to him a part of myself, a part of my life that I'd never revealed to anyone else. No matter what happened, he would always have that piece of me. I hoped he knew how much that meant to me, to share that part of myself with him. Maybe he would never know, but I did and that's what I held onto.

Jack squished his release into me even more, and I moaned softly in his ear. He kept moving, grinding his hips against mine, until—to my complete and utter shock—I felt myself start to climb again. This had never happened, not even with him, not in my entire life, but as he ground into me, I knew he was going to make it happen. I knew he was going to bring me another orgasm and he wouldn't stop until he did it.

"Jack," I moaned. "Oh god, I'm going to come again."

"Me too," he panted. "Fuck."

"Don't stop. Don't ever stop."

"Never."

We moved like that together for several minutes, and after what felt like an eternity of being joined with him but also no time at all, we were both coming again, crying out into each other's skin, whispering desperate words to each other as we reveled in this moment.

When Jack finally pulled out of me, he pulled back onto his knees and stared between my legs. I knew what he was looking at because I could feel it trickling out of me. He'd come so much both times that I knew that even hours from now, I'd still feel it there. It wasn't just a first for him if that's what he'd meant earlier, but it was for me as well. I'd never had sex without a condom. Ever. But somehow, sharing that with Jack felt like the most natural thing in the world. It felt like we were always supposed to have this moment with each other.

Jack climbed off the bed and went into the guest bathroom. I heard the faucet running and then he came out with a wet rag. I could see he'd already wiped himself off, so when he climbed back onto the bed, his attention was all on me. He cleaned me carefully, his eyes on me the entire time.

After he tossed the rag on the floor, we both moved and slid under the covers. I felt boneless and relaxed, and we just stared at each other in silence for a long time. After a while, he put his arm around my waist to pull me closer, and he leaned back so I could lay against his chest. I was exhausted after our love making, but I wanted to stay in this moment forever. Feel him swirl his fingers on my bare back, feel his warm skin under mine, bask in the afterglow.

When sleep finally started to win out, I let it wash over me. I closed my eyes and burrowed even further into his chest. I thought I heard him say something, but I couldn't understand it as I let sleep claim me.

Chapter 21

I could hear the faint sound of voices.

I turned over in bed and checked my phone and saw that it was just after three in the afternoon. Jack and I had gotten back to the house around eleven, so I had slept almost three hours. I also had texts from Catrina and Isaac, but I didn't check them just then. I felt so relaxed and at peace, and I didn't want to think about the real world. I smiled into my pillow remembering the morning with Jack. We'd never made love like that before. With that kind of depth and fervor. I wanted to keep basking in it. I wanted to have him again.

I turned back over to cuddle next to him only to find that he wasn't there. When I came out of sleep a bit more, I recognized his voice on the other side of the door and realized he was talking to my mom.

The events of early that morning came rushing back. The hurt. The anger. But then I remembered Jack, and it all immediately fell away. I wanted to hear what they were talking about, but I wasn't quite ready to deal with that yet. Instead I grabbed my phone.

Hope Vermont is amazing! Text me or call me and tell me all about it whenever you can.

I texted Catrina back.

Hi.

Omg, hiiiiii. Tell me everything. How's Jack? Getting along with Monica?

He's amazing. Okay, I know you're going to call me as soon as you read this, but I can't talk! He might hear. But I have to tell you... I'm officially his girlfriend.

TALIA!!!!!!!!!!!! Omg, you cannot do that to me. You can't tell me the biggest news of our fucking lives and expect me not to want to call you and find out everything omg omg omg I'm so happy for you I love you I love Jack I love this ahhhhh

I giggled when my best friend's text came through. Her excitement and joy and love was contagious.

I swear I will tell you about everything when we get back. Also... you'll never guess who came to my mom's diner this morning.

Who??

Kenny.

Kenny, your dad Kenny??? Oh god, Talia. Did you see him? Did you talk to him?

Saw him, barely talked to him. Basically told him to fuck off and then went for a drive with Jack.

I'm so glad Jack is there with you. Wish I could be there to tell that asshole to go to hell.

My eyes burned, and I loved Catrina so much in that moment. I loved how much she wanted to protect me even when I resisted it.

Thanks, Cat. How's trimester one treating you?

Still miserable. I can't stop puking. Brody is stressed, but I keep telling him to get over it. This is normal. Trimester 2 is coming next week so hopefully things get better. Ugh. No one tells you how much pregnancy sucks ass.

Right? I hope you feel better soon. Let's hang out when I get back in town. I'll call you Friday, okay? Love you.

Love you most. Say hi to Jack and Monica.

I smiled as I went to look at Isaac's text next, but the smile immediately slid off my face.

Hey. Hope you're enjoying your vacay. We need to talk about Chuck. It's getting bad.

Okay. Shit. I get back Friday. Wanna meet up before the show Saturday and talk?

He didn't reply right away, so I put my phone back down on the end table next to the bed and tried not to panic. If Isaac thought Chuck was getting bad, it was probably a nightmare. Chuck had been struggling with his substance abuse issues for almost as long as I'd known him. But it had never gotten in the way of the band, and he was talented as hell so we always let it slide. If it was getting to the point where it was going to interfere, then Isaac was right. We needed to have a conversation and fast.

I sighed as I turned to sit up in bed. I could hear my mom and Jack still talking, and I wrapped the blanket from the bed around me before I tiptoed over and pressed my ear to the door.

"...she doing?"

"She's okay," I heard Jack say. "She was better after we went for a drive, but I'm sure she's still upset." He sounded hesitant in all of his words, like he wanted to please my mom but also didn't want to betray my confidence. He was right, though. I was way better now— Jack obviously wasn't going to tell my mother that he fucked the stress right out of me, but he was right that after our morning together, I felt okay. I was still pissed at my mom and at Kenny, but the ache in my gut had disappeared.

"Did she tell you about him?"

"A little." That was all Jack said, and I was grateful for him. God, I lo—

Wait. Fuck. No. No no no. I didn't... I couldn't... We'd only just started speaking again two months ago. He had only been officially my boyfriend for two days. No. I didn't... I couldn't even think the word. I *liked* him. A lot. A helluva lot. That was it.

"She doesn't hate me, does she?" My mom's voice sounded so small and sad. I almost walked out of the room right then, but instead I rushed back into the bed and laid the cover out over me without even hearing Jack's response.

I wasn't ready to deal with this right now. I just wanted to think about my week with Jack. About our day on the lake and the way he'd made love to me this morning. So ferocious, so profound. And I wanted to think about the fact that I could still feel his release inside me.

Damn, that was sexy. I shifted in the bed, feeling it shift around inside me and then I moved over so I was on his side. I could smell him in the sheets, and I inhaled deeply.

A few minutes later, I heard the front door open and close. Then light drifted into the room before it became dark again, and a second later the bed was dipping as I felt a warm, hard body at my back.

Jack kissed my neck and cuddled into me. He'd gotten dressed again, and when I felt his clothed body against my naked back, I wished it was his skin against mine.

I pulled his arms tighter around me, and he moved even closer.

"Hi," I said quietly.

"Hi." His breath was hot on my neck, and I turned my head so I could find his mouth. When we broke the kiss, Jack shifted me so I was on my back and he was on his side next to me.

"Your mom asked how you were," he told me.

"What did you say?"

"Didn't really know what to say, but I told her you seemed okay." He searched my face with his eyes. "Are you? Okay, I mean?"

I nodded. "Better when you're here."

He gave me one of his soft, private smiles before he kissed me again.

"You should talk to her," he said when he pulled back.

I sighed. "I know."

"She went back over to the diner," he said. "She just came to check on you."

I looked at Jack. "Do you think I should just let it go?"

"I don't know, baby," he said, his quiet tone echoing mine. "I think you should each say your piece, and then you decide what you want to do from there."

148

"Have I told you how glad I am that you're here?"

I could get so used to putting that delighted look on his face. "You have. But I will love hearing it every time you say it."

He ran his fingers through my hair. "You okay?" his voice was raspy and quieter. "I went a little rough earlier."

I shifted in the bed and licked my lips when I saw the heated look on his face when I moved. "I'm awesome. It was incredible. You were incredible."

"You better go talk to your mom before I decide not to let you leave this bed."

After a quick shower, I got dressed in a Klein sweatshirt and jeans before walking over to the diner. When I spotted my mom, she was chatting with a customer at a table in the corner. She looked up when the bell tinkled.

"Welcome to Mon—hola, mija," she said when she saw it was me. She looked nervous but happy to see me. She filled up the customer's coffee mug and walked over to stand behind the counter as I took a seat at one of the round, swiveling chairs.

"Estás enojado?"

"I'm not angry, Ma," I replied. She pulled out a glass and set it in front of me. She turned to the refrigerator that was under the counter and pulled out a gallon of chocolate milk. She'd done this even when I was little. We always kept chocolate milk in the house because my mom believed all problems could be solved with a glass of chocolate milk.

"I'm sorry it blindsided you today," she said as I took a drink of my milk. "We really are just friends, though. I've known him for almost thirty years, and he's your dad. But I set that boundary with him years ago. We haven't had a relationship since before you went to college." The unspoken part of that was, *since before the day you went to his work.* Before the day that had almost broken me.

"I just don't trust him."

"I know."

"And I don't want him to hurt you."

The tears stung my eyes before I could stop them. My mom leaned on her elbows on the counter and grabbed both of my hands.

"He doesn't have that power anymore," she said so only I could hear. "Over either of us."

I nodded quickly and took another drink just to occupy myself with something else.

"I should have told you I was still in touch with him," my mom said.

"No." I shook my head. "You were right. It would have just made me stress more than I need to. You can take care of yourself."

"Talia." She squeezed both of my hands again. "I love that you want to protect me. We take care of each other. We always have, yes?" I nodded, and she brought her hand up to cup my face. "El amor de mi vida. Siempre."

I stood up from my chair and hugged my mom over the counter, and she held me back tightly. It was something she'd always said to me. When I was younger and I would ask her why she didn't date, she would always just smile at me and say in Spanish, "Why do I need a man? *You* are the love of my life. Always."

My mom had the cook, Enrique, make me an omelet with grits and a short stack of pancakes. When I told her I didn't need the calories, she just rolled her eyes and put syrup in front of me.

Her and I were talking just as the door tinkled again, and when she looked up, my mother's face reddened. For a second, I thought Kenny had come in again, but when I looked over my shoulder, I saw a big, hunky forty-something *lumberjack* making eyes at my mother.

"Hey, Monica." The man sauntered up to the counter and sat in a stool two down from mine, and I looked between him and my mother as they interacted. He had blonde hair that matched his blonde beard, and he was wearing jeans, work boots, and a big flannel coat that he shrugged off and put on the counter next to him, only to reveal a massive upper body that was almost bursting through his white t-shirt.

"Hi, Matthew," my mom said. She was trying to act extremely casual, but I knew something was off. "Coffee?"

"Decaf," he said. "Caffeine's bad for the heart, you know." He glanced over at my mug and then up at me and did a double take. "This has got to be Talia!"

He knows me?

If possible, my mom got even redder.

"This is her," my mom told *Matthew*.

"Well, I'll be." He had a thick New England accent and a big white grin that he flashed as he scooted over to sit next to me.

"I'm Matt," he said, holding a hand out. "I've heard so much about you."

I looked at my mom, who was studiously looking away, and then back at him. I shook his hand.

"Well, I have heard nothing about you, *Matthew*. How do you know my mom? You a regular here?"

Matt laughed boisterously. "Sure am," he said. "Been coming here almost every night for years. My wife died five years back, and I'm hopeless in a kitchen. If it weren't for your mom, I'd likely starve to death."

"Yeah, she's a good cook, for sure." I could feel my mom's eyes on both of us, but I ignored her.

"That, and she's the most beautiful woman from here to Georgia."

I almost spit out the milk I'd been drinking. I gaped at my mom, who looked like she was about to pass out.

"She's my favorite girl, your ma," he said. Then he smiled at my mom like she hung the moon, and I texted Jack to get his ass over to the diner and help me grill this hot older dude who was *apparently* my mom's *boyfriend.*

◆ ◆ ◆

"I'll just drop this off here for you. Let me know if you need anything else."

The couple smiled at me as I dropped off their check. They were my last table of the night and then I would close up and wait for Jack to come pick me up and take me back to his place for the night.

It had been a crazy week or so since I'd come back from Vermont. Isaac and I had a talk with Chuck, who decided to leave the band so he could focus on his sobriety. We'd gone with him and his family to drop him off at rehab, and I'd hugged him tightly and told him how proud I was of him. Isaac and I started frantically searching for Chuck's replacement after that but had absolutely no luck, and I was just trying not to panic about that.

The past week and a half with Jack had been like a dream. I was either with him at his place or he was at mine. We spent the entire day texting or talking on the phone. He would often leave work to either come have lunch with me or at Gia's if I was working. On Saturday after we got back, Isaac and I had to cancel our show since Chuck decided to quit Flora and Fauna, and Jack had taken me to dinner with Catrina, Brody, Callum and Carver instead, and had treated all of us.

Yep, that's my man, I wanted to say when they all looked at him in awe.

Catrina and I had a lunch date so I could tell her everything about Vermont, and she told me we would have to have a girls' night soon to celebrate me no longer being an idiot.

I had a wonderful best friend.

Last night, I'd had the evening off, and Jack had taken me to see Catrina's *La Bohème* performance. He got us box seats, and I'd blown him in his car on the way back as a thank you. The way he moaned and shook showed me I wasn't the only one who was thankful. Catrina would be done with the show by the end of the week, and she was beyond excited to be able to kick up her feet and relax for the rest of her pregnancy.

I was happy. Happy in this perfect, amazing way that I couldn't even properly explain.

I was cleaning up my tables and doing sidework after my last table left when I heard the door to the restaurant open. Shit, I'd forgotten to lock the door. I rushed around the corner to tell the person we were closed, but when I saw the person who was standing just inside the restaurant I froze.

"Hello," she said, an unreadable expression on her face. I couldn't find it in me to respond, so I just stood there, gaping like a fish. "Do you remember me?"

"Yes," I barely managed.

"He told you we were engaged?" she asked. "Or you knew?"

God, she was gorgeous. Even with her long dark hair pulled in a ponytail, hardly any makeup, and just a simple white blouse, black pea coat, and black pencil skirt, she looked like a runway model.

Rachel, who was the opposite of me in every way imaginable, was standing in Gia's, her hands folded tightly in front of her as she stood there stiffly, watching me with cold eyes.

I shook for a moment and then took a deep breath. I wasn't going to let this woman intimidate me. I had no idea why she was here, and I wasn't all that interested. I was shocked and caught off guard, but whatever she had to say to me I knew was going to be something I didn't want to hear. I knew that all it would do is poison me against Jack because I had known women just like her my entire life. I had known *people* like her, all genders, who felt entitled to someone else and felt like they should have the ultimate say.

The truth was that Rachel had no power over me or over Jack. He and I had done nothing wrong. They'd broken up months before we got together, and it wasn't until she realized he'd moved on that she decided to insert herself back in his life.

"Yes," I answered finally to both of her questions.

She regarded me coolly, eyes scaling over my body, and it took every bit of my power not to cross my arms in front of me. I wouldn't let her think she had any type of effect on me. She didn't.

Rachel was silent for so long that I thought she was going to just leave. I started to think this was some twisted game she was playing with herself—get a good look at her ex's new partner to prove to herself that said partner didn't hold a candle—that she just needed to see with her own eyes that I would never compare.

We stood there, me right next to the bar where I'd turned when I'd heard the door open, her standing right in front of the glass door where she'd come in, waiting for the other to strike.

When she finally spoke, her voice was so icy it could have sliced through my chest cavity if she'd let it.

"His family will never accept you."

My stomach plummeted, the pain her words caused like a living, breathing thing roaring to existence in the pit of my gut.

"I'm not sure what you think is going to come of this," she said, each word twisting the icy knife. "But eventually Jack will realize the mistake he's made. He'll grow out of this silly phase and realize what he has to do. He's going to realize what's right for himself and for his family, and when he does, you're going to nothing but a memory. You'll just be put into a box and shoved aside like all trash is."

"Get out."

I knew deep down that all of her words were said from hurt. Despite the curl in her lip and the disdain written all over her features, it was her cool blue eyes that betrayed her. It was sadness and despair I saw in those orbs that stopped me from moving forward and taking a swing. She wanted to call me trash? I would show her exactly what a Puerto Rican girl from Queens was capable of. Because even though I knew she was in pain and wishing things were different, I wasn't going to let anyone talk to me that way or make me feel like that. Ever.

"It's time for you to go before I do something both of us might regret."

Rachel scoffed, but I reveled in satisfaction at the small shimmer of fear I saw skate across her pretty face.

"Just remember what I said, Talia." She spat my name like it was a curse. "You know Jack and you don't fit. I think you've always known it."

"Goodbye, Rachel."

When she turned her back and pushed out the door, it wasn't until I saw her turn the corner around the block that I rushed to the door, locked it, and turned to slide my back down the glass. I sat on the cool tile, put my head in my hands, and tucked my knees up to my chest as I shook. I didn't cry—I was still too shocked—but I could hear every single one of Rachel's words ringing in my head as I sat there and stared at a spot on the floor.

I didn't know what to do. I was so shaken by the encounter that I couldn't think straight. I wanted to call Catrina and tell her what happened so we could plot our revenge like I knew she'd want to do. I wanted to go see Jack, tell him everything, and have him deal with Rachel like I knew *he'd* want to do. But more than anything, I wanted to forget this ever happened.

God, why didn't you lock the fucking door, the voice in my head snapped at me angrily.

153

This entire situation was a ridiculous mess. I was still trying to deal with my own shit, and the last thing I needed was to have to deal with Rachel's shit, too. I didn't have to own this. I didn't have to let her words have any impact on me or my relationship with Jack.

No.

Rachel's words were about her, not about me. She didn't know anything about my relationship or my history with Jack other than the tiny nuggets Jack had given her. She knew nothing about how we felt about each other and nothing about how Jack's family would react.

But when the image of Kenny's father approaching me that day on Wall Street flashed in my mind, I couldn't stop my brain from imagining that it was Jack's father telling me what Kenneth Emery Sr. was implying. What Rachel had said.

I don't want trash around my son.

I fought those thoughts and feelings while I swept the floor by reminding myself what Jack had said to me while we were in Vermont. He wasn't slumming it with me. I meant something to him. I meant more to him than his fucking pedigree. I knew that. I trusted Jack, and I trusted what we had together. I had to believe in him. In us.

An hour later, when I was finished with my sidework and was about to lock up and Jack called to say he was outside, I decided to keep the incident with Rachel to myself at least for now. I knew Jack would react poorly and it would set us back from all the progress we'd made over the last weeks we'd been together. I wanted to put it out of my mind and forget it had ever happened. I didn't want Rachel's hurt or my own fear that there was truth in her words color what I knew Jack and I had.

As soon as I unlocked the front door and let Jack into Gia's, he was grinning, and I was immediately wrapping my arms around him as he held me back just as tightly. I needed his arms around me to remind me that *this* was the truth.

We kissed for a long time standing in the doorway—the doorway Rachel had stood in only an hour ago while she told me I'd never be what Jack needed. But here, in his arms, I felt like everything he wanted and needed, and he felt exactly the same for me. Eventually, he pulled away from our kiss, and I noticed how excited and giddy he looked, making thoughts of Rachel slip from my mind at least temporarily.

"What?"

Jack's grin got wider as he pulled back, grabbed my hand, and walked me over to the bar. I giggled when he lifted me up, and then he sat me down on the bar, his eyes bright with some unnamed emotion. I knew something was up.

"What happened?" I asked, holding his face in my hands as he stood between my legs, hands on my hips. "Are you okay?"

"I... um..." Jack ran a hand down his face but then let out this small stunned giggle. "I quit my job."

I gasped and brought both hands to my mouth.

"What?"

"Yeah, I um..." He shook his head in disbelief. "A friend of mine from law school wants to expand her firm and she asked me to join her and I said yes. I gave my dad my two weeks' notice today. My friend does criminal defense and immigration. She got a grant so she can provide free legal services to undocumented immigrants. It's... Talia, it's my fucking dream job."

I stared at him in bewilderment for a few more moments before I dragged him back to me for a hug. "Oh, my god, Jack."

I pushed him away and held onto his shoulders to look at him for a moment before yanking him back to me. He laughed into my neck.

"I'm so proud of you," I whispered into his hair. I truly was. I knew how miserable he was working for his father, and I knew how much he wanted to do something to make a difference. Several of my mom's cousins from the Dominican Republic had been undocumented up until a few years ago, and knowing that Jack would be helping people like them made my already full chest want to burst with joy.

We stood there wrapped in each other's embrace for a while before Jack pulled back. He looked at me, studying my face for a long time with this look of joy and wonderment on his face.

I tightened my legs around him. "What?" He didn't say anything, and I grinned and nudged him. "What? Do I have something on my—"

"I love you."

It felt like someone had dumped a bucket of ice water on me.

"Wh-what?"

"I'm in love with you, Talia."

No. Fuck. Not tonight. Not now. No, no, no, no, no.

"Jack—" When I tried to squirm away he grabbed onto my biceps. Fuck, I needed to tell him about Rachel.

"Just listen, please."

"Jack—"

"You are the most important thing in my life," he said before I could stop him. "Having you back in it has been the best thing that's ever happened to me. I love falling asleep next to you. I love waking up with you in my arms. You were the first person I wanted to tell

155

about this. The only person's opinion I cared about. I've loved you since I was twenty-one years old, and I've only just gotten the courage today to finally tell you. I love you."

I stared at him in shock for several moments before I pushed him away from me and jumped off the bar, Rachel's words bouncing off the walls of my brain.

"Eventually Jack will realize the mistake he's made."

"Talia—"

"How can you say you've loved me since we were twenty-one?" I said angrily when I made my way around the bar. I needed distance from him.

"Because it's true."

"How can it be? You were engaged, Jack! You can't say you've loved me for almost eight years when you were engaged to be married to someone else."

"His family will never accept you."

Jack began to walk slowly around the counter, and I backed up through the restaurant, trying to maintain some space from him. His words gutted me. They scared the shit out of me, but they were also the words I'd wanted to hear for so damn long. I wanted to be loved. I wanted to be loved by him, but I didn't want to love him and then lose him if Rachel was right after all. If he ended up being like the two men who'd done the same thing. And the fear was stronger than any joy the words might have given me.

"I never stopped thinking about you. Not once."

"Don't say that." The thrill and the terror were equal measure.

"It was the day of our engagement party when I ended it—"

"Jack, don't—"

"I woke up that morning, and instead of being excited to marry this woman who was lying in bed next to me, instead of looking forward to our party and celebrating with my friends and family, all I could think about—"

"Please—"

"You'll be nothing but a memory."

"—was you."

Chapter 22

I couldn't believe I was driving north on Route 2 again so shortly after my last trip.

It was raining, and I could barely see through the water and my own tears, but Catrina's voice over the car's Bluetooth was calming me down.

"You need to tell him about Rachel. You should talk to him."

"I can't," I said miserably. "I kicked him out of the restaurant and sat there and cried for an hour like a pathetic loser. I think I fucked everything up, Cat. For good this time. He won't want me after that. I'm a mess, and he deserves better."

"Maybe."

"Thanks, Cat."

"But he wants you. He loves you. And you're all twisted up about fucking Rachel." Catrina sighed angrily. "It's so obvious that she's just a jealous ex trying to get her man back. Come on, Tal."

I knew Catrina was right, but it wasn't just about Rachel. Of course it wasn't. Yeah, Jack's confession of love was epically bad timing considering what had happened earlier last night, but if I was entirely honest with myself, I would have had to admit that I probably would have freaked out whether she'd said what she said to me or not.

Now that the fear had tamped down a bit, though, Jack's words were beyond elating. Jack loved me. He didn't care that I was a poor girl from Queens. He wanted me. He loved me. *Me.* And if what he said was true, he always had. It didn't matter what Rachel thought or his parents or anyone in the entire goddamn world.

"I love him."

Nothing changed around me when I whispered the words. The sky didn't fall. Trees didn't collapse onto the road in front of me. Birds didn't suddenly drop out of the sky. The rain kept falling. The car kept moving forward. Life went on. But inside me it was like something fundamental had shifted.

Being the woman who loved and was loved by Jack felt like everything good in the world rolled into one. Like chocolate milk, like having coffee with my mom, finding the perfect string of notes to a song that had been swirling in my head for weeks, getting the last cherry pastry at the bakery, a hot shower after a long day. It was joy and comfort and peace and rightness. It felt like the most simple and easy thing in the world, like it made the most sense of any truth I'd ever known. I loved Jack. He loved me. We loved each other. And I was fucking it all up.

"I know," Catrina replied gently. "I know you do."

The torrent of tears started again. "FUCK!" I screamed in the car. "Tal—"

"I have to go," I told Catrina abruptly. "I'm so sorry. Thanks for talking to me. I'll be at my mom's place soon."

I hung up before Catrina could respond and pounded on my steering wheel.

I wanted to check my phone, but I didn't want to risk it in the rain and I also knew what I would find. When I left that morning, I'd had about twenty calls and texts from Jack.

Talia, please call me. I'm sorry I freaked you out. I didn't mean to say it, but it came out. I know it's too soon. I know you're worried. Call me.

Baby, talk to me. Please. Let's just talk through this. I won't take back what I said, but I won't say it again until you're ready to hear it if that's what you want.

I just need to know you're okay. I'm starting to worry.

Talia, seriously, are you okay? Should I send Catrina to your apartment?

I'm not running away from this. From us. I want to be with you even if you're scared. Even if you don't love me. I don't care.

It was the last one that ripped me apart the most.

I love you. I always will. I'm tired of pretending I don't. Call me when you're ready. I love you.

It was when I got that message that I called the rental car company and left. I hadn't planned on going to my mom's for Thanksgiving. It was always a crazy busy time of year for her at the diner, and I was planning to go with Cat and Brody to Cat's huge family Thanksgiving. I was even going to ask Jack if he wanted to come even though I was scared he was going to say he couldn't because he had to be with his own family.

Instead, I was imposing on my mom even though she said over and over that it was fine, to please come. She'd even offered to close the diner and drive down, but I refused to let her lose business because of me. Not when it was my own mess that had gotten me here.

♦ ♦ ♦

The moment I trudged up the stairs that led to my mom's house, the front door opened, and she walked out and enveloped me in a hug. The tears that had subsided came back in full force. We stood there on her porch as she held me and I sobbed into her shoulder for I don't know how long. Eventually she was able to coax me into the house. I sat down on her plush sofa, and she put a plate of chocolate chip cookies on the coffee table with an enormous glass of chocolate milk next to it. Then she put down a glass of whiskey in the center of the table, and when I looked up at her, she just lifted one shoulder.

"Thought we might need that."

Was it possible to love her even more?

I told her everything, and she didn't interject until I got to the part about what had happened the previous night. She let me spew all of the dumb things I'd done along with all my worries and fears, starting from when I was with Jack at Klein until now. I told her about Rachel and she cursed in Spanish for almost five full minutes before she finally let me tell her the rest. What it finally came down to was that I hated that I kept hurting Jack, hurting myself, but I didn't know what else to do. I felt so lost and helpless.

When I confessed that I loved Jack, I started sobbing again. My mother folded me into her arms, and I cried harder. I didn't deserve her love and comfort, but I took it anyway. The last time I'd cried like this had been over Vincent, but this time it hurt even worse and I didn't know why.

No, that wasn't true.

I knew why.

Because this time I'd guarded my heart so closely, tried desperately to protect it, but it was cracking in my chest anyway. The barriers had been shattered along with my heart, and the ache that devastation caused was unlike anything I'd ever felt.

After a while, I was able to calm down. My mom handed me a cookie and I managed to eat it despite how much my stomach was churning. Then my mom cracked open the whiskey bottle and we each took a large swig. The burn was soothing—calming in a way that removed the ache in my chest if only for a moment.

Then my mom crossed her legs on the couch and faced me.

"Tell me," I said quietly. "Tell me how badly I'm screwing this up. Because I need to hear it."

"That's not what I want to say," she said. She looked so sad and serious. I wanted to start crying again but I barely managed to stem it as she started talking. "First, I want to tell you that nothing that woman says matters even a little." I sniffled and she said, "No, I mean it. Imagine how you would be if you knew you lost Jack for good. Almost how you feel right now. That's where she is, and that's

159

the place her words come from. But that's not important right now."
My mom sighed. "I need to apologize, mija."

I frowned. "You don't have anything to apologize for."

"I do," she said with a nod. "I'm so sorry I didn't protect you from
the pain your father caused."

No words she could have said would have shocked me more.

"Ma—"

"No, let me say this." She took a deep breath and grabbed my
hands in hers. "I let him hurt you for too long. I let him come in and
out of our lives as he pleased, and I want to believe it was because I
wanted you to know him, but that isn't true. Not entirely. I wanted
him near for my own selfish reasons. Because even after everything,
I loved him, and even though I knew we would never truly be
together, for so long I was just willing to take whatever he would
give. I didn't think about how much that would hurt you then or in
the future."

"Ma, th-this isn't about that."

"Isn't it?" she asked softly. "He made you believe that all men
would do what he did. And that stupid boy just reinforced that.
Those two made you believe that men were only capable of deceit.
That all they would do is leave. But that isn't true."

"I—"

"Jack is not him." She said it firmly, like she was trying to make it
really sink in. And when she repeated it, tears flooded my eyes.
"Jack is not Kenny. Jack is not Vincent. Jack is Jack." I looked down
at my lap as the tears slid down my cheeks. "Talia, look at me."

I looked up, and when I saw my mom's eyes were glistening, I
choked out a sob.

"Look at me and listen to me." I nodded. "Jack is not them. Do
you understand?"

I didn't know if I did. And if I did understand, I didn't know if I
believed it. I didn't know if I was capable of separating all the men in
my life. They would all hurt you in the end. They would use you as
they pleased, and they wouldn't think twice about it. I didn't know if
Jack would want to be with me forever. Maybe I would end up a
memory, just like Rachel said. I didn't know if he wouldn't keep me a
dirty little secret hidden away from his family the way Kenny had
done to us for years. The way Vincent had done to me.

What about Brody?

The voice in my head interrupted my dark and sad thoughts, and
I paused. He was a man I knew could stay. I saw the way he loved
Catrina with all of his heart. Sure, he'd fucked up when we were in
college, but since then, he had always been there for Catrina. They
were married. They were going to have a baby. Brody had stayed.

Jack had stayed. Despite how much I had tried so hard to push him away at every turn, despite what Rachel thought, Jack stayed, and when I forced him to leave, he came back. He'd loved me even then. I didn't want to believe that he'd loved me the past six years, but in all the time I'd known him, Jack had never once lied to me. He'd loved me since then. And maybe... I didn't want to dare hope, but maybe he would love me for a long time. Maybe even forever.

He stayed. And I loved him.

That night, I cried in the bed Jack and I had shared until I fell asleep. Around three in the morning, I woke up with an idea in my mind. I must have been dreaming about it or unconsciously forming the idea in my head long before that because it was so urgent that it had woken me from a deep sleep.

My eyes were puffy as I reached to the side of my bed and pulled my tablet out of my bag. I scrubbed both my hands down my face, and opened my email app.

I really hoped he had the same email, but even if he didn't, I needed to get all of this out. I refused to look for him on social media because I knew it would only do more harm than good. So it had to be email. If he never saw it, then so be it. But this note, these words, had been in my heart for so long that the only way I was truly going to be able to move forward was if I sent the email I should've sent years ago.

Vincent,

I don't know if you'll ever see this. I don't care if you do. You don't even have to respond. But I need to say this.

What you did to me was evil and cruel. You told me you loved me, made me believe that you wanted a life with me, and the second you got the chance, you tossed me aside like I was nothing to you. Like I was trash.

You never saw me after that, so you'll have no idea how much pain you caused. I could try to tell you, but my words won't do justice to the devastation you left behind. It stayed with me. For years, I never believed men when they told me they wanted to be with me. I believed they were all like you. I believed they would all somehow do to me what you did to me, and I didn't think I could live through another heart break like that.

It wasn't until recently that I finally began to see that not all men are like you. I finally see that there are other men out there who are capable of being honest and true, who are capable of showing real love, and not a "love" that's predicated entirely on lies, deceit, and ugliness.

I thought it was my fault. If only I'd loved you more, changed for you, been exactly who you wanted me to be, then I could have the love I wanted. And if I couldn't change who I was, then I would just have to avoid love entirely. You made me believe I didn't deserve to be loved as I am. That no one could possibly love me, because if that was possible, you would've stayed.

I know now—only just now—that that's not true. What you did was about you, not about me. It was about what you wanted and who you were. I am worthy and deserving of love. Maybe you didn't see that. Maybe you aren't capable of seeing that in others. Maybe now you are. I hope so. I hope you're happy and that you've found what you wanted.

I'm not expecting a response. But these words have been inside me for so long, and they belong out in the world. They belong out of my head and out of my heart. I don't have room for them anymore. I wish you all the best.

Talia

I ended the email with the exact words he'd texted to me so long ago. Almost a decade ago. I didn't know if he would notice or care that I'd thrown his words back at him. I still didn't even know if he would see it. But I needed him to own those words. I needed those words to not be part of me ever again.

Because even though Rachel's words had crawled inside me, it was the damage done by Vincent and Kenny that was truly stopping me from being able to move forward.

When I hit send, the sense of relief that washed over me made me feel almost light headed. But I needed to do one last thing.

I printed the email. As I heard it sliding through the printer that my mom kept in the guest room, I slipped shoes on my feet, and I took the printed email off the printer and walked into the living room. My coat was on the hanger on one of my mom's closet doors. I put it on, and quietly made my way across the small house and into the kitchen. As quietly as I could I slid open a drawer. When I found what I was looking for, I tiptoed to the front door.

The water near my mom's house was just a short walk away. I crossed the deserted street and pulled my coat tighter around me as I felt the wind pick up as I got closer to the water's edge. I pulled the lighter I'd found in my mom's kitchen drawer out of my coat pocket along with the email. I unfolded the paper, held the lighter to the corner of the page, and watched as it ignited. I let it burn about halfway through before I dropped it into the water.

I stood there and watched the ashes float away, along with the painful memories of a past I didn't need to let burden me anymore.

I wanted to be free. I was free. Nothing anyone had said or done could be my burden to bear anymore.

My mom was sitting on the porch steps when I walked back to the house. Neither of us spoke as I sat down next to her. She wrapped her arm around my shoulders, and we sat there together in the cold November night air, while I looked up at the stars and hoped that Jack was okay.

♦ ♦ ♦

I was exhausted when I woke up the next morning. My eyes felt swollen, my mouth was insanely dry, and when I opened my eyes, the first thing I thought about was Jack and my plan for the rest of the day. I would spend the day with my mom at the diner and then make the drive back to Boston. I wouldn't even stop at home, I would just go straight to his place and hope like hell that he was there and that he would even talk to me. I would tell him about Rachel and Vincent and how I had finally let all of that shit go.

I didn't know if I was ready to tell him I loved him yet because some of the fear still lingered, but I knew I wasn't afraid for him to love me. And even if I couldn't say it, I would do my best to love him in every way I knew how.

I was jonesing for coffee after I got dressed and pushed open the bedroom door. I knew my mom would already be at the diner, and I was hoping she'd just made a fresh pot so I could drink every last drop.

I grabbed my coat off the hanger on the back of the door, but yelped and dropped it before I could even put it on.

"J-Jack?"

He stood up from where he was sitting on the couch. He ran his hands nervously down the front of his jeans.

He looked more beautiful than anything I'd ever seen. He was wearing black jeans and a black sweater that did nothing to hide his beautifully ripped body. His hair wasn't done, and he looked like he hadn't slept in days. He had dark circles under his eyes, which were rimmed red, and there was a generous layer of stubble on his jaw. But he was a vision. And if I was still in doubt about how I felt about him, it all would've washed away in that moment.

"Hi."

"What are you..." I trailed off as I took several steps closer to him.

"I had to know you were okay." His voice was hoarse. I hated seeing the proof of the pain I'd caused, but I couldn't take my eyes off him. "I needed to see you. Catrina called."

"What?"

"She told me about Rachel coming to Gia's."

Oh.

"Oh." I nodded but didn't trust my voice to say more than that.

"Why didn't you tell me?"

"I..." I swallowed and took a deep breath, hoping it would stop my voice from shaking while knowing that it wouldn't. "I didn't get a chance."

Jack nodded. "I talked to her. She's not... we don't need to worry about her anymore." All I could do was nod and trust him because then he was talking again. "I'm so sorry she did that, and I'm sorry I freaked you out," he said slowly. "But I won't apologize for what I said, and I won't take it back." I nodded stupidly again, and he walked closer so that we were only about a foot apart. "I'm in love with you. And I don't know what I'll have to do to prove it to you, but I'll work my ass off to do that. I want to be with you in whatever way you'll have me. Even if it means you'll never tell me you love me back. I don't care because I know that you do even if it scares you. I'm not leaving this time." He stood straighter. "I won't let you push me away again. I'm staying. Let me stay, Talia. Let me be the guy who stays."

We held each other's stares for a long time. I could see every bit of love and honesty in his eyes, and I hoped he could see mine.

"Please stay," I whispered.

His arms were around me a moment later. We stood there embracing, just hugging each other, and I refused to let him go.

"I'm sorry I ran," I said into his ear.

He just shook his head and I held onto him tighter. I slid one hand up into his hair and pulled his head down onto my shoulder. His arms were so tight around my waist that I was on my toes.

"I need to say something," I said into his neck.

After a bit, Jack pulled back and guided us both to the couch. We sat down facing each other.

"Do you remember Vincent Cunningham? The guy I dated freshman year?"

Jack frowned and nodded.

"Did you ever know how we broke up?" When he shook his head, I told him the whole story, and by the end, Jack looked like he was ready to spit fire.

"He told me he loved me the day he left for New York," I murmured. "He'd told me he loved me so many times before that. Kenny told me he loved me, too. 'Love you, Tally,' he would say. And I believed him. I believed them both, and I *thought* that's what love was. I thought Vincent loved me. But now I know he never did.

"Love is about truth and honesty, and that was something neither of them ever gave me. Love is about putting the other person first, and neither of them did. I wanted to be what they wanted me to be. I wanted to do whatever it took for them to love me enough to stay, and it didn't matter. Whatever they felt for me wasn't love. Not without conditions. You have never tried to change me. You have never asked me to be or expected me to be anyone other than me. You have loved me unconditionally." My voice broke on the last word, and Jack scooted closer and took one of my hands in his.

"I don't know if you'll love me fifty years from now," I continued, my voice raspy with emotion. "I don't even know if you'll love me tomorrow. I've been so scared of you leaving that I didn't even think about how it would be if you stayed. But I want to be in this *now*. With you. Who knows what will happen? Maybe one day you'll wake up and realize you want something—someone—different." He opened his mouth like he was going to interrupt, but when I kept talking, he closed his mouth.

"But I don't care. I don't care if you want to leave one day because right now I just want you here. With me. I want to be with you. I don't want to worry about tomorrow anymore. Just stay today. We'll worry about tomorrow when it comes."

I was in his arms again. And when he snuggled into my neck, I giggled and fell on my back, and he was on top of me. I spread my legs for him, and he looked down at me, one arm braced next to my head and the other on the back of the couch.

"I love you."

His whispered words were like a prayer.

It was true. I didn't know what tomorrow would bring, but I would take all the love he would give me until he wasn't willing to give it anymore. I wasn't going to let the past haunt me and rule over me. I was going to be with the person I loved for as long as he would have me. For as long as we were happy. Because for the first time in my life I knew that a man truly loved me. Without conditions. And it was perfect.

Chapter 23

"'I t's so wonderful to hear from you, Talia,'" I read to Catrina. "'I've thought about you so much over the years. What I did to you was unforgivable. I would give anything to change what I did, but I can't. You deserve every happiness in the world. If you find in your heart to forgive me one day, I would love to reconnect. I'm sure you're even more beautiful than you were ten years ago.'"

"He is such a fucking skeeze!" Catrina said when I finished.

"Right? I just told him he ruined my life for a decade, and he's trying to fucking flirt with me."

"So gross," Catrina said, shaking her head. "Are you going to reply?"

I shook my head and put my phone face down on the table. "Nope. No need to. I let all that shit go up in Vermont. I'm happy. And I don't need anything from him ever again."

Catrina put her head in her hand and looked at me dreamily. "Your love story is so epic."

I chuckled and rolled my eyes at her. "You're a hopeless romantic."

She smiled. "I totally am."

"So, how's that little monster treating you?" I asked, gesturing toward Catrina's stomach. I loved the way she rubbed her small stomach when she looked down happily and then back up at me.

"So much better now," she replied. "No more puking my guts out, but I'm hormonal as hell. I alternate between crying and being horny at all times."

I laughed loudly, and Catrina was giggling until suddenly her face turned incredibly serious.

"Holy shit."

I looked over my shoulder to see what Catrina was looking at.

The restaurant we were in was relatively empty since it was four o'clock in the afternoon on the Friday after Thanksgiving. There was a couple sitting on the other side of the dining room, and a woman with short blonde hair sitting at the bar.

"What?"

"That's Holly."

I looked over my shoulder and back at Catrina again.

"Who?"

"Holly Goldsmith," Cat whispered. "From college."

I gaped and looked back again. I could only see the dark blonde hair. "Are you sure? Didn't Holly have super long super blonde hair?"

Holly Goldsmith had basically been Catrina's and my archnemesis at Klein. During our senior year, Holly had teased Cat about being a virgin and then proceeded to post on social media about it. It had ended up striking up a no strings relationship between Cat and Brody that had ended in them falling in love, but Holly had been a huge jerk to both Cat and I way before that. Every time we'd see her, she'd whisper to her friends about us and then laugh loudly enough to draw attention. She always sarcastically complimented my clothes, and told Catrina how much she loved red heads, even though her tone dripped with insincerity. She was the definition of a mean girl.

"I'm going to go talk to her."

I looked at Catrina like she'd said she was going to join the circus.

"What? Why? She's evil."

Cat rolled her eyes. "She's not evil."

My jaw dropped. "Okay, obviously you're suffering from some memory loss. Did you forget she called you out for being a virgin in room full of people? Do I need to pull up that Facebook post where she talked about finding out someone was a virgin? Do you I need to remind you of when we were out at the reservoir and she asked in front of everyone if you were *still a virgin*?"

"That was six years ago," Catrina hissed. "You didn't see her face when she turned around earlier. I did. She looked really, really sad."

"So? Even wicked witches get sad sometimes! Remember when the Witch of West's sister died? She was all broken up over that."

I could tell Catrina was trying not to laugh, and she tried to give me a stern look. "I'm serious, Talia, she looked really sad and tired. And." She shrugged. "I probably wouldn't be married to Brody and pregnant with his child right now if she hadn't been such a rotten B word."

I snorted. "Ugh. Fine! I'll go over there with you, but I'm not going to talk to her."

"Yes, you will," she said as she stood up and grabbed my arm. "Come on." She dragged me through the restaurant around several tables until we were standing behind the woman.

"Holly?"

She practically jumped out of her skin when Catrina said her name. When she looked over her shoulder she looked like a scared rabbit, ready to scamper away at the smallest sign of danger.

"Catrina?" She looked at me. "Talia?"

"Hi," Catrina said with a smile. "We saw you from over there and thought we'd come say hello."

Holly looked suspicious, but Catrina was right about everything else. Her skin was pale and had an almost gray tint to it. She had dark circles under her pretty blue eyes. She looked exhausted and more than just sad. She looked downtrodden, like the years had done a serious number on her. I tried to harden myself to the pang of sympathy in my stomach, but it was impossible. I may have hated her in college, but this woman sitting in front of us was clearly hurting.

"Are you back in Boston now?" Catrina asked.

Last we'd heard, she'd moved back home to Virginia.

"Just got back last month."

Catrina waited for her to say something more, but she didn't.

"What are you doing now? Where are you working?"

"I'm a nurse," Holly told Catrina.

Catrina looked at me for help and I just shrugged. Then she looked back at Holly and seemed to think something over.

"Talia's in a band," she said, and I frowned at her, unsure of where the hell she was going with this. "She plays shows pretty much every weekend. She's doing a solo show this weekend because her band is still looking for a new guitarist, but you should come."

I sent Catrina a wide-eyed look but she gamely ignored me and kept looking at Holly with a kind look on her face. What the fuck was Catrina doing?

"No thanks."

"We should go," I muttered to Cat, but she ignored me.

"It'll be fun, I promise," Catrina said. "Talia's really talented and the evening is always super low key. Not a ton of people usually, but the places do get fairly packed. But we get there early so we have a place to sit. Anyway, Brody and I could pick you up even. I'm sure he'd love to see you, too. I could probably force Gabe to take a night off work." Catrina looked earnest and hopeful, and Holly just watched her for almost a solid minute of unbearably uncomfortable silence.

"Okay."

Catrina pumped one of her fists when Holly agreed. She gave her all the details, and I knew there was no way in hell she was going to actually show up. But I wouldn't burst Catrina's lovely little bubble until I absolutely needed to.

"You just invited Holly Goldsmith to my show this weekend," I groused as soon as we paid our bill and walked outside.

"I sure did," Catrina said brightly. "It's going to be awesome."

I took an Uber to Jack's apartment when we left. Patrick, his doorman, let me up, and when I went into the door that Jack had left unlocked for me, I saw him lying on his huge leather sofa, eyes closed, snoring softly with a book on his lap.

I took that moment just to study him. The planes and angles of his face, the slope of his cheekbones, the curve of his mouth that I could sometimes just stare at absently without realizing it. His long, hard body was draped across the entire expanse of the sofa. He'd still gone to work today to close out many of his clients or transfer them even though his dad had been so furious when he told him he was quitting, that his dad had told him not to bother coming back. So, he was still in his work clothes, and his collar was undone several buttons, his tie hanging loosely around his neck.

He looked edible and perfect and everything I'd ever wanted or needed. Seeing him there, knowing he was all mine, knowing he loved me, made my heart feel too big for my chest. This man—this perfect, beautiful, smart, sexy man loved *me*. He was mine and I was his. After everything, he'd found his way into my heart even if I'd resisted it, even if I'd pushed him away. He'd never given up on me. On us.

I sat next to his legs on the couch and pushed back the dark brown hair that had flopped onto his forehead.

His eyes fluttered open, and the shy, soft, gentle smile he gave me almost made my heart stop.

"Hey, gorgeous."

I didn't reply. I pushed my fingers further into his hair and leaned down to kiss him softly. Just a brush of lips. He was still smiling that smile when I pulled back.

"I love you," I whispered.

His eyes widened almost imperceptibly.

"I do." My voice was barely there. "I love you."

Saying the words was the greatest joy and rush I had ever known. It felt like I'd been swimming against a current for hours and then all of the sudden, I was on dry land; like a piano that had been out of tune until someone had laid their hands on it and brought out that one crisp clear note after a perfect tuning. It felt safe and right and wonderful. I loved Jack. I'd loved him for almost as long as he'd loved me, but I'd been so scared to let myself. I wasn't scared anymore. Saying the words was so simple that it almost made it feel like I'd been saying them forever. I was exactly the same person I was before I said them, except the entire world had opened up in front of me.

Jack just watched me for a long time before he finally sat up and pulled me into a hug.

"I'm sorry I didn't say it before." I whispered the words into the crook of his neck.

"I wanted you to say it when you were ready," he replied into my hair. "I would've waited forever."

A tear slipped out of the corner of my eye, and when Jack pulled back he kissed it away.

"I love you, too."

I kissed him for real this time. I didn't try to hide myself from him. Both of our eyes were open, and I didn't try to stop the tears. I let him see everything—all the wild, intense, passionate feelings I had for him. He kissed each tear off my cheeks, holding my face in his hands as he did so. I choked out a small sob and buried my face in his neck again. We held onto each other tightly, and I reveled in his whispered words in my ear as he began to undress me. He told me how much he loved me, how beautiful I was, how he would never leave me, how much he needed me, wanted me, cherished me. The words went directly from his mouth into each crevice of my heart, filling me so full of him that I felt like I couldn't breathe.

I'd never known anything like this. Before him, I'd never known what it felt to be loved like this, to need someone and to be needed by someone like you were an extension of them. To be as necessary to their existence as a vital organ. That's what Jack was to me. He'd been a part of me since I was a girl—a young woman in her early twenties who had let two men shape how she saw all the other men who came after them. But Jack had found his way in even then, even when I denied him, even when I pushed him as far away as I could. Now, I'd finally let him in. He'd been there all along, but my willingness to open myself to his love made it so much sweeter.

Jack Harding was the love of my life. I'd fought it for seven years, and I was finally done fighting. Instead, I would fight *for* us, never against. Not anymore.

I was on my back on Jack's sofa. He'd stripped off all my clothes piece by piece the same way he'd stripped down all the walls I'd put around my heart—slowly, delicately, carefully. He had one knee on the couch between my legs, the other on the floor as he looked down at me and took off his clothes, his eyes on me the entire time. I was panting below him. I didn't know where to put my eyes or my hands. I wanted to take in every bit of him, show him all the love I had for him, and that made it impossible to be still. I ran my hands down the skin of his torso as soon as he lifted his shirt. Then down his arms, loving how his muscles felt under my hands. I wanted to look at his face, but I was desperate to drink all of him in, so my eyes flicked back and forth, over and over, between different parts of his body and then back to his eyes. I couldn't get enough of him.

His name tumbled from my lips like a benediction. We held each other's eyes then, conveying through our gazes all the things we felt for one another. The moment felt too big to be real, too massive for Jack's living room, his apartment, the entire city. How could I hold onto this moment? How could I keep it with me and let it sustain me for the rest of my life? I didn't know how, but I would try like hell.

He leaned in to kiss me as he slid inside. I whimpered into this mouth—a desperate, needy sound that I couldn't hold back—and Jack made a small noise in the back of his throat.

Our bodies were plastered together as we moved against the leather. My limbs were shaking as I wrapped them around him and clutched him to me as tightly as I could. I knew it wouldn't take long before I came. He was deep inside me, his thick length filling up every inch of me, but it wasn't even that. It was the emotion of this moment that was taking me higher.

It felt like there was a bright, burning flame right in the center of my chest, and the heat was radiating out to my limbs, crawling across my skin, making me a captive of that feeling, holding me in its thrall.

"I love you," I breathed against his mouth. "Jack, I love you so much."

"Baby," he moaned as he sped up his thrusts, tunneling in and out of me, almost leaving my channel completely each time only to sink back in harder each time.

He buried his face in my neck, our sweat making us stick together as I wrapped my arms tighter around his hot, damp back. I whispered the words in his ear again and again, moaning as I did so, and the choked sounds coming from him were turning me on even more. I tightened around him and he grunted loudly, so I did it again. And again. And again and again until I knew he was close, until I knew he wouldn't be able to take much more. I was right there with him.

"You're mine," he growled in my ear. "You are mine, Talia." I moaned loudly at his words, letting them wash over me, burrow inside me even deeper than he was. "You've always been mine. You'll always be mine."

"*Jack.*"

"I love you." He leaned back only enough so he could look at my face. His eyes were heavy lidded with lust and desire, and his face was glistening with sweat. I'd never seen him look so beautiful.

171

"I love you," he breathed again. He slammed into me over and over. "Come for me. Please, Talia, I love you, come for me."

I came as soon as he told me to. I screamed into his mouth as he kissed me while I came. I was trembling hard, my body quaking as he I came harder than I ever had in my life. The feeling almost frightened me. I worried it would never end—that I would just lay here forever lost to the sensations, lost to him.

The blood was roaring in my ears and my vision dimmed, but vaguely I registered the sounds coming from Jack, the feeling of his hot release flooding me. I knew he was right there with me, lost.

◆ ◆ ◆

"How was your dinner with Catrina?"

We were a sweaty, sticky mess on Jack's couch, but both of us were too worn out to move. So instead he pulled the small blanket from the back of the couch over our cooling bodies as we laid there still trying to catch our breaths. The blanket didn't even cover below Jack's mid-calf, but it would be enough until we both forced ourselves up and into the shower. Our legs were tangled together, and I was running my fingers through Jack's sparse chest hair, my head on his arm, as he ran his hand up and down my back.

"It was good. I missed you today."

He leaned forward and kissed the tip of my nose.

"Same he—"

"Oh, my god, you'll never guess who we ran into."

"Who?"

"Holly Goldsmith."

Jack looked like it was the last person he was expecting. "Seriously? Did you talk to her?"

"I didn't really. Catrina did. And she invited her to my show tomorrow."

Jack gaped for several seconds and then burst out laughing. I shoved at his shoulder.

"It's not funny!"

"Oh, it's hilarious," he said, still chuckling. "I can't believe she did that. I didn't think they were friends."

"Um, they're not. Remember how I told you all the shit that happened with her making fun of Cat for being a virgin?"

"Wow, yeah." Jack shook his head. "So, why did she invite her then?"

I sighed. "Well, she did look really sad, or whatever."

"Aw," he said. "That's sweet." Then he narrowed his eyes at me. "Oh, my god, you totally feel sympathy for her."

"No, I don't."

"You do! I can see it. You feel bad and part of you wants her to come so you know she's okay."

I began wriggling in Jack's arms, but he just laughed and held me tighter.

"It's okay," he said, kissing my neck. I couldn't stop the sigh that escaped as I tilted my neck to give him more access. "You're a big softie. I always knew it."

"Whatever, Harding."

Then he was kissing me, making me momentarily forget about Holly and my show and every other thing in the world but him.

Epilogue

Five Months Later

Talia

"Good set tonight, Talia."

I looked up from where I was sitting on Jack's lap on a couch in a sectioned off VIP section of the club and I could feel his hard cock pressed against my ass.

I didn't recognize the person who stood on the other side of the rope, but I looked up with a grin and a wave.

"Hey, thank you so much. What's your name?" Jack ran his hand up my inner thigh, and I shivered in his hold.

"I'm Travis."

"It's nice to meet you, Travis. I'm so glad you enjoyed it."

When Travis walked away, I turned to Jack and grabbed his face in my hands so I could kiss him hard.

The venue we were at tonight was unlike any I'd ever played before. It was a large, nationally known blues club that had featured bands and artists I'd admired for much of my life and had been open for over thirty years. When I was on stage, playing to all the people packed in the music hall, who were singing songs I wrote along with me, it was one of the most surreal experiences I'd ever had.

Ever since Flora and Fauna had gotten our new guitarist, Adrian Lord, several months ago, we'd all decided to get more serious about how we showcased ourselves and how we played music. I'd resisted a lot at first—especially when Adrian wanted to get a bassist so I could focus on writing songs and being our vocalist—but eventually I'd agreed to the bass player, Faron James, and we'd hired a manager and released our second full length album in that time that featured the song Isaac and I had written together the day after Jack and I had made love for the first time in six years. It was called "Don't Let Me Tell You to Go," and it was the last song on the album. We'd tried different styles with it, but ultimately all three of us decided to strip it down and have it with just Isaac on the piano and my voice. When I'd played it for Jack and saw the tears shimmering in his eyes, I'd fallen in love with him all over again.

"I can't wait to take you home," Jack murmured huskily in my ear. His hand was traveling further up my inner thigh, and my short, black leather dress was doing nothing to hide what he was doing.

"Me too," I breathed. "Need you."

His thumb brushed my clit and Jack gasped when he realized I wasn't wearing any underwear.

"You were up there all that time without anything under this dress?" he growled.

I shook my head. "I took them off after the show." I bit his ear lobe. "Just for you."

"Fuck." His hand traveled higher until his fingers were lightly toying with my clit. When he felt how wet I was, he cursed again. "As soon as I get you alone, I'm going to fuck you so hard."

"Yes. Please."

"I'm going to pound your wet, tight little pussy until you can't walk."

The loud music pounding through the club was the only thing that covered the sound of my moan.

"First I'm going to fuck you over the couch," he whispered. "Make you come on my cock." His hot breath on my neck and ear was driving me as wild as his fingers and his words. "Then I'm going to take you to our bed and eat you until you scream. And then I'm going to fuck you again." I whimpered and clutched the back of his neck.

I loved how he said *our*. It had only been two weeks since we'd moved in together, and it had been blissful. Jack hated how I left globs of toothpaste in the sink on occasion, but other than that everything was beyond perfect. Coming home to him, waking up to him, going to bed next to him every single day and night was a dream come true. I loved him more every day.

Jack and I had had dinner with his parents exactly once. It hadn't gone as horribly as I'd expected, but when Jack's mother started to make comments about the country club or her donor list for her charity and remarking how I "probably wouldn't know anything about that," Jack had made our excuses and we hadn't been back since. I told him I didn't mind the snide remarks and that I'd be fine to give it another try because I knew it wouldn't be easy, but he'd just sighed angrily and said we could give it another go in six months.

His sister, however, was a different story. Julianna and I got along amazingly. She asked me questions about my family and told me she couldn't wait to meet my mom, and she'd even taken me out shopping and to lunch just the two of us several times over the last five months. Jack's nieces, Sophia and Ainsley, were every bit as amazing as Jack had sworn they were, and he and I had gotten to babysit them for a night while Julianna and Elliot had a date night. We'd watched *Moana* twice and then made a choreographed dance to "You're Welcome," that made Jack laugh raucously.

Jack took his hand from off my back and shifted so my back was against the arm of the chair. He brought that hand up to toy with the diamond bracelet on my wrist that he'd given me three months earlier on Valentine's Day. I'd protested at first, telling him it was far too expensive and that I couldn't take it, but later, when he'd fucked me in nothing but that bracelet, holding me down by my wrists reminding me I was his, I wouldn't have given up that bracelet for anything.

I wouldn't call myself a romantic, but Jack definitely was. He showed me romance as much as he could, and I'd grown to adore it. His small gestures—flowers sent to the studio, a card left on my bedside table telling me he loved me, breakfast in bed—were often even better than the way he made me feel when we had sex. That's how much and how deeply those gestures made me feel.

I gasped when Jack slipped a finger inside me, still lightly touching the bracelet on my wrist.

"You look good in diamonds," he said against my mouth before he kissed me—a soft, teasing kiss, where he only faintly brushed his tongue against mine. He slid his hand up the back of my hand until one of his fingers brushed my ring finger.

"You'd look better with one right here."

I was barely registering what he was saying, I was so fucking horny. I just wanted him to take me home already. Stop teasing me and just fuck me.

"Would you wear my ring, Talia?"

He slid his finger out of me, and I finally became slightly coherent again.

"Jack?" I was breathless and confused and turned on, writhing on his lap and staring into his green eyes.

He pressed his forehead to mine and I inhaled his scent, pine and him.

"We should get married."

My heart sped up. I didn't know if it was the lust and whiskey talking or if he really meant it. I tried to huff a laugh, but the speed of my breath and my heart made it more of a strangled sound.

"Is that how you ask a woman to marry you?" I tried to joke, my lips brushing his.

He wrapped his arms around my waist and dragged me impossibly closer to him. When I pulled my face back, Jack wasn't smiling and his eyes had cleared. He didn't look like he was riding a wave of sex and alcohol. He looked like the genuine, honest, sincere Jack that I'd fallen in love with.

"Are you being serious?"

Jack nodded. *Marry me*, he mouthed, and then brought me closer still as he whispered, "Be mine. Like you always have been. Like you always will be. Be mine forever. Marry me, Talia."

I opened my mouth to respond, but just as I did, Brody rushed over, yelling my name. He and Catrina had been on the dance floor, grinding despite her huge, pregnant belly. They'd come to the show with Gabe, Callum, Carver, and Michael, all four of whom had left shortly after my set finished, while Brody and Catrina stayed with Jack and me.

"What's wrong?" Jack asked when I looked up at Brody's frantic face.

"Where's Catrina?"

"She's standing at the bar. She told me to come get you."

I clambered off Jack's lap and looked over to see Catrina leaning against the bar heavily, clutching her stomach. She smiled up at me, but it looked more like a grimace.

Brody looked at me when I looked back at him, and said, "Her water broke."

The four of us rushed to the hospital, Brody in the front seat and Jack in the passenger seat, while Catrina and I sat in the back. She was turned with both her feet up on the door, her head against my chest while I tried to murmur words of comfort as she held onto both my hands. Every time she had a contraction she squeezed both my hands so hard I thought they were going to break.

"How're you doing?" Jack looked back at us. He was exuding calm, unlike Brody who was clutching the steering wheel and staring straight ahead, his jaw clenched tight.

Catrina was deep breathing, so I said, "Okay, I think," and gave him a soft smile.

He wanted to marry me. Jack Harding had asked me to marry him. Talia from six months ago would have been shaking with fear and worry, but Jack had changed me. Fundamentally. I wasn't scared of him anymore. I wasn't scared of us. I knew he loved me as much as he said he did, and I knew beyond a shadow of a doubt that he wanted a life with me. And I knew I wanted one with him. Jack had helped me open my heart again. With him, I didn't need to be afraid. I was ready to build something with him even more than we already had. I was ready for whatever was in store, just as long as he was with me every step of the way.

♦ ♦ ♦

Jack

When we got to the hospital, Catrina was rushed to a room so that a doctor could check on her. She was still contracting pretty badly, but Talia had sent me a text from the room to let know she wasn't dilated enough to start delivery. I could see down the hall Brody pacing outside the room on the phone, running a stressed hand through his blonde hair.

I was staring down at my phone, playing a random game, when I looked up and saw Talia walking toward me.

Goddamn, she was gorgeous. And mine.

Sometimes, I would catch myself looking at her and it would almost steal my breath. I was a lucky son of bitch, and I knew it.

Over the past few months, she'd gone back to looking like the Talia I'd fallen in love with so long ago. She'd cut her hair into a long bob and let the natural dark color come through, though it wasn't the black she'd had in college. I loved whatever clothes she wore and however her hair looked, but this was the Talia of my dreams—the one I'd seen when I closed my eyes in the six years we were apart and let the memories of her wash over me.

I'd fallen in love with her on a Sunday morning our senior year of college. I'd taken her out for brunch after a night out of drinking, dancing, and fucking. I was telling her a story, and she was laughing until she snorted so hard chocolate milk almost came up her nose, which only made her laugh even harder. I knew I loved her then— seeing her so happy and carefree and open in a way she so rarely was.

I knew even then that there had to be a reason why she wouldn't let herself be in relationships. I knew she dated Vincent Cunningham, but I never knew how badly he'd broken her heart. And I'd known nothing about her father. But knowing what I knew now and seeing that after all that she was finally willing to give her heart to me made me want to guard and protect it even more. I couldn't promise I would never hurt her, but I could damn sure try.

I'd meant what I said to her earlier that night. I had a ring in my underwear drawer at home that I'd bought two months ago. I knew how hard it was for Talia to even say I was her boyfriend months ago, so I was scared shitless of giving her a ring and seeing her run for the hills. But tonight...

The words were out before I knew they were. And when they were out, they just felt so right. So necessary. I wanted to spend my life with the girl I'd loved since I was twenty-one. I loved her even more now than I did then. Seeing her walk toward me now, her petite curvy body still in the clothes she'd worn to her show made my cock stand at attention.

She was wearing a short, tight, sleeveless, black leather dress that I knew she wasn't wearing panties underneath. The V at her chest dipped sinfully low showing a significant amount of the round mounds of her stellar tits. She was also wearing *very* high-heeled thigh-high boots that still didn't bring her to my eye level. She was desire personified, and I wanted to spend the rest of my life with her.

"Hey," she said as she plopped on the waiting room chair next to me. There were wooden chair arms between us, but she still angled her body toward mine, hooking one of her boot-covered ankles under my calf and wrapping her arms around my bicep.

She yawned widely and sunk as far into me as the chair would allow, resting her head on my shoulder. It was after two a.m. now and I was exhausted and still fucking horny from earlier, but there was no place I'd rather be than right here with her.

"I'm glad you're here," she said through another yawn. I put my hand closest to her on her inner thigh in between her crossed legs.

"Me, too."

"Guess who's here?" she said.

"Who?"

"Holly. She's a nurse here on this floor, did I tell you that?"

I shook my head. Talia and Catrina had slowly started trying to become friends with Holly over the past few months. From what I knew, Holly was very guarded and really unlike the person they used to know, and Catrina was determined to befriend her. And because Talia was her best friend, she was just along for the ride.

"You don't have to stay," Talia murmured sleepily. "Emily and Amos just got here. Derek's on his way," she said, referring to Catrina's parents and brother.

"Are you staying?" I looked down at her. Her sleepy, sexy, caramel-colored eyes did things to my insides when she looked up at me. God, I was crazy for her.

She nodded. "Cat wants me to. We always talked about it, us being in each other's rooms when we had kids. It'll be me, Brody, and Emily in the room when the time comes."

"I'll stay."

She looked at me with a smile before she leaned up and pressed her lips to mine.

"I love you." She breathed the words into my mouth and gave me life along with them.

"I love you so much," I whispered back.

When she pulled away just a bit, she looked down at the floor.

"Did you mean it? What you said at the club?"

I turned toward her and touched her chin to gently tilt her head up toward me. Her eyes were slightly wide and she looked nervous and vulnerable. I didn't know which of my answers she feared more, but I could only tell her the truth.

"I've loved you for eight years. I'll love you for eight hundred more. Yes, I meant it. I want to marry you, Talia. I want you to be with me for the rest of our lives." As subtly as I could—because I knew she would hate the attention it drew—I shifted so I could move down to one knee in front of her. Tears filled her eyes as I grabbed both of her hands in mine.

"I promise I'll stay. Will you marry me?"

"Yes," she gasped, a cry falling from her lips. "Yes, I'll marry you."

We were both on our feet a moment later, and she was kissing me like she wanted to crawl inside me. I wanted her to. I wanted her to be a part of me in every way.

Behind us, a throat cleared. When I turned I saw Holly Goldsmith standing there in pink scrubs.

"Talia, Catrina is asking for you."

Talia gave me one last, lingering kiss before she followed Holly away. I watched her go, and when she was almost down the hall she looked over her shoulder and gave me a look that was full of promise. Promises of love and forever. The promise of everything she would let me do to her as soon as we got home.

She was my everything. The only love I had ever truly known. I had roped her in and she had done the same to me, wrapping that rope around and between both our hearts that would tether us together forever. All we both had to do was stay.

J.C. Hayden

Acknowledgements

Talia and Jack's story was a true joy to write. The experience was made even better by the following people. Thank you to *Josh* who helped guide this story to where it ended up with his thoughtful editing/review. Josh, thank you for encouraging me and convincing me I'm a real writer. Big thanks to *Sam,* for always being down for a brainstorming session and for your help with the paperback cover. I would be hopeless without you. As always, thank you to my mom (who is now allowed to read my stories), for pushing me to put myself out there.

And of course, thank you to every single person who read *No Strings* and who read this book, too. Sharing my work with you all is one of the greatest joys of my life.

About the Author

J.C. is a writer from St. Louis, Missouri. When she's not writing she's spending time with her cat and doing her full time job as an advocate.

Your feedback is so important to indie authors! Please leave a review wherever you like to leave reviews. You can always shoot me an email at jchaydenwrites@gmail.com

Find me online:
Website: jchayden.com
Instagram: @jchaydenwrites
Facebook.com/jchaydenwrites